THE LEGEND OF

MODOC
The Lost Years

Also by Ralph Helfer

The Beauty of the Beasts

*Modoc The True Story of the Greatest Elephant That Ever
Lived*
*Zamba The True Story of the Greatest Lion That Ever
Lived*

Mosey

The World's Greatest Elephant

Zamba The World's Greatest Lion

The Legend of Modoc
Modoc
The Lost Years

Ralph Helfer

Published in the United States.
Published by Legacy.
Books may be purchased for educational, business, or sales promotional use.
www.ralph-helfer.com
info@ralph-helfer.com

First Edition

Book design by Tana Helfer Herbert

Library of Congress Cataloging-in-Publication Data

Helfer, Ralph
	The Legend of Modoc: The Lost Years / by
Ralph Helfer. — 1st ed.
	p. cm.
	ISBN Paperback:	979-8-9912786-1-4
	ISBN Hardback:	979-8-9912786-0-7
	ISBN Ebook:	979-8-9912786-2-1
1. Modoc (Elephant) 2. Animals, Freedom 1. Title
LCCN: 2024920872	2024
	Biography and Fiction

Credits for Image, photo insert and jacket

Sketch
Courtesy of Chala Cadot art called "Modoc and child"
(Chapter's Emblem)
Watercolor art work
Courtesy of Chala Cadot art called "Modoc's Family"
(Cover Image 2nd layer)
David Costa Art
(Digital Artist - Cover Image 1st layer)
Tana Helfer Herbert
(Created final Cover Image)
Jacket Design © 2024 Tana Helfer Herbert
Cover Image © 2024 Tana Helfer Herbert
Layout by Tana Helfer Herbert
Author photograph by Spearhead International
Courtesy of Ralph Helfer:
(Picture of Modoc standing tall)
p.V

Dedicated to my daughter

Tana

Foreword

Ralph Helfer and I were kids together back in the early 1940's. We lived in the same apartment building on the corner of Yucca and Wilcox, one block north of Hollywood Boulevard. I remember roller skating up and down Wilcox, flying kites on a nearby (small) hill, and climbing the Hollywood sign.

Ralph, however, was always into animals… all kinds… even snakes! My grandmother, Nanny, would make him a "snake bag" out of a pillow case, with a drawstring at the top that would close it tightly. Ralph would go into the desert and capture a snake, put it into the pillow case and bring it back to the building to show to all the neighborhood kids.

Once he brought home a King snake and the whole bunch of us sneaked into the back yard where I remember holding it and wrapping it around my arm. When I put my arm in the sunlight, the snake would squeeze it tightly, releasing its grip when I put my arm in the shade. Thrilling! (That might have been when I first started doing the "Tarzan" yell).

Years later, after we were all grown up, my family and I visited Ralph when he had "Africa USA." Africa USA was a training compound and a provider of animals for Hollywood. Some of its most famous animals were Clarence, the cross-eyed lion, the bear in "Gentle Ben" and Zamba, who was "Leo the Lion" in the MGM logo. By now, Ralph was famous for creating what he called "affection training", which replaced the whip, gun and chair of the old way of training animals, with love, understanding and respect. We spent the day mingling with all sorts of wild animals. I even rode on an elephant with Ralph. We met his lovely wife, Toni and his adorable daughter, Tana. We reminisced about the old days…

We went our separate ways for many years, with Ralph spending much of his time In Africa, a land he loves with all his heart. Recently, we've been in touch via emails. He sent me his book based on a true story, "The Legend of Modoc." He is a magnificent writer and I was enthralled from the get-go! The story is about Modoc, the "Greatest Elephant That Ever Lived" and a young man, Bram, born on the same day as Modoc. The two grow up together and Bram follows in his father's footsteps of learning to train elephants in the circus, "Wunderzirkus", where all the animals are taught their routines through love, patience and nurturing. Bram and Modoc became inseparable.

Fate intervened and the two of them embarked on adventures that were exciting, frightening, scary, uplifting, heartwarming and unforgettable.

There were times I found myself crying... not just because of the horrific encounters they were faced with... but with the way the two of them survived because of the love they had for each other... they survived because of an unshakable bond... a belief that love conquers all.

Modoc and Bram win at the end.

There were several major hurdles Bram and Modoc had to overcome, but I'm not going to go into detail. I leave that to the brilliant story teller... my dear old friend, Ralph Helfer.

Carol Burnett

Acknowledgments

Three designers attempted their handy work to create a book cover that could capture the special image needed to truly embrace the spirit of this book. While deeply talented, they were not able to capture it.

It was my daughter, Tana, a seasoned and skilled writer in her own right, and my constant guide and mentor, who was able to crack the code and create the perfect cover. She knows me well.

She designed the cover, and in doing so, was able to capture the spirit of all that this book is.

Being a writer has many hurdles, and what's needed is that special person who can get you through the rough times when you hit that well-known writer's block, are searching for the perfect word, or need guidance as you debate killing off an important character. For me, that is my daughter.

Throughout our lives, she has been there to guide me. When my hand was writing erratically, and my style went off in its own flamboyant direction, Tana was always there - a steady northern star to bring me back to my sanity. While we had our disagreements, our shared mindset meant that we always produced the right results.

I am honored to have had her on board.

Thank you so much.
Love you always,
Dad

I was fortunate to have two editors who worked together and saw to it that the manuscript read the best it could. Kudos to Mike Valentino and Bunny Garrett. Thank you so much. It's truly appreciated.

Thank you, Kellie Rendina and Bethany Brown for guiding Tana through the process of book publishing, and helping us to get The Legend of Modoc out into the world.

Author's **Note**

Please read

There was a time not told, in the writing of Modoc, when she and Bram vanished from the eyes of those who followed. No one knew of their whereabouts.

I felt that a few strands of her life had been lost in the sands of the desert, the primeval forest of India. That there was more to Modoc's life that needed to be told. It was then that I decided to return to India to see if I could pick up her life trail...I had to go back. It had been years since I had been there, and I knew that to trace her life would be nearly impossible, but I had to try.

Where to look? Who would know? The police and hospitals would be of no value. They had been approached long ago to no avail.

But there is a place known to all who traverse the inner world, a place where an invisible line carries the mumble of a thousand voices. Twisting through arched corridors, over sleeping bodies, past dancing troubadours. Weaving by the cobra swaying to the flutist, bare-chested Shamans sitting cross-legged in a trance, and turbaned men sitting around Hookah Shisha pots with smoke billing, carrying the essence of the sweet smell of bhang, perhaps opium, filling the passageways.

The Bazaar.

The people of the Bazaar. Yes, they would know. The mystery of their whereabouts would be found in the bazaar. It was there that the mystery could be unraveled at last.

And so, for a few rupees, stories were told by the ancient, bearded ones, the nomads in from their camel caravan; the beggars in the bazaars. The thieves of the back alley.

Most spoke of them in a loving way. Those who would have seen them, talked to them, lived in the shadows for a night. Some swore that what they told me was the truth, others weren't sure. I watched their eyes. Those that looked straight at me, some with shifting eyes. Others were quite convincing. One old woman cried as she spoke, "I knew them well," she said. I think most of those who might have truly known of them were long gone. There were wisps of truth here but who was telling them? The beggar? Perhaps the camel herder? Yet I felt that perhaps there was just enough truth that would pull the drawstring together and weave a story from the treasure of her life. Most pointed which way they last saw them going. These stories were in some ways different from the ones I had heard on my previous trips. Therefore, I have chosen to write another version, the one told to me by the locals. Although perhaps the beginning and end are similar to the original Modoc story, their tale tells of a journey not known before.

Do come with me back to India on an adventure of Modoc and Bram's life. Perhaps some of it's true, some not, but which part is fact, and which is fiction? I leave it to you, dear reader.

The Legend lives on

CHAPTER 1

Deep in India's subtropical Randipur forest, the trumpet of elephants was heard signaling the awakening of morning. A mist had come, and with it a patter of light rain that brought out the essence of the forest; its scent was overwhelming. The woody aroma of the damp moss from the sandalwood and the jasmine overpowered the senses in the heavy, humid air and lingered in the stillness.

Nestled in the middle of the forest lay the GANAPATI TEAK LOGGING CAMP, a clearing cut by the machetes of men who fought each day to keep the advancing forest at bay.

The river Tamu, large and swift, flowed past the camp waiting to carry the hundreds of logs downstream to the town of Kishna, where they will be cut into sizes buyers have ordered.

The mahouts, a breed of small, tan-skinned men dedicated to their way of life, had gathered for their morning chai while grouped together around a smoking fire in hopes of keeping the mosquitos away. A cup of water was poured on the fire to increase the billowing smoke. They wore only burlap shorts, knowing the sweltering heat would soon come and the mosquitos would quickly go. Their elephants stood nearby scratching bug bites itching their legs and blowing air because that's what elephants do. Another used the tip of his trunk to tickle his brother's ear. All waited impatiently to begin their day of pulling, lifting, and loading logs. Suddenly, their trunks rose in unison searching the breeze as their ears thrust forward. Something was thrashing through the forest and creating chaos. The swiping of machetes, falling bamboo, and murmuring voices were carried on the faint breeze.

Emerging from the humid forest came Naxalite rebels on the run from the Indian Army close on their heels. Dressed in stolen Army camouflage fatigues, with rags for turbans, and sporting thick beards, their sweating bodies neared exhaustion from tramping through the humid, thick undergrowth; curved machetes were swung by the leaders or hung from their belts. All were heavily armed with guns and equipment. Several with war injuries of severed arms and twisted legs limped along behind. Some with missing limbs hobbled with bamboo crutches; others with open wounds that had not healed suffered flies stuck to their dark, sticky, oozing blood.

The mahouts went quiet, and the elephants grumbled and stomped nervously as the strangers approached. A large, sweat-drenched, fat-bellied slob of a man wearing a stolen Indian Army colonel's cap carried a bazooka over his shoulder. Flanked by two of his men, he sauntered over to where the mahouts huddled. Apparently, he was the leader.

"Hey, elephant man, where is your Sahib?"

"I'm here." The firm voice came from a medium height, slender, but muscular Caucasian within the mahouts. Out stepped a man dressed in a kurta, a short wraparound skirt. A cropped blond beard and mustache graced his youthful face. Behind him stood an exceptionally large elephant. Up top sat an Asian girl of her late teens and was an outstanding beauty. Her long, jet-black hair, dark eyebrows, and slim body caught the eye of the rebel. She threw her leg over and slid down the elephant's side to stand closer to the Sahib.

"My name is Bram, and this is Sian, my girlfriend. The elephant's name is Modoc. And yours?" he said, offering his hand.

The rebel brushed it away and spit a thick wad to the ground, the dribble lodged in his beard. "Ah! I am not interested in knowing your names or giving you mine. But you are too young to be in such a position," said the rebel while giving Bram the once over.

"Mr. Ja, the owner, has gone to Bombay. I am in charge." At age twenty-two, Bram was used to people thinking he was years younger. It was a curse he endured.

"Yes, well of course you are," said the rebel, a bit snidely. "And you are white?"

"I was born this way," Bram answered a bit condescending.

One of the mahout's, thinking Bram was in danger stepped forward in a protective stance with his machete in hand. A battle scarred rebel soldier knocked him to the ground with one blow of his gnarled fist.

"There is no need for that!" Bram declared as he helped the man stand. "You can have whatever you want."

"Ha, I do not need your permission—your camp is now ours! You will provide food for us and a place to sleep. HUH? Yes?"

"Yes, of course, whatever you wish."

"I have decided to tell you my name... it is Mohammed. I was named after the great prophet and spiritual leader of my people, so do not use it in vain."

"I am honored!" Bram said, trying to appease the brute.

"So, I will expect a good deal of respect."

"Of course, you will be given all you require," said Bram.

"Now then, I am aware the Army is not far behind us, so me and my men must continue our journey till we reach our destination."

"Which is where?" asked Bram.

"Sanapur. Once we reach there, the Army will not be able to find us."

"But it is a long way and far up the mountain," countered Bram.

"Yes, it is, but I have heard of a trail close by that would get us back up to the Sanapur region in the shortest time. Is that not true?" asked Mohammed.

"Yes, it is true. It is called the Dullirah Pass, but it is an exceptionally arduous journey. Few travel it, but I am sure you can make it," said Bram, hoping they would leave quickly.

"My men are weary and in no condition to trek a long distance." He walked over to the elephants.

"So," he continued, "we will take your elephants."

"Huh? You what?"

"Yes, yes. Of course. We will be taking them. They can carry us and your storage supplies as well."

Bram knew the consequences of such a move. "My dear friend, that is impossible! The trail is too narrow for the elephants. I have traveled it," said Bram, terrified at the thought of it.

"Ack! I am not your friend! Now you are trying to trick me, huh? I am sure we can make it."

"How can you say that? You have never been there," Bram said while trying to control his voice so as not to show his despair. "I must warn you the trail you speak of becomes too narrow and not passable with elephants."

"Ah! You lie!" Muhammed exclaimed.

"But I speak the truth. It is passable only by foot," Bram replied, desperate for Mohammed to believe him.

"If it is true, I will pray, and Allah will see us through," Mohammed responded. He waved his hand to show Bram the subject was closed and strutted toward Sian.

"Hmm … and this delicate flower is yours you say?" He walked around Sian eyeing her in a lecherous manner, then reached out to touch her. She slapped his hand and stepped aside to stand beside Bram.

"Ha! A feisty one! When I am ready, I will take her as my own." Bram's face turned crimson, but it was not the time for a confrontation. He knew for the safety of the mahouts, elephants, and most importantly, Sian, he'd have to bide his time.

"So, we will leave as soon as the elephants are loaded. That will give us time to rest while you prepare the elephants to carry all our equipment and all that is in your storage. My men can get proper rest as they ride."

Mohammed saw the look on Bram's face.

"Hey! Hey! Mr. ... Ba ... Bram ... whatever your name is? Do not fail me! I am too tired to play any games. The Army is close by, so nothing will stop me from leaving with your elephants and their mahouts. You hear me?" He poked Bram with the barrel of his gun. "Huh, Huh?"

Bram grabbed the barrel of the gun and knocked it away. For a long moment, things could have turned for the worse.

"Yes," Bram agreed. "We will have them ready." He grumbled while his mind raced trying to figure out what to do.

"How many elephants do you have?"

"There are thirty," replied Bram. "Besides a breeding bull."

"And my men are forty-nine, so there are enough to carry them and the equipment—but the bull! Why is he not with the others?" demanded Mohammed.

"He is too dangerous and exceedingly difficult to handle," Bram replied.

"But that's only when he is breeding," challenged Mohammed.

"Zarifi is a killer elephant and is always unmanageable," replied Bram trying to convince Mohammed.

"Ah! I don't believe you! You are playing games with me and for that you will have to pay!" He pointed his pistol at one of the village women and pulled the trigger. A shot rang loudly as the woman dropped with blood running from her thigh.

Her husband screamed, "Dear Allah!" and ran to her.

"What have you done?!" Bram yelled at Mohammed.

"Aha! You don't know who you are talking to. I am Mohammed, named after the great prophet and spiritual leader of my people," he repeated. His arms flailed as he yelled for all to hear. "Do not cross me! Besides, this is of your doing! Not mine! So, get the bull! I want to see him in the lineup when we leave. If you fail, the next time I will aim a little higher and at two of your people."
Mohammed leveled the gun at Bram's head and his tone changed to a shrill yell. "Get him—now!"

"Very well." Bram ignored the gun as he walked away with his face a darker crimson.

Mohammed chuckled to some of his nearby men. "This elephant, Zarifi, he sounds like he is much like me! Huh?" His men joined him as they broke out in hysterical laughter.

Bram realized he was dealing with a fanatic, a crazy man. Best to tread lightly until he could hopefully figure out a way to expel the rebels from the camp.

Once Mohammed left, the mahouts gathered around Bram mumbling their concerns. Ja always treated the mahouts as his own family, caring for and protecting them. Now it was Bram's job to be there for them.

The atmosphere in the camp was stifling. Everybody wanted Mohammed and his men to be gone, but to take the elephants was stealing the life blood of the village. Above all was the fear of taking them on the Dullirah Pass trail. They all knew it turned into a small, dangerous path barely suitable for humans only. But for now, they were faced with another dilemma—handling Zarifi.

The mahouts squatted around Bram waiting to hear what he felt needed to be done.

"My friends, you all know what we are up against with Zarifi. Putting him in the lineup is a dangerous thing to do. But we have no choice. We have changed his ropes many times but to move him from his place, well, that we have not done. Zarifi is a killer; the first chance he gets, he will try to grab one of you. So go easy. Gather all the rope and chains that are not being used and a dozen men who are willing to work with Zarifi. And bring Kulba; next to Modoc, he's the biggest elephant in the group, and we will need him after we restrain Zarifi. I will bring Modoc as we will need her, too, to engage him as we work. Now, let's get Zarifi down here." Bram tried his best to give off a calm demeanor, but he was wondering, was he trying to convince the mahouts or himself that this was the proper course of action as he told them the plan.

Sian sat with the mahouts and heard every word. She had been raised at the logging village by her father, Ja, and was quite aware of Zarifi and the danger Bram and the mahout were about to face. She went to Bram and took him aside.

"My love, what are you going to do? Zarifi is so dangerous. How can you handle him?"

Bram saw she was shaking, and he tried to calm her fears.

He took her away from where the men were packing and went to the edge of the forest where he could embrace her and soothe her worry.

Bram had met Sian while he and Modoc were swimming in a small lake hidden in the forest near the camp. He remembered hearing a giggle. It was Sian. She was sitting at the edge of the lake braiding her hair. Bram had left his clothes on the shore and was embarrassed when he saw her.

Since that time, they had been as one and never left each other's side.

"I realize to handle Zarifi is dangerous, but we have no choice." Bram embraced her. "I will do everything I can to keep the men and myself safe." He combed his fingers through her long shiny hair and kissed away the tears welling in her eyes.

"I know, my love, I know. I will pray that all goes well." She wiped away the tears trickling down her cheeks.

"Now, I must go. Best that you stay and help the mahouts but stay away from Mohammed. He is one extremely dangerous and ruthless man."

Long before their arrival, Zarifi sensed they were coming. As a punk (baby) he had been brought up as a logger, hauling teak with the others while being given all the needs his life required: food, water, housing, friendship. Then, his testosterone kicked in and he morphed into a killer. Not all male elephants turn into maniac killers. But those that do leave a path of slaughter and death. Such was the case with Zarifi.

He stood rocking back and forth, his trunk rolled up in a tight ball ready to loosen at anyone who dared come too close. Even with one leg shackled in the back and one in the front, he was still quite formidable.

The men arrived, ropes were laid out, men positioned. They knew what to do. They stripped naked, then helped each other pour coconut oil over their bodies. Zarifi would find it difficult to grab them because the oil made them slippery as an eel. In the last five years Zarifi had been able to grab two men. One poor fellow had gone back to recheck a knotted rope when his body was grabbed and beaten against Zarifi's leg. The other man tripped. Neither had bothered to drench themselves with oil.

Bram gathered the men and explained, "We need to rope the two back legs together. Just give him enough room to jail walk."

Bram knew there was nothing to prevent Zarifi from trying to grab a mahout. It would be their trained ability to stay away from a kick that could kill or a trunk that could grab them and throw them under his foot where they would be crushed.

The men moved in quickly to get a rope around his back leg as Zarifi ranted and trumpeted and reached back with his trunk trying to grab the oiled men. Time and time again he thought he had an arm or a leg, only to have it slip off. He could not hold a grip on their slippery bodies. Once done, the men prepared to move to the front legs. First they would have to deal with Zarifi's long, sharp tusks.

Zarifi proudly carried two huge tusks eight feet long with spear-like daggers at the tips. More dangerous than his trunk, he had bloodied the tips on careless people more than once.

The men successfully getting his back legs under control infuriated him and drove him into a frenzy as he pounded his trunk against the ground and threw dirt high in the air.

Bram knew if Zarifi was to be in the lineup, his tusks would have to be compromised.

"Now, get the Naariyals," said Bram.

Two men approached; each carried a Naariyal (coconut). A hole had been chiseled on one side of each. Hot pine tree sap, called jungle glue, was poured into a gourd along with sticky jungle gum and the concoction mixed into a foam until thoroughly blended. Then the mixture was poured into the coconuts. A third mahout appeared with a small carved and jeweled narrow-lipped bottle. He opened the bottle and steam rose from it as he poured a few drops in each hole.

"What is that you have?" Bram inquired.

"We believe a sprinkle of woody scent of myrrh sprinkled in the hole will allow the forest nymph to see to it that all goes well."

"Hope it works!" said Bram.

All was ready. Standing in front of Bram were two of the mahouts, Puran and Jalaj.

He put his hands on their heads, whispered a prayer that the Gods would protect them followed by a namaste. Then, he spoke.

"Now comes the difficult part. You must work together. I will have Modoc keep Zarifi's attention by entangling her trunk around his. That will keep him busy, so you two can get those Naariyals in place. Remember, there will only be a split second where you will be able to shove them onto the tusks."

The men stood ready. Modoc moved in to engage Zarifi. Trunk tangled with trunk, as Puran watched for the right instant, then rushed for it, slamming the Naariyal onto the tusk.

Next, Jalaj stood poised with the Naariyal cupped in his hands ready to push it on the other tusk. Suddenly, Zarifi lurched and knocked the Naariyal out of his hands. Jalaj, instinctively, reached down to get it. Zarifi saw what happened and broke Modoc's hold on him. He dropped his trunk and quickly encircled Jalaj's body. In a fraction of a second, Zarifi raised his foot, slid Jalaj's limp body underneath, and with a jerk, Jalaj was decapitated. Zarifi bellowed as he threw the headless body into the bush as a final disdainful gesture Zarifi kicked the Naariyal away.

"Oh, good Lord!" exclaimed Bram. Everybody stood in shock. It had happened in an instant. Jalaj's brother standing nearby became hysterical. He let out a gut-wrenching scream, picked up the Naariyal, and raced toward Zarifi. Standing in front of him for an instant screaming his lungs out, he slammed the Naariyal on the remaining tusk, turned, and walked away.

Zarifi did nothing. Whether it was the screaming or the defiant stance in front of him, one will never know. Things happen that have no logical explanation, perhaps the wood nymph...?

The mahouts, each in their own way suffered the loss. Most gathered around Jalaj's brother clutching, hugging, whispering words of faith, comforting him, offering their condolences mostly in their own language. A few mahouts with the help of the brother went into the bush, gathered Jalaj's remains, and wrapped them in a sisal blanket.

As was their tradition, the mahouts sat in a circle around the body and together chanted the mantra 'om'.

Bram tried to remain composed as he thought to himself that the madman Mohammad had indirectly claimed his first victim. He took the shawl he had tucked under Modoc's blanket and placed it over his head. It had been left with him by Ja before he departed. The black shawl made of Persian lamb's wool with many mantas written in Hindi on it was used at times of religious needs.

"There may be an occasion where its use will be needed," Ja had said before leaving.

Giving the sign of the namaste, Bram stood in the circle of the mahouts and spoke. "A golden light has come and lifted our dear friend Jalaj up and away to the realm of God's domain.

There to feel the hand of God on his shoulder, to give him a new life of love, and to be welcomed into his domain. The gates of heaven will open wide and welcome Jalaj."

Zarifi stood quietly as his trunk rested on the ground. He seemed exhausted from the struggle of getting his back legs and tusks secured as well as the killing of a human. Surely, he felt something. For him to have murdered a human some emotion must have gone through his mind. It had to mean something to him. Remorse? No? Perhaps a feeling of accomplishment.

Nearby, Modoc was doing a slow methodical rocking. She knew. Not the details of the death but that something had occurred to depress Bram. She always felt Bram's emotional trauma. How? No telling, she just knew. Perhaps she was privy to the human's waves of intense sorrow.

With the Naariyals in place, and Modoc keeping his attention, the men were successful in getting Zarifi's front legs secured. Bram brought Modoc to one side of Zarifi and Kulba to the other side. With them confining him, both leaned in, pressed him tightly, and headed down to the river's edge where equipment and supplies were being loaded on the elephants.

CHAPTER 2

Bram arrived in the early afternoon with the mahouts, Zarifi, Kulba, and Modoc to find the area in total chaos. Elephants ran loose trumpeting and dancing and not letting their mahout load them. Baggage was hanging from their backs, women sobbed while grasping their husbands' legs, begging them not to leave. Children cried for their fathers.

Guns, ammunition, and equipment were scattered everywhere. Fights broke out as rebels attempted blatant gropes of the mahout's women. The massive amount of food and supplies taken from the storage area was overwhelming. They had taken the year's supply and emptied the storage completely and piled it into large sisal wraps in hopes of getting it up on the backs of the elephants. The loads were sloppy, oversized, far too wide, and in danger of sliding off.

Up and down the row, mahouts tried to load their elephants properly. But the rebels kept pulling them down and hoisting their weapons up and securing them on the elephants' backs where the shooters could lay with a pile of ammunition.

Bram saw a heavy .50 caliber machine gun being mounted on one of the elephants and many boxes of ammunition surrounding it.

The rebels had found a bunch of Persian pillows in the storage and laid them around the machine gun for their comfort and making it look like a giant bird's nest. Packed below the 'nest,' the illiterate rebels had strapped enormous bundles of miscellaneous goods creating precarious loads.

Bram stopped the melees and organized the workers, then with the help of some of the mahouts, he was successful in getting a load strapped to Zarifi's back.

He was trying to figure out where to put Zarifi in the lineup when Mohammed, who had been walking up and down inspecting the loads, appeared.

"My my, such a big fellow," said Mohammed as he strutted around Zarifi.

"Now you see, I was right. You have brought him here," he said in all his arrogance. "Agh! You white people. You know nothing about doing the impossible. And tomorrow, I will show you that we can cross the mountains on your so-called 'path.'" Then, he stared at Zarifi. "Put him behind my elephant. He can be my protector," Mohammed said. He then chuckled loudly for all to hear. He pointed. "You, Bram, will lead the way. Your pretty girlfriend can ride alone on her own elephant as only a princess should." He smirked salaciously and then shouted, "We ride at dawn!"

That evening, most of the rebels slept under the stars. It wasn't the first time. They had been doing so since being on the run from the Army. But it had been the first time in a while that they had full bellies while doing so, filling their stomachs to the brim on some of the camp's supplies. Some of Mohammed's higher-ranking lieutenants kicked the mahouts out of their homes and took them for themselves for the evening. Those who were allowed to remain in their homes opened their doors to those who had been displaced, while others still were cherishing their time together with their loved ones. The camp felt like there was an ominous cloud over it, knowing that nothing would be the same after tomorrow. Bram and Sian were enjoying a simple meal of chicken and rice together when the door to their home was kicked open. It was Mohammed.

"This is my home for tonight," he proclaimed. Bram had enough and got up from the dinner table and stepped towards Mohammed.

"Wouldn't you rather sleep with your men, like the great leader you are? Show solidarity before the long ride tomorrow?" Bram said, continuing to try to play to Mohammed's ego.

"I'd rather sleep with your girlfriend," Mohammed said with a belly laugh.

"I'm afraid that is impossible," Bram said as he took another step closer to Mohammed. The smell of his rotten breath and sweat was almost enough to knock Bram out, but he stood firm.

"Do you need another demonstration of what happens if you resist, white man?" Mohammed said with all joy now gone from his face, replaced by a look of lunacy behind his eyes, his hand instinctually drifting towards his pistol.

"You need a guide through the path, don't you? You'll also need your energy in the morning. It's a long ride to Sanapur, even with the shortcut," Bram countered.

Mohammed mulled this over for a second and then reason seemed to return to his eyes, and he smiled a yellow-toothed grin. "That is a fair point. I will concede you this final evening with your woman."

Mohammed then began to turn as if to leave but stopped before speaking again. "But know this: when we reach Sanapur and I have no more need of your or your elephants, you are dead and your girlfriend will be mine," he hissed at Bram as he finished his about face and left the doorway of Bram and Sian's house.

Bram let loose a long sigh as the adrenaline that had been pumping through his veins finally receded like the tides of the ocean. Sian then looked at him again with tears in her eyes.

"What are we gong to do?" she asked meekly.

Bram again rushed over to Sian and took her in his arms. "We must have hope. Mohammed is bullish and insane, but he cares primarily about his survival. When he sees the pass is impassable with the elephants, surely, he'll see reason. And hopefully by then the Army will catch up to us and end this nightmare."

They finished their meal, prayed, and tried their best to sleep as they held onto each other as tightly as they could.

The following dreary, early morning amidst an occasional trumpet from a forlorn elephant, the long line disappeared into the gloom at dawn, a solemn caravan moving out on a trail of doom.

Two days later fog rolled in as the caravan inched its way up the treacherous pass; thirty-one strong, sweat-soaked elephants spread over a half mile along the trail, swiping their trunks against the dense fog hoping to see the ground below.

Further on their upward trek, the trail narrowed until it became a mere path. A small, frightening, serpentine route across the Himalayan Mountain range known as the Dullirah Pass.

Some behemoths swayed their heavy tusks to keep their balance on the treacherous, narrow trail. On one side stood a crumbling rock wall; a sheer drop of 1,000 feet lay opposite it to the rocks below. The truth of what Bram had described came to light. Each rebel knew it, Mohammed above all, but no one would dare speak of it. Mohammed would never admit his being wrong. Stubbornness mixed with insanity is a frightening combination. The width of their enormous loads of renegade equipment, guns, ammunition, food, and camping supplies was far too wide for the narrow passage as they scraped against the vertical side of the mountain. The gunner with his machine gun and ammunition mounted up top made his elephant's load top heavy. They had been warned but to no avail.

At the higher altitude, the fog thinned. Modoc, with Bram's help, cleared the path as best they could of fallen debris by pushing boulders aside that had rolled down the steep embankment. Fearing not being able to see the edge of the precipice in pockets of dense fog and falling over the rim, she would locate the edge of the path by running the tip of her trunk along its edge.

A strong breeze from uplifting air currents rose from the valley below. The fog became patchy, and the mahouts could sometimes see the elephant in front of their own as the caravan bunched closer together.

Suddenly, out of the eastern sky loud sounds were heard. Three Indian 580 fighter planes came in over the mountain range in formation flying low under the cloud cover to scout the area. They could barely make out the caravan through the drifting fog. As they flew over, Mohammed lost his building temper and unleashed his frustration. He snapped. He stood on the back of his elephant raging his anger, waving his hands and gun while screaming his fury and shooting at the planes.

"Shoot the imbeciles! Kill them, kill them all!" he screamed.

Those within reach of his voice manned their guns.

As the planes circled around, they opened fire to strafe the caravan.

There was sheer panic as the elephants stampeded, mahouts fell, and equipment slipped around to the bellies of the elephants. Two elephants went down, blood spurting from their multiple wounds. One stumbled and fell into the chasm while the other was never to rise again. Others limped on, terrified of slipping on the crumbling edge of the path and falling into the chasm. mahouts cut the cumbersome packs off their elephants in hopes of getting through. Supplies were scattered underfoot and over the edge. The heavy machine gun and its ammunition were pushed over the edge to clear the path. Through the chaos Bram saw Sian slide from her elephant and disappear into the fog. "Sian! Sian!" he yelled. Sliding down Modoc's leg he was immediately engulfed in the wispy mist she had faded into.

The march up the trail had been too much for one of the oldest elephants in the group, Molly. She was far too old for the stress and exertion. Her legs gave out and she stumbled along the crumbling trail when bullets found her. The bullets that brought her down came as a sort of relief. It was her time. She collapsed hard and lay on her side. The load on her back split open knocking two rebels and their gear over the edge. Realizing their fate, their screams faded to the rock below.

Her mahout knew. When the bullets rained down, he knelt beside her and laid his hand on her eye and did a prayer namaste, then stood and walked into the wispy fog.

A third rebel was furious. He had no idea of Molly's demise. "Get up, you lazy cow!" he yelled and poked her with his machete, but she didn't budge. God had opened His golden gates for her.

"She's dead!" yelled another frantic rebel. "And she's blocking the path."

The word came down.

"Mohammed said to push her over the ledge. Use your elephant."

The mahout behind Molly brought his elephant in line with Molly's body.

"Dhakka den! Dhakka den! Push! Push!" The elephant dropped her head low to the ground, balled her trunk, and gave all she had to push the giant carcass over the cliff.

"Can't do it. She's too heavy." The mahout on the elephant in the front of Molly, seeing what was needed, managed to turn around and together with the other elephant heaved and pushed until they finally got Molly's body over the cliff; with a frightful roar, a big chunk tore loose from the edge of the path. It became even more treacherous than before.

Bullets were flying and ricocheting off the rock wall. Zarifi panicked. A low belly rumble coupled with him rocking back and forth warned he was at a breaking point. He let out a bellowing trumpet and started to shake. He shook till the straps holding the pack on his back broke, sending the equipment and a rebel shooter over the precipice. The man's shrieking was heard fading all the way to the bottom.

In an attempt to rid himself of the coconuts, Zarifi slammed his tusks again the ground over and over until the coconuts cracked open and flew off.

Zarifi felt a sting. Something had bitten him, or so he thought. He reached back and scratched it with his trunk. It made his whole leg burn. He didn't understand. Several more stings irritated him. He felt weak. He wanted to leave. Why wasn't Mohammed's elephant moving? With the coconuts gone, he bellowed an agonizing trumpet. Then he whipped around and with his full force rammed Mohammed's elephant with his razor-sharp tusks sinking them deep into her thick skin. She screamed a blood curdling trumpet and shot ahead nearly throwing Mohammed off his roost.

Then Mohammed saw it. The tip of Zarifi's mammoth trunk was snaking its way up the side of his elephant toward him. As it approaches his leg, Mohammed grabbed his Army rifle and beat the advancing trunk with the butt of the gun. Unfazed, the tip of the trunk, like a giant snake, felt its way up his leg, his arm, around his ears, eyes, touching here and there. Then with a lightning whip-like move it wrapped itself around Mohammed and squeezed.

A muffled cry was heard.

"ALLAH! DEAR GOD! HELP ME!" A thick coil wrapped around his face. He couldn't see, he couldn't hear. He felt himself being lifted and carried off. An instant later he felt a rush of cold air rising from the canyon below, then there was nothing. The trunk was gone, and he plummeted down to the rocks below, screaming all the way.

Zarifi felt several more painful stings. Something was wrong. Another and he felt himself falling. He didn't understand why he couldn't stand. He was not to rise again.

On the second 'fly by' Modoc felt bullets hit hard enough to knock her to her knees. She tried to stand, but everything twirled and spun. Blood poured from the bullet holes in her head and into her eyes blurring her vison. The elephant behind her was pushing and trying to climb over her to escape the horror. The mahouts were yelling, "Drop the packs! Maybe we'll get through!" She heard the thud of bullets hitting around her. Struggling to right herself, she finally staggered to her feet; her body shook uncontrollably as she tried to get her bearing. She took one step then another. An updraft of a strong breeze of cold air rising from the canyon below told her she was standing on the edge of the precipice! With a lurch she whipped herself around landing back on the path against the secure wall of rock. She rubbed the blood from her eyes with the tip of her trunk till a ray of light came through. All was hazy and blurred. She stretched her trunk out to locate Bram. She trumpeted for him. He had always been there for her in times of need. Then, using her trunk she felt for the edge of the path. Occasionally pockets of clear air came and went, showing her the way.

Modoc awoke lying in a field with many others of her kind. She remembered having staggered down a road helped by mahouts who kept her from falling. All around her, she heard the moans, the tweaks, the slapping of trunks of those trying to alleviate their pain. A man was soothing her with a cool towel while telling her she would be alright, then darkness fell.

CHAPTER 3

The war had ended. The battlers all lost. It lasted but a year
before the rebels brought it to an end. The year was 1970.
Religious violence had broken out between the Naxalite rebels,
a strong Maoist sect, and the Indian government with each
believing they were right. Bodies murdered in massacres were
strewn in the streets. Golden temples lay crumbled, their
archways previously encrusted with fine gems ransacked,
sculptures of the Indian gods Brahma and Vishnu were smashed
into pieces. The towering spheres of the mosques, many
enriched with the etched symbols of their religion were toppled.
Neither side had won. The Indian government had hopefully
brought the tribe into a peaceful agreement in an attempt to
settle the dispute. But it had turned hostile. To agree, one had to
favor the other and neither had the mind to do that. So, neither
had won, both had lost, defeated on all fronts. The Army finally
carried the battle into the foothills of the Himalayas, an area
well known by the rebels. Every trail, rock crevice, and gully

were familiar to them. They left the Indian Army far behind to come again another day.

There was considerable loss to the Indian Army. Makeshift tent hospitals had been set up throughout the border of the war zone where the wounded were taken for emergency treatment.

Once treated, if needed, they were flown to a major hospital in Jodhpur.

Bram awoke to the sound of people hustling about, things being moved, people talking, the whir of a sputtering fan as it swept a wave of hot air across his body. July was humid and temperatures were well above one hundred.

Bram heard a voice close by.

"Well, I see you are awake and feeling better, are you?" Bram opened his eyes to see a man bending over him. He was dressed in an immaculate white hospital uniform with a turban to match and was checking Bram's heart with a stethoscope. He stood back, stroked his thick beard, and adjusted his tortoise shell glasses. A name tag indicated Dr. Shah was the head physician at the hospital. Shaking down a thermometer, he slipped it under Bram's tongue.

"Where am I?" asked Bram.

"In a makeshift hospital near the defunct war zone. We were going to ship you out to the major hospital in Jodhpur, but your recovery has been quite good, so we have kept you here." Tell me young man, what is your name?"

"Bram. Bram Gunterstein," he blurted out.

The doctor then continued, "Apparently, you were caught up in a terrifying ordeal that was not of your making and have spent the last month healing from the multiple wounds you suffered. Although none are of major concern, you lost a considerable amount of blood and the infections had left you weak and fatigued."

"Modoc, is she...?" mumbled Bram. "And Sian. Are they okay?"

"If you mean your elephant? Now don't you worry. She, like you, suffered a number of wounds but none were life threatening. However, it's the infection that has us concerned. As for this Sian you speak of, I know nothing of her whereabouts."

"I've got to go. Where is Modoc? Got to find Sian." Bram was delirious. "I must ... go!" Bram swung his legs off the cot in an effort to right himself.

"You'll never make it," said a nurse as she caught him as he collapsed. A syringe was quicky filled and injected; Bram settled back in his bed. Dr. Shah removed his glasses and stood looking at Bram. A puzzled look crossed his face.

"Look, Mr. Bram, I don't know how a young white person like you can have your own elephant, but that is not my concern. She...? What's her name?"

"Modoc." His voice was weak, but he seemed alert.

"Yes, Modoc, well, she had a few bullet holes in her upper cranium. But there is nothing there but skeleton fiber. You know, many people think that's where the brain is but it's not. It's far down between the eyes. Many a hunter has learned that the hard way."

The good doctor put his hand on Bram's shoulder. "So don't you be troubled. Be assured we are doing all we can for her and many others who were injured. Give it a few more days and then I am sure you will have the strength to see her. Just stay rested and we will get you both on your way."

"But you're a doctor of people and Modoc is—"

"An elephant," Dr. Shah said, then laughed. "My friend, when we are so far from civilization, and when we are called to help, we 'change our shoes.' It doesn't matter whether our patients are two or four legged because they're all God's creatures. We do all we can to assist them.

"My assistants and I make the short journey every day to care for her and the others. It's not far from here, just down the road." He pointed at the tent's canvas opening, "About an hour's walk. Just this side of the U.S. Army air force field. The Army has been gracious enough to let us use their jeep.

"But now, rest. Don't worry, I will look in on you later."

"Doc, my girlfriend, Sian, is she okay?"

"I know not of this person. Perhaps she was taken to another facility."

"Please, please, can you find out for me?"

"Yes, of course, I will have my staff find her. Now sleep."

"Doctor Shah, if you will, please take this to Modoc." Bram removed a medallion from his neck. It was a silver nugget with the elephant god Ganesha set in gold.

"My goodness, such a strange request," mumbled the doctor. "Yes, well. Of course. But how do I give it to her?"

"Just have her smell it then put it around her neck. She will know."

"It's too small a necklace, but I will find some cord. Yes, I will do this. Now rest."

Dr. Shah retrieved the thermometer from Bram's sweating face. It read: 102. Bram was still a very sick fella. Dr. Shah felt Bram's concern for his girlfriend and the elephant was responsible for his temperature rising. He left instructions for the nurse to keep him informed of any change.

The realization of what had happened on the trail started to materialize in Bram's mind. He drifted in and out of sleep due to his weakened condition. He dropped off into a nightmare of anguished slumbering as he relived the terror he had experienced. His mind was trapped in a frenzy of horror jumbled together in a montage of machine guns, elephants slipping off a cliff to fall to a valley below, murderous rebels, and Modoc and Sian disappearing in the fog.

"I told them the path was too narrow. I told them! They wouldn't listen!" he yelled aloud while tossing and turning in delirium, reliving the chaos of terror unfolding in his mind.

"Sian, come back! Sian!" Two nurses were there, one kept him from flopping out of the bed, the other swathed his sweating body with cool towels to keep his temperature down. Then, a needle injection wiped away the thoughts that caused the pain. In his delirium he murmured, "I'll see you tomorrow, won 't I? Tomorrow, to..."

"Who is Sian?" asked one of the nurses.

"His girlfriend. They can't find her. I think she must be dead."

Bram slept for twenty-four hours. He awoke smelling a sickening odor of sweat and an overpowering deodorant coupled with the rancid stench of cigarette breath! He found it unbearable. Someone was breathing in his face. From out of his nightmare dilemma now came another. Only one person carried the stench of the devil. A demon from his past. Was it possible after all these years?

He opened his eyes to see its face inches from his own. Mr. North! A tall, fiftyish, bald, tight jawed man with small beady eyes looking through a pair of thin framed prescription glasses balanced on the tip of a long narrow nose. He munched the hairs of his mustache, something he did whenever he was excited. North was the epitome of Ebenezer Scrooge. He was smoking a cigarette as brown juice bubbled from his mouth while smoke kept one eye closed. His clothes were of a past era. A worn and too tight grey flannel pin stripe suit with a mismatched bow tie. There stood the man Bram had been running from for many years! Bram could tell North was ready to bite his head off. The first words stormed out of his mouth, "Checking to see if you were still breathing, you bastard!" he yelled. "You owe me big time!" He grabbed Bram's bedgown and pulled him up even closer to his face. Bram could see his cracked, blackened tooth decay. "You are a liar and a thief, and when I get you back to the States, I will turn you over to the authorities."

North, seeing the nurses looking concerned as to what was happening, dropped Bram back to his pillow. Then without a pause he feigned compassion, "How do you feel?"

"Just weak," Bram said. "As though you care."

North blew a cloud of smoke in his face. "Strong enough to make the trip back to the States? Huh? Huh?" North was losing it. His face turned a mucky red. "Maybe all that has happened will teach you a lesson. Stealing my elephant! Damn near got her killed. I'll find someone else to work with her. Yes, that's what I'll do. You'll see."

"She is not your elephant, and she won't . . ." Bram said struggling to raise his voice.

"Won't what?" North asked.

"Won't work for anybody else."

"Oh yeah? We'll see about that! Maybe a whip or strong bull hook will change her mind."

North hated being contradicted by anyone let alone Bram.

"Modoc just won't work for...." Bram turned his head, too weak to go another round with him.

"Ach! You imbecile!"

Bram just didn't have the strength to stop his put downs.

"Well ... now look," said North, "I have arranged for a plane to take you and Modoc back. It's going to cost me a fortune, but it will be worth it in the long run."

Inch long ashes from his cigarette fell on the bed sheets. He lit another stick with tar-stained fingers.

"Your smoking is going to kill you," said Bram, waving the smoke away.

Ignoring the remark, North ranted on, "I would have her go back on a ship, but in her weakened condition she would never make the long journey. And anyhow, it would take forever to travel that far. Besides, we have a big celebration planned for her return. I'm having a stage built outside the big tent and a large sign painted in red and gold letters:

'NORTH'S WUNDERCIRZUS'

'WELCOME HOME,

    MODOC'

"Why a stage?" asked Bram.

"Ach! You're such an idiot," stormed North.

"Careful with your words!" said Bram, feeling his face flush.

"Yeah well," he rebuffed, sluffing it off, "we are having the mayor come and present an award to Modoc. It will be a big celebration. We are inviting big-name movie stars, maybe the Governor will come? Why, she's a hero!" he boasted.

Bram had heard enough.

"North, you have really lost it. The Governor? Really. You'll get some animal lovers who will show up, but it's not going to be as big a deal as you think. Besides, how will Modoc accept the award without me there? Next thing you will want her to give a speech! And all this for what? She didn't do anything. She's not a hero. She simply survived."

"Survived... Survived! That's it! I can see it now!" His hands traced his thoughts against the backdrop of the hospital tent.

"'ELEPHANT SURVIVES THE DESERT'

"The celebration is for her return!" He went on. "She's a survivor!" It was like an awakening!" He stalked around the bed as his hands waved in the air imagining what could take place.

His ranting and raving were causing the hospital staff concern for their other patients.

"Please sir, you will have to leave." The head nurse spoke. "You are disrupting the other patients."

"A minute please," he said. "Just a moment more."

She looked at her watch. "Just one."

North sat on the edge of the bed and leaned close to Bram. He tried to whisper but what came out was a strange dissertation of high and low squeaks.

"Then inside the tent a tribute to her," he continued.

"You can't have two?"

"Two what?

"Tributes."

"Well, we'll figure something. Heinz will put on a special act with his tigers, Appelle, the clown with his chimps for a few laughs and then a spectacular performance by the flying Zafforli family." He thought for a moment. "As a finale I will have the police arrest you on camera."

"What for?"

"You stole my elephant!"

"But it's not true; you know that!"

North, not listening, was creating a story as he went. "And you made a deal with the rebels to take you across the mountains. What great PR. It will turn this whole thing around. Ha! I'll make a lot of money off this yet."

"Not when I tell them what really happened."

"By then I will have cleaned up."

"You should stick to running your circus," said Bram, exhausted from his rhetoric.

"I can do that with my hands tied behind my back. No problem. The circus runs itself . . . well, kind of. Everybody knows their job."

Bram knew if it wasn't for the dedicated people who, working together, had given their all to be there, North wouldn't have a circus.

"And besides, I have never heard of an elephant being carried in a plane. Sounds impossible; how can a plane carry an elephant?" asked Bram.

"You're such an idiot"! Err. . .. Whatever. Now you just shut up and listen." He lit another cigarette from between his lips and nearly burned his fingers. Then, he moved up close to Bram's ear to be sure he heard every word. "With the war over, much of the used Army equipment is being sold off, including some planes and field equipment. They had this old jc-130b back loader plane sitting out in the field. It's a smaller version of the ones the Army used to carry small tanks, trucks, you name

it. So, I figured an elephant shouldn't be much of a problem."
His coughing interrupted his point.

"Where was I? Oh! It has seen a lot of action, but they
assured me they had patched it up and it was airworthy. I
offered to buy it if they would fly you and Modoc back to the
States. They said they would supply a pilot and copilot if they
could put some vehicles and equipment on board to be dropped
off in New York. So, we made a deal, and I bought a plane! I'm
not sure I would fly in it though! HA! You get the honors." He
took another puff, then dropped the cigarette on the canvas
floor, snuffing it out with his foot. "When it arrives in New York,
I'll sell it for scrap." He lit another cigarette. "So, get yourself
ready. Modoc too. I don't want any more shenanigans from you
or so help me I'll. . .." He broke into another coughing spell. His
face turned crimson with black edgings. He looked a lot like a
picture Bram once saw of the devil.

"Now look, I can't wait around for you and your
elephant to get better. Gotta go back and see that the circus
revenues aren't misused."

"Time's up, Sir." It was the head nurse. This time she
was accompanied by two, stern Indian Army M.P.s.

"Okay, okay," said North.

"Before I go," he sputtered, "I've got a little surprise for
you. Ya see that big guy over there?" He pointed with a grubby
finger.

Bram rose on one elbow. Standing under the mesh tent
was a huge, as in fat, fellow dressed in a pair of pink and orange
New York style shorts and a tee shirt that read 'I'm special.' With
his arms folded and his legs spread, he looked like he had just
come out of a ward that kept loonies. He wore a felt hat with a
narrow brim over a fat face with jowls. Bram lowered himself
back on the bed.

He wished North would leave so he could get some rest.
"So what? Did you bring him to beat me up?"

"Look, smart ass, I can't risk you running off again.
Malcolm is here to stay—with you."

"Malcolm? His name is Malcolm?" Bram snickered.

"Yeah, he's my nephew. So don't get out of line."

"That figures. What's he going to do then, sit on me?"

Ignoring Bram's remark he added, "Don't underestimate
him. He will do whatever is necessary if you try to escape."

By then the two security men had North by his arms and were heading out of the tent.

North took a big puff on his just lit cigarette then tossed it in a bed pan. Over his shoulder he yelled, "See you and Modoc when you arrive in New York. I'll have Modoc's new trainer with me. I'll expect you to show the new guy Modoc's commands," he yelled over his shoulder.

Bram was exhausted from it all. He turned over in the bed tired of listening to all of North's snide remarks. There was no way he would go back. He had successfully avoided North for years. The thought of losing Mo to another trainer was unbearable. He had to find a way. He dropped off into a delirious sleep knowing his nightmare of the past would be waiting to recount the horrors he had encountered.

CHAPTER 4

It took several weeks for Bram's body to catch up so he could get out of bed and handle mundane things. His mind had allowed some peaceful night's sleep from the terrors he had experienced, and he felt much better.

He had repeatedly asked about Sian, but nobody knew anything about her. His thoughts took him from her falling over the cliff to being lost in the mountains. Maybe even held captive by the rebels. He would never give up hope of finding her.

The doctor had permitted Bram, with the help of a nurse, to sit outside on a veranda next to the hospital where he could relax, read a book, or talk to the locals.

He had just finished his lunch of tandoori chicken, pilau (rice) and a cup of masala chai (tea) when a man in an Army uniform approached. He was a 50'ish, well-manicured officer, sporting a row of hash stripes across his chest. By the looks of them he must have seen a lot of duty. His Army cap tucked under his arm showed a gold eagle on the brim. He scrutinized a tablet he carried and then focused on Bram.

"Are you . . . Bram?" he questioned.

"Yes, I am," said Bram putting his book 'The Origin of Buddhism' in his lap.

"Well, good, I found you."

Just then the head nurse approached.

"Mr. Bram isn't having any visitors, sir. He needs to rest." Her thoughts were of Bram's last visitor.

"I'll be but a moment. It's important," the visitor promised.

"But sir?"

"It's okay, nurse," said Bram.

She left with a disconcerting eye.

"I'm Captain Tyler with the US Army air squadron." They shook hands. "A Mr. North told me to see you and check when you will be able to be on board for our flight back. I'll be flying you and your, err ... elephant to the States."

"Her name is Modoc. Glad to meet you."

"This will be a first for me. Probably should go into the Guinness Book of Records. What in the world ... may I ask, is happening? Are you o.k.? I mean well enough to fly?" The captain seemed totally confused by his assignment.

"Didn't Mr. North tell you?"

"No, he just made a deal with the Army transportation division to fly you and an elephant to New York."

"That's it?" asked Bram.

"Yeah, that's it."

"Well, there's a lot more that goes along with that."

"Like what?"

"Look, if you don't mind, not right now. I must get myself out of this hospital and go see Mosey." Bram was not about to relive the same horrors his nightmares had kept him from getting a much-needed rest over.

"But of course, how thoughtless of me. Maybe another time. I'll look forward to hearing what happened. Get well, and the next time I'll see you will be at the plane. We're just down the road a bit stationed at the American Military air strip."

As he turned to leave, he said, "But, if I may ask, who's Mosey?"

"Mosey? That's Modoc's nickname, sometimes we just call her Mo."

"So where is Mosey now?" asked the captain.

"In a place where they put all the elephants that were shot."

"What? Was she in that caravan of elephants some rebels stole trying to escape over the mountain? I hear many were shot by the Indian Air Force. Bloody shame it was. They just got it wrong." He thought for a moment. "So that's why you're here? You were caught up in that fiasco?"

"Yeah. We sure were," said Bram remembering. "She's recuperating but I don't know what condition she will be in to travel," said Bram. "Once I see her, I will know."

"Gotcha. No problem. Look, stay well, I'm ready when you are." And the captain was off.

Dr. Shah arrived to give Bram a shot, check his heart and read his temperature. "Well, young man, you're feeling well, are you?"

"Much better, Doc."

"It looks like you're just about ready to see your friend, Modoc. But let's give it a couple more days."

Bram was so excited. Never before had he been away from Modoc for that long and he was anxious to see her. The nightly horrors had given way under the doctor's care and treatment and had moved on, perhaps to bring havoc to others in their sleep.

It was early morning when he awoke to someone standing at his bedside.

"Good morning, Bram." It was the head nurse. "You have a visitor."

"I do? Where?"

"He is waiting for you just beyond the garden."

"Thank you."

Wondering who it might be, Bram quickly donned his clothes and walked out into the blazing sun through a small garden area the staff had put together for the wounded to enjoy. He followed the path through a grove of acacia and euphorbia, past a patch of lantana and sweet-smelling oleander shaded by the sacred Keji trees, then he arrived at a Zen Garden. Covering a fairly large area, he marveled at the intricate raked desert sand design and artistically placed boulders. The staff surely had an eye for the beauty of nature. At the end of the path was a small wooden door. Bram entered onto a grass covered circular clearing. In the middle stood a large, ancient, beautiful mimosa tree, its branches full of pink flowers. A large golden Buddha statue sat in front of it. A cool breeze stirred the long tentacle like branches sprinkling its blooms on the Buddha. Stone benchers sat on either side.

The lone figure of a man dressed in a tan tunic and dhoti pants with a matching turban stood at the Buddha. A black band was draped over one shoulder and crossed at his hip where a gold medallion was pinned. His beard and brows were thick and black and blended well with the dark eyes of an Asian. He stood with his hands in namaste. He was flawless.

It took a minute for Bram to gather his senses.

"Ja, is that you?"

He turned.

"Yes, my son, it is I."

"JA! JA! YOU'VE COME!"

Bram ran and embraced him. Ja had been like a father to Bram. He was Bram's mentor, his friend, but more, he was the father of his dear Sian.

"Now, now," said Ja, "come, let's sit a moment." He pointed to one of the benches.

"Ja, it was so horrible! The poor elephants were in shock. They didn't know what to do. And then the planes came and... and—"

"Easy, Bram," Ja said, putting his hand on Bram's shoulder. "Let's not awaken the ghosts of the past. Ah! How horrible all this has been. But you have survived and that is all that matters."

Bram pulled him close.

"Ja, Sian... They can't find her. Do you think she fell over the rim? I am so worried."

"I know, I know," said Ja.

Bram looked around. "Why have we met here? This seems like a place of worship." He felt the black band.

Ja said nothing. He got up and knelt before the Buddha, his hands clasp in a namaste. Bram sensed something was amiss.

"Ja, what are you doing....?"

Then, the realization came to him as a warm shock wave coursed through his body.

"Ja, Ja, no it can't be." Ja stood and embraced Bram.

"My son, it is true. Sian has passed on."

Bram could not hold back his pent-up emotions. The months of not knowing had weighed heavily on him, and now it was like a retching of those hopes and aspirations. They were all dead, never to be realized.

His sobbing seemed to radiate all around him.

Were the plants to wilt, the Buddha to weep, there was no greater sorrow.

"Ja what will I do? I miss her so much. She was my life; we were as one."

Ja thought for a moment. "Bram, I have physically lost my daughter, but I keep her essence in my heart and in my thoughts. She shares with me my life. My thinking of her still keeps her alive."

"But is it not all illusion?"

"But what is illusion, but her thoughts given to you?"

Bram let the tears flow down his cheeks. "But I want to hold her, to kiss her."

"Then go to your dreams, she will be waiting to be smothered by you in your love for her." Ja took Bram in his arms to let the sorrow empty itself of grief and the tears run dry.

"The pain of loss is so unbearable," sobbed Bram.

"Tomorrow will bring a new day, and we will speak of the pain of you losing your loved one and me my daughter. But for now, let us leave our grief here under the mimosa. It will be cleansed and returned fresh and new," said Ja. "In a short time, you will be with your friend Modoc. She will fill your heart with all the love life has to give. So come, she is waiting."

As they left, Bram reached out and touched the Buddha. He felt a warm energy flow and nestle in him, and then he knew she would always be with him to give him the comfort and love of times gone by.

They arrived back at the hospital.

"For now, you must rest. We have a lot yet to do," said Ja.

Ja summoned the nurse who saw to it that Bram was comfortable. She placed fresh cool compresses on his head.

"I can't believe I will finally get to see her. I kept trying to see Modoc since I have been here, but they won't let me. It has been so long since I've laid eyes on her. She needs to see me, feel me touching her. She needs to know that I'm even alive!"

"I am sure she knows. Her connection to you is so strong, she knows when you are able you will come to her. You must trust her as she trusts you. This whole ordeal has been a living nightmare and she and many others of her kind are recovering. So tomorrow, if you're well enough, we will go and see her, and she will be so happy to see you." He smiled; his eyes sparkled in anticipation. "But it has been a long journey for me, and I must leave you now to rest for our walk tomorrow."

Bram clasped his hand, feeling the warmth and affection of the man he so dearly revered. "I am so pleased that you have come. You have given me the strength I have been longing for."

Ja smiled. "Till tomorrow." And with that he backed away, did a namaste, and was gone.

Bram settled into the comfort of his bed. For the first time it felt inviting. Ja had come.

The following morning, Bram, although still quite weak, was ready. The nurse helped him out of bed; the doctor gave him a quick checkup and wished him a good day. The head nurse gave Bram one of the hospital blankets. "This is for your big friend," she said. "The nights have been cold."

"She will be back to thank you in person," Bram said, blessing her with a namaste. "You are too kind."

Ja had come and had been talking to the doctor.

"You still have the doctor concerned about your health. He asked that you don't overdo it."

"I have you to watch over me," Bram said, then smiled.

"Yes, of course, and that I will do."

At the end of the tent was a rack of mahogany walking sticks for those who needed a bit of support after recuperating from their illness or injuries. Ja took one and handed it to Bram. "Our morning's walk could be a bit tiring," he said handing it to a reluctant Bram.

It was time to see Modoc.

CHAPTER 5

A morning chill brought a wet mist that gave life to the spring flowers blanketing the hillsides. No one kind appeared more than another. Marigold, pansy, sunflower, petunia all graced the landscape as far as Bram could see. It reminded him of his days in the flower fields in Germany.

As they walked down the dirt road, Ja noticed an obese man standing off in the bush peering directly at them, his expression one of intense concentration. "Who's that?" he asked.

"That's Malcolm. He is one of North's cohorts. He's supposed to keep an eye on Mo and me, so we don't try to escape. He comes with the package North sent."

"Malcolm? What package? North is here?"

Bram took Ja over to some boulders. "Sit for a moment, there is something I've been waiting to tell you."

Ja sat most concerned about what Bram was about to say.

"North has found me, Ja. I don't know how, but now he wants to take Modoc and me back to New York. Modoc to perform and me to go to jail."

"What! No, no, no, my son, that cannot be."

"But I have no choice. He has already hired a plane to take us back."

Ja rose and paced back and forth. "There has got to be a way, something we can do. When do you leave?"

"In a couple of weeks. The doctor tells me Modoc will be well enough to travel by then."

"Bram, this North is a fanatic to have traveled this far to find you. He is so determined. We must think of a way—"

"There is nowhere to run to, Ja. I have given up and am resigned to go. And with this guy watching every move I take, making sure Modoc and I don't run away, well it's not like I have a choice."

"He doesn't look like he could run very fast," said Ja, sarcastically.

Bram waved to Malcolm. Best to stay friendly at this point. Malcolm waved back and smiled showing his two missing teeth.

"I'll have to deal with him when I get my strength back," said Bram. "I think it will be most difficult." Bram felt an underlying hostility radiate from Malcolm. He was not as portrayed.

"Let's hurry on. I am so anxious to see Mosey," Ja said.

As they walked, Bram noticed three small boys at the side of the road, two seemed to be arguing with the smallest one about the elephants. All were barefoot, dressed in the customary loin cloth and nothing more. The little one was in tears. Not more than five years of age, he wore a red headband holding back a thick mop of black hair. Bram had heard that the children of a nearby village had been assisting in the care of the elephants. These were undoubtedly some of them. Bram saw in the little boy's eyes that he was taken by all the horror and saddened by it all.

"Here, here now, what seems to be the trouble?" Bram asked.

"It's not so," he sniffled. "Mr., Sir, it isn't true."

"What isn't true?" asked Bram.

"They," he said, pointing to his two friends, "say when an elephant dies, maggots come and, and…," he whimpered, having trouble saying what he didn't believe, "eat them and that God can't help them."

The other two nodded their heads. "Yeah, it's true. The maggots and the worms," they confirmed, "eat them all the way up."

Bram could see he would have to use a little diplomacy to satisfy both views. He took them to a nearby grassy knoll where they all sat.

"Now then, what are your names?"

"I'm Aarav," said the little one.

"And you?"

"Muhammad."

"And you?"

"Sai."

"Well, I am pleased to meet all of you. Now then, I can see you love elephants, so my answer is most important." They all nodded their heads in agreement. "Let me say that you are all correct."

A giggle broke out among them.

"No, no, that is impossible," said Sai.

"Well, now let me explain. When an elephant dies here on earth, the maggots and worms come, so you, Mohammed, and Sai, are correct. However, when elephants go to heaven, there are no maggots or worms. They arrive at God's gate whole and as beautiful as when they were born. So, you, Aarav, are correct too."

"Yes, yes!" cried Aarav. The boy could not hold back his tears and wept openly. His tears were now of joy. "See, I told ya," Aarav said.

Bram hugged him and said, "Go now and be happy."

His little voice rang out to his friends standing nearby. "It's ok. God is going to help them," he said. "I told you He would." and he walked away,

"But the maggots do come," said Sai.

"Yeah, but it doesn't matter. Further—"

"You'll see."

And their young minds kept it going all the way down the road.

Watching the discussion, Ja was impressed with the way Bram handled it. "You have learned well, my boy. Very well," he emphasized.

The walk had been a bit far and some boulders under a mimosa tree afforded a place to rest.

"Another mimosa tree, Ja. It must be an omen."

"They are God's inns. Places to rest and leave your worries," said Ja.

It had been a trying time those last few months, and neither man spoke but instead took in the fresh air, the sweet smell of the Mimosa, and the warmth from a giving sun. Ja saw the tears on Bram's cheeks.

Bram spoke. "I believe my love will always be with me, but I can't forget the horror of it all."

"Neither can I, but you must begin to tell your mind what to think," said Ja. "You can't change what happened, nor can you ever forget it, but you can give your mind no room to think it."

"How?"

"You must put up a 'No Vacancy' sign. Think of other things. Don't let it in. The room must be occupied with only the good things in your life."

"Like what?"

"For a start, think of all the things in your life that made you happy. Your growing-up years with Modoc. Things that made you laugh. Your act in the circus. How about your friends in the side show?"

"Yes, I do remember many."

"Like?"

Bram chuckled. "Well, there was the time when Modoc was invited to award the winner of a beauty contest a silver chalice. As this quite lovely girl was handled the trophy, Mo let out a fart. The stage was quiet for a spell and then everyone broke into an uproar of laughter. I shouldn't have let her eat all those berries before show time."

Ja laughed nonstop for quite a while as did Bram.

"You see, for just that moment you were back at a time when life was good. You had put out your 'No Vacancy' sign. Your mind occupied itself with good thoughts. It's just 'thought,' Bram, and it's yours to do with whatever you have, pardon the pun, in mind. The mind is best when it concentrates on one thing at a time."

"Good thoughts," Bram said. "Good thoughts."

Ja interrupted him. "Let us leave our grief here under the mimosa. It will be cleansed and returned fresh and new," said Ja. "In a short time, you will be with your friend Modoc. She will fill your heart with all the love life has to give. So come, she is waiting."

Bram and Ja topped the rise and looked down to the valley below, this place of death where only a few of the elephants were recuperating. The others had passed on. The villagers called it 'The Valley of Stones.' Rows of elephants lay like heavy grey boulders, some never to rise again, others being treated by the same doctor who treated Bram.

The Mahouts were there, each caring for their elephant as one does for a family member. Some wept openly, all applied gels, cleaned open wounds, and gave them the most important thing they had to give, love. Speaking in their ears, saying calm and comforting words they knew would be recognized. Many had gone to 'God's Gate' whole and beautiful and were draped with sisal cloth and richly colored Hindu blankets. Others were still in the healing stage.

An old gaunt Mahout, who had lost his elephant many years earlier, stood as the overseer. He saw to it that the many children from the village and farms cared for the elephants. He had set up a small shack in the middle of the rows where he could pray to his gods for guidance. It consisted of a sisal drape hung over a few tree branches. A brass candle holder which held a half-burned candle sat on a small wooden table and a rolled-up piece of canvas for a bed lay in the corner.

Doctor Shah had graced his palm with many rupees to watch over Modoc and the other elephants and see that the village boys carried enough canvas bags of water to quench their thirst, care for their bodies, clean wounds, wash eyes, and remove poo.

Local farm boys brought enough fodder from the farms to hand feed them. Some had brought healing gels and porcupine quills to dig out intruders on their skin that were not meant to live there. The good doctor saw to it that the children were compensated as well.

Here and there, colorful cloths hung from tall bamboo poles to mark their faith, their home, and their people. Some had written God's words on their elephant's skin and drawn pictures of their deity to bring love and health to them. A small path led them down the rows of elephants where they could walk between those living or not. Bram searched each row hobbling from one to another looking, calling her name.

"Mo, where are you? Mosey, come on, girl."

From the far end of a row where five lay deceased, he heard her chirp, weak, but yes, it was her. Bram dropped his cane and ran as best as he could, sidestepping those who were still recovering and others that had the wreath of the dead placed on their bodies.

Mo lay, like the others, on her side. Wet burlap bags had been placed over her eyes to keep them from burning in the searing hot rays of the sun. When she heard Bram's voice, she searched the air with her trunk hoping to touch the man who meant so much to her.

"Mosey, Dear Mosey!" yelled Bram. He eased himself across her body. A weak belly rumble could be heard. Modoc always let Bram know when she was happy. Either by a tummy gurgle or a bird-like chirp. Bram's tears flowed down his cheeks as he spoke in her ear.

"Mo, dear Mo, I have missed you so much. How is my big girl?" He pulled the burlap aside and laid his head against hers and stretched his arms from ear to ear. He hugged her as best he could. Tearing a piece of cloth from his shirt, he wiped her eyes. He saw her eyes move back and forth until her vision cleared, and then she saw him clearly. She touched his face with the tip of her trunk and tried to rise. Her belly rumbled; her legs flailed.

"No, no dear Mosey. Stay and rest. We'll soon have you get up and about. We have so much to do. So much." Bram noticed his chain around her neck. The doctor had hung it on a piece of rope and put it around her neck. He smiled, feeling it would have let her know he was near.

Ja and Bram, with the help of some village boys, bathed and treated Modoc's wounds. Each bullet hole was washed, medicine applied and, in some cases, rebandaged.

Fifteen sets of hands swarmed over her, massaging her body to help her blood circulate.

But now, she had to stand... or die. No large animal could lay in the same spot for an extended period as their body weight would cut off blood circulation to vital organs and death could come quickly. She, like the others, had to be coaxed to stand. There was no other way. Dozens of mahouts and villagers would gather and physically push, shout, beg, entice with food, anything to get them to stand. To stand was to live. Long, long poles had been brought in and sunk six feet in the ground with ten feet showing. Elephants, once standing, could lean against the poles for support and allow the blood in their body to circulate. In some cases, those that were too weak to stand and were less than two or three years old needed to be rolled over by hand. Elephants at that age could weigh a ton. Trenches were dug running parallel along their back where they laid. Some 12 feet long, six feet wide. Not more than three feet deep. Dozens of mahouts and children all lined up on one side pushing to turn an elephant over with its back in the trench where they would have the balance to roll it over to the other side. A colossal job but necessary.

But Modoc had to stand. Each day she had risen to stand a longer period of time. Adult elephants spent most of their lives standing. And so it was for Modoc.

"Okay Mo, it's your turn. We need to get you on your feet. Come on, girl."

Twenty mahouts and twenty children gathered around her. First to get her in a sphinx position. With the help of many she rocked back and forth two or three times till on the final one she managed to right herself.

"Good girl. Mosey, we're halfway there."

Next came the front. When elephants stand, their front end rises first then the hind section. Everyone formed a half circle and on a command from the old mahout, they pushed. And pushed.

"UP MODOC, UP GIRL. COME ON, YOU CAN DO IT."

To help, Modoc balled up her trunk and pushed it on the ground helping to raise her front. After a few tries she got her front feet up under her, then everybody rushed to her back end and heaved! And heaved. Slowly she rose! The strain caused her to poop! "Look out!" someone yelled. Those near the back end had to move quicky.

"Ha! Modoc. So good. Huh!" Surely thirty pounds littered the dirt.

A chorus of laughter broke out with everyone yelling and praising her for her accomplishment.

"GADAGI! (POOP) Ya! Ya! Good girl. Nice poopy."

Modoc was standing!

The children hugged her legs. They were so proud.

Mo did her chirping. She was happy to be standing too.

Ja came up. He reached up and touched Modoc's head, then pressed his palms together, thanking God for having blessed Modoc and given her life. Bram saw the blanket the nurse had given him lay on her back. She straightened it with her trunk chirping all the time. Far too small but well meant.

"Bram, Modoc is going to be alright. She will just need a lot of rest and care."

Bram sat down between Modoc's legs and looked out over the bodies of elephants. Some had died where they lay, others were recuperating, all were being cared for by their dedicated mahouts and the villagers.

An elephant meant everything to a mahout. It was the means of support for his family. Their well-being depended on it. For one to die was like a member of the family passing. The death would be mourned the same as for a human. They would be buried where they lay.

A few mahouts could not accept that their beloved elephant had died. They were crying, moaning aloud. Bram was choked with tears as he listened to those who had lost their loved one.

"Come, come, now, Sarus, we have to get you home. There are logs to drag, you can have a good swim in the river." He pressed his head to the elephant's and sobbed.

Another cried, "Get up, big one, nothing can hurt you. Everybody is waiting for you. Mama made your favorite treat so come along." He was tugging on its ear.

A few elephants had begun to rise on their own. Others, still moaning in pain, struggled to get their feet under them.

Ja had come dressed to work. His clothes were the same as the workers in the field. When the mahouts realized it was Ja, they gathered to greet him. They circled him, some kissing his feet, a sign of respect, others murmuring God's words. It was Ja's lumber camp that gave their elephants work; work that paid for the family to exist, put food on the table, and gave care when needed. He was their mentor, a father figure, a friend, but above all their Guru.

Ja spoke. "Your hands have God's energy of love and devotion running through them that will heal our friends. For their brothers who are not destined to rise, God's golden gates will open to them and there will be a light to shine the way."

Bram was so pleased to see Ja had come to his people. Such a warm and loving person, he was so like his daughter. He knew Ja would see to it that their needs were met and would arrange for them to return to the village. Many rupees were given out to the mahouts, the villagers and many more to the old overseer. He knew Ja would give those mahouts who had lost their elephant a punk elephant to start anew and to raise as family.

On their way back, Bram told Ja that he and Mo would be flying to America.

"What? How in the world can you fly an elephant in a plane? They don't make them big enough. Besides, how do you think Modoc will take to it? She has never even been close to an airplane before."

"Yeah, I have no idea how she'll react. But I think once she gives it the once over, she'll board."

"What happens if she won't?"

Bram thought for a moment. "I think North would rather have her dead than to not return."

Ja thought it best to change the subject. "Flying? My boy, it is truly a miracle that one so large can be lifted off the ground."

Since Modoc had seen Bram, her healing took on a dramatic change. She stood on her own and even played with some of the children. It was amazing what emotions did for a healing heart. And so, it was a grand day when Bram made the trip with Modoc from the Valley of Stones to the hospital. The staff had set up an area for her where she could rest, get plenty of food and water and be close to Bram. Now that they were together the weeks passed as one. Sometimes the staff noticed Bram sleeping with Modoc.

Each day Bram noticed Malcolm was always there watching, smiling his toothless grin. What did North think I would do? thought Bram, just take Modoc and walk off into the bush?

It was time to leave. Modoc's injuries were well on their way to healing, and the doctor had given his approval to both of them. They were in good shape to make the trip back to the United States.

Mo had enjoyed her stay back at the hospital. Her belly bulged from all the fruit and vegetables the staff had provided. Bram packed what little he had in a sack and hung it around Mo's neck. The staff had assembled to say their goodbyes as had the mahouts who were still recovering or waiting for their elephants to recover. Bram went to each one, his hands clasped together in a namaste.

"These have been sorrowful times, my friends, but now each day will bring a new life, one I am sure will bring back the happiness you once knew. May God be with you." He thanked the staff for their care. "Modoc and I will not forget your devotion to the healing of those in need. Thank you from both of us."

Ja arrived and was there to send them on their way. "Bram, I have brought you and Modoc gifts." He handed Bram a beautiful choon. Made of the finest mahogany with a silver tip, it had the deity 'Ganesh' carved on it to protect and guide Modoc on their travels.

"May it guide her where you choose to go and ease your journey through life," said Ja.

"Oh! Ja, how beautiful. It is a gift I will always treasure."

"And for Modoc, I brought this neckpiece for her to wear." A silver medallion of the Ganesha deity hung from a woven sisal thong. "It can join the one you gave her. It will protect her from harm and keep her in good health as it does you. It is meant to lay on her forehead in time of peril." He turned to Modoc. He, as always, spoke to her as though she understood. In her way, perhaps she did. "My dear friend, although my words go through you, their love remains. And this token of my friendship shall keep you safe and strong, keep you in good health, and protect you from those who wish to do you harm."

Modoc lowered her head so Ja could put the necklace around her neck. She shook her head so the medallion would adjust itself into the right position and chirped her thanks. Bram was in tears having to say goodbye.

"Ja, I go with a heavy heart knowing you will not be there to guide me in this world of turmoil. You are the father of my love, Sian, and I will keep her in my heart forever."

"My son, let her be our link to one another. I, too, will always remember my dear child. When you are in need, summon her and she will let me know your thoughts. The three of us will live on within our love for each other. It can never die."

Ja's words cast a light in Bram and he realized the three of them were bound with their love for each other. He hugged Ja with tears of devotion.

There was no more to be said. Mo raised her foot without being asked. Bram mounted, and they left heavy hearted but with the knowledge of being in God's hands.

CHAPTER 6

Once back on the road, and not sure as to which direction the base was, Bram asked a few children walking on the road which way to go.

"We'll show you if we can have a ride," giggled one of the kids.

"Sure, come on."

Out of the bush came a bunch more, all clamoring to go for a ride. They formed a ladder of kids up the side of Mo, climbing over each other, those who were last were pulled up by those above. When finished, there were kids from Mo's head to tail all cheering and having fun. Off they went, Mo swaying her gait while the kids laughed, some nearly falling, singing a childish song of elephants.

They passed large agricultural farms stretching as far as his eyes could see, all squared off like checkerboards, each a different color according to the crops they produced. Some of the pickers came to the road with their produce: melons, carrots, berries, even onions. The pickers were having as much fun as the children, throwing the veggies up to the ones who could catch it. Mo kept a wary eye for those who might fall to the ground.

The rhythmic ambling of Mo's sway put Bram in a nostalgic mood to reminisce about the years he had been running from North while always looking over his shoulder. Which was worse, he thought, submitting to North or trying to escape? He exhaled a deep sigh, his thoughts turning to Mo. He knew he could never be separated from her. And now, every step brought him closer to a plane that would take him back to a life of misery. Bram looked back and saw Malcolm far behind moving not unlike Mo, his belly rocking out of step with his legs. Was this where his running from North had taken him? To being watched like a prisoner.

As Bram scanned the farms, the thought suddenly occurred to him that maybe this was his last chance to escape. The farms would give him plenty of water for Mo and a huge variety of food to keep her fat and content. Surely when the farmers heard of his dilemma, they would take him in.

Yes! This was his chance. Just ahead Bram saw a dirt road that snaked through the farmlands. A quick look back showed Malcolm, quite a distance behind, ambling along, not seeming to be in any hurry. Up ahead Bram saw a large sign:

UNITED STATES AIR FORCE

BATTALION 46

He made his decision. He would go for it! He stopped at the dirt road.

"Okay, off you go," said Bram, clapping his hands for the children to dismount.

The kids scampered in every direction. Some slid down Mo's side, others jumped, little ones were lifted down. They gave their namaste, then raced away. Modoc clicked after them, swinging her trunk and trumpeting. She had always had a soft place in her heart for children.

Bram turned off the main road and started down a well-worn dirt road that headed into the fields of vegetables. Modoc was in her glory. All the vegetables she could ever imagine stretched out field after field. She couldn't hold it in and let out a trumpet.

An Indian farmer, hearing her trumpet, appeared from around a farmhouse and approached Bram. A thin, muscular, middle-aged man wearing a dirty black turban that hung in shreds and a skirt-like dhoti as dirty as the turban. A thick, unkempt beard was joined by a massive head of long hair hanging down his back. His deep-set dark eyes gave him the look of a wolf. In one hand he carried a long-curved kukri generally used for hacking fruit from the trees. A large black dog walked at his side, his fur covered with burrs and mud. Bram offered his hand.

"Hi, I'm... ."

There wasn't any greeting from the man. "Where did you get the elephant?"

It was asked in a note of distrust. He ran his mud-caked hand over Modoc' s belly. Mo shuddered at the touch.

"She's mine," said Bram.

"Ha! Yours? Na can't be. Where did you steal her?" the farmer asked belligerently.

"I told you, she's mine."

"Where would a young white boy get such a fine animal?

"Maybe you'd better get down," said the farmer while looking quite hostile.

His hand clinched Bram's leg and pulled. Bram drew out the choon Ja gave him from his wrap and stabbed the man's hand.

"Yeow!" The farmer pulled his hand away causing the choon to leave a long thin cut spurting blood across his hand. Furious at being stabbed, he yelled at Bram, "You Gaandu (asshole). I'll have the police after you. Stealing an elephant, have you!"

The dog, smelling blood and sensing the man's anger, lunged at Mo and bit her on the leg. A swift kick sent the squealing canine tumbling far into the brush.

The horde of pickers in the nearby fields heard the commotion and grabbed their rakes, shovels, or machetes and ran to see what was happening. Once they saw the farmer's bloody hand and chest where he had wiped the blood and the bloody choon in Bram's hand, they became a force to be reckoned with. Where before they were friendly pickers feeding the kids, now like a swarm of bees, they grabbed at Bram trying to pull him off Modoc.

"Modoc!" Bram screamed.

It was a call of distress. She knew it well. Blasting an ear-piercing trumpet, she bellowed with rage and whipped around and furiously waded into them. The pickers flew in all directions. Her trunk snapping like a whip tossed bodies and farm tools in the air. But there were so many. From the fields they came like a pack of wolves, circling her, stabbing, beating, raining blow after blow on her body. Hands were reaching up to Bram trying to pull him down.

Then Malcolm appeared. He waddled down the road totally unaware of the fighting until he saw the bunch of pickers trying to pull Bram off Modoc. His first thought was to protect Bram. He launched his three-hundred pounds into the fray scattering pickers in all directions. A mass of bodies and farm tools flew in all directions! Through the tangle of arms and bodies, Bram saw dozens more pickers leaving their work and coming from the fields yelling at the top of their lungs. Malcolm fought back but, even for him, the odds were overwhelming. There were just too many. It was then that Bram feared for his life. It was time to go.

But he couldn't leave Malcolm. Using the choon to guide Modoc, he moved her into the middle of the fracas. Malcolm was pinned down under a swarm of men.

"Mo! Pick him up!"

For a moment she stood bewildered. Which one? She knew what 'pickup' meant but which one? She reached and grabbed one of the pickers.

"No, No! Not that one! Him! Him! " Bram yelled, pointing with the choon.

She dropped the man, moved to Malcolm, wrapped her trunk around his fat body, and picked him up. His weight was not a problem. Malcolm, covered in blood and drained of his strength, hung on.

"Modoc! Now, let's go! Move up! Girl, Move up! "

Using the choon he guided her to a fast pace. She turned, and like a locomotive trashed whoever got in her way; then they were out of there. It was a good distance to the Air Force base sign before they could catch their breath. Bram looked back to learn nobody was chasing them.

"Easy, girl," said Bram.

Modoc slowed to a stop at the side of the road. She was still holding Malcolm in her trunk.

"Put him down, Mo."

She set him down on a grassy knoll where he sprawled out on his back exhausted. Bram, anxious to check Modoc's wounds, carefully slid down her side and put her into a sphinx position.

"You did good, girl, really good," he said, hugging her trunk.

Mo laid her trunk on Bram's shoulder and put the tip of her trunk on his cheek giving him a slurpy kiss! She knew when she had done good. As he walked around her, he ran his hands over the bruises, cuts, some deep, and scrapes. She winced when he touched the deep ones.

"Some of these are pretty deep, Mo. We need to get you to a doctor. They should have one at the Air Force base." He gave her a hug and walked over to join Malcolm on the grass. Malcolm lay belly up, clothes torn, cuts and wounds scattered throughout his body. He was wiping the blood on the lawn.

"Sure, appreciated the help back there," Bram said.

He looked at Bram. "Uncle said not to, uh, let anything happen to you and your elephant. Huh? Yes, well, so I did good, huh?"

"Yes, I'll say. You took a lot of those pickers off Modoc and me. That was quite a tussle."

"Yes, tussle. It was a tussle," he said, playing with the word.

Bram extended his hand. "Well, thanks a lot."

Bram was trying to figure him out. He was of course illiterate and yet cunning. Not a friendly person. More like a robot told to do certain things and oblivious to all else. He grasped Malcolm's fat, sweaty, limber hand that had no grip and it slipped away from Bram's grasp. "Modoc's good. Huh. Yes, she picked me up. Huh?" he giggled.

Bram tore off a piece of his shirt to stop some blood from dripping down Malcolm's shirt, but Malcolm pushed his hand away and threw Bram a look to kill. Bram looked away not understanding the brewing confrontation.

"You sure have been keeping a protective eye on us," said Bram changing the mood.

"Uncle said to watch you. Maybe you will run away."

"Still afraid I might try?" asked Bram.

Malcolm sat up and looked Bram in the eye. "I don't think so." He flopped back on the grass.

"You're right, I won't. Best to just go back and face the music," he murmured to himself.

"North will be proud of you, Malcolm. You have done a good job."

"I keep an eye on you."

"Yes, you have," said Bram.

Bram realized Malcolm no longer needed to be concerned about him. The farmer was the last escape plan and that sure didn't work out. There would be no more running. He was resigned to his fate.

It occurred to him that Malcolm never mentioned the plane. Did North not tell him? Was he planning on going with them? Bram realized he and Mo needed to put as much distance as possible between them and Malcolm. Even though his chances of escaping had gone with the farmers' attack, he felt an impending danger from Malcolm. There was something else. Sometimes people who possess mental irregularities are more dangerous than those with a civil mind. Whatever it was, he made a note to himself to keep a watchful eye on Malcolm.

Bram got up slowly. His bruises and wounds were taking their toll and he noticed some of Malcolm's injuries were bad as well. They were both covered everywhere with bruises and gashes, some deep. Rivulets of blood still oozed from the deeper cuts.

"We had better move on. Our wounds need attention. We can wash up at the Air Force base and find a doctor."

As they started down the road Malcolm asked, "What was that?"

"What was what?

"Back there. The farmer people."

"Well, let's just say there was a misunderstanding."

"So, okay?" Malcolm was struggling to understand.

"Yes, everything is okay." A hundred yards down the road was another sign with an arrow pointing the way to the Air Force base entrance. Half an hour later, they arrived at the base gate. A large, battered sign outside the post read:

USA AIRBORNE COMMAND
O'BRIEN AIR FORCE BASE 21
DIVISION 7
NO ADMITTANCE

The gate to the base was broken and lying lopsided. Mo picked it up and set it aside as they entered.

"Looks like they'll be evacuating the base pretty soon," said Bram to nobody in particular.

Ahead was the giant airplane hangar where Bram saw a number of planes being worked on by Army personnel. Walking towards them was Captain Tyler.

CHAPTER 7

"Well, well, what do we have here? One elephant, one young man and—who is this?"

"Captain, meet Malcolm."

Malcom stood with his customary poise. His belly bursting over his shorts, Legs spread, baseball cap, hair tousled. his torn Hawaiian shirt, and that ingratiating smile.

The captain stood with hands on hips looking at Malcom like he was a rookie just joining the Air Force. He started to speak but only one word came out.

"Amazing," he said.

Then, looking at Bram, he said, "Hmm! Well good lord! You look like you've been in a brawl." And in the same breath, "Good to see you're up and around." He gave Bram a warm handshake. "But this is not how I remember you," he said looking at the extent of his injuries. The captain walked over to Modoc. "I wonder which of you is called Modoc?" he teased. When Mo heard her name, she chirped. "Guess you're Modoc," he said giving her trunk a pat, careful not to touch her cuts. "Now then, what in the world happened?"

"Well, we had a disagreement with a few farmers."

"That's it?" said the captain clearly wanting more.

"One didn't believe Modoc was mine."

"Well, I can understand their thinking, but they shouldn't take matters into their own hands, which it looks like they did. It doesn't look like it ended well. Sorry about that. I'll get a medic to take care of your wounds. Some of those cuts should be looked after right away." He waved to a nearby M.P. "This man can show you where the infirmary is. They'll take good care of all of you and treat those wounds. Ha! Wait till they have to treat Modoc." He laughed walking away.

"Thanks so much," yelled Bram.

Once at the hospital, a group of paramedics went to work on the three of them. Cleaning, patching, giving shots, and suturing.

Bram heard one who was working on Modoc say, "Wait till I tell my wife I treated an elephant. She won't believe me."

"You look funny, Mosey, with all those patches on you. Now, you keep your trunk in your pocket, so you don't touch them! Ya hear me?" Bram ordered.

When Bram would tell her to put her trunk in her 'pocket' she would put it in her mouth and hold it. But the urge was irresistible. The first chance she got when Bram wasn't looking, she explored the bandages by tearing a few off to see what was underneath. When Bram caught her, she quickly 'pocketed' her trunk.

"MOSEY! What did I say?" he admonished, holding the choon over his head in a threatening way.

Mo lowered her head, puffed some air and did a chirp. Being quite coy.

"Okay, no more. Be good."

She knew how to get to him.

A medic walked over to Bram. He carried a rather large syringe and a bottle of medicine.

"I understand you and your elephant will be flying with the captain?"

"Yeah, looks that way."

"Would you hold your elephant while I give her a shot?"

"Should I put her in my lap?" answered Bram.

The medic seemed embarrassed. "Sorry sir, I just mean that animals feel more secure when their owner is with them."

"Well, you are absolutely correct, however why would you be giving her a shot?"

"It's a tranquillizer. Some animals panic when they fly. This will keep her calm."

Bram squinted. "Calm meaning oblivious as to what is happening? That means in an emergency she wouldn't even know me. She would have to act on her own natural behavior."

"Right."

"Like run?"

The medic stood, syringe in hand, in a stupor. "Oops! I see what you mean. Sorry," he muttered and left sheepishly.

Malcom hadn't heard the conversation about flying nor had he mentioned it. He seemed to have no idea that Bram and Modoc would be leaving.

Seeing as Malcolm had still not mentioned the flight, Bram was sure North had not told him. Whatever the reason, Malcolm had no idea that Bram and Modoc were going to fly away in a plane. Best not to mention it, he reasoned.

Their next stop would be in New York City, so it really didn't matter. But the thought kept coming back to him. Maybe a miracle would happen, and they would land someplace before New York, maybe to refuel? A place where he could escape. Bram was a positive thinker, so miracles were always within his reach. Had his life not shown him they were possible? Over and over again miracles had favored them. Best to leave Malcolm behind just in case.

The medics were patching Malcolm when the captain approached.

He took Bram aside. "Now, you see that plane just over there?" he said, pointing to a four-engine Army transport plane sitting off the runway. "That's the baby that's going to take you back and—"

To Bram all planes looked alike. He was more concerned about Malcolm. "Captain," Bram interrupted. "About Malcolm. Sir, he won't understand us leaving without him. I think that could create a problem."

The captain smiled. "Hmm. I understand. He did look a bit weird to me. But don't worry, I'll take care of him. I'll let you know when we board. My co-pilot will see you before we take off. Meanwhile, head over to that hangar," he said pointing. "The plane will be brought there to load equipment. That's where you will board. She's kind of an old relic but seems fit enough. I'll meet you after supper at the plane. You can eat at the mess hall," he said, again pointing, "over there before we leave. There won't be any meals served on this flight."

Once the medic finished with Malcolm, he along with Bram and Mo, headed toward the mess hall.

"What is happening, huh?" asked Malcolm.

Bram didn't know what to tell him. "Just looking," he said. A stupid answer, but to Malcolm it made sense. Bram had no idea what plans North had for Malcom, but it might be best to leave him there. North would set him straight.

It wasn't long before the plane was taxied over to the hanger. Bram, Malcolm and Modoc met it there.

Bram walked Mo up close for her to get a good look at it. Bram was amazed that this plane of solid metal would be able to get off the ground. When Mo saw the four big engines with giant propellers, she backed off, not sure what they were. She tapped the metal with her tusks, ran her trunk over the windows, and felt the tires. When it didn't move or show aggression, she felt it was safe. And when Bram heard her chirp, he knew she felt comfortable with it.

The captain arrived and walked around Modoc. He took Bram aside. "She sure is a big one. Will she be okay? I mean, with the rocking and bouncing movement and all?"

"I don't know, sir. We've never been in an airplane before. But I think so. She didn't mind being in a stormy sea and that was pretty rough riding."

"Another thing. Mr. North said to watch you, that you can be a troublemaker. Is that so?" he said, casting a wary eye on Bram.

"No, sir, Mo and I will not cause you any problems."

"Good. I have learned to like you both. I just want to get you back safely on the ground. Right. Now look, we have never flown an elephant before so it's important that you lock her down tightly. We don't need a loose elephant in the sky. Kapeesh?"

"Kapeesh who?" said Bram.

"It means, 'Do you understand?'"

"Oh! Kapeesh. Yes, I do."

The whine of a motor coincided with the ramp lowering at the back of the plane. Some men drove a jeep and a small tank-like vehicle on wheels up the ramp. Containers, boxes, and Army supplies followed and were tied down. A couple of hours passed before everything was locked down and the captain waved for Bram and Modoc to go in. They walked up the ramp past the tank. Mo, a bit hesitant, stopped when she heard a sound, then squeezed by. Her trunk was into everything she could touch. The jeep was gone over thoroughly, as was the tank, the boxes, and supplies. They all got her stamp of approval before she would pass. They stopped at a narrow door with a sign that read:
COCKPIT

NO ENTRANCE.

Malcolm had hesitated, then followed closely.

Three big, tough looking MPs, as big or bigger than Malcolm, appeared from around the corner and blocked him.

Malcolm tried to push his way through, but the MPs didn't budge.

"Hey, Mr. Bram, they won't let me through." He sounded like a cub missing his mother. "Where are you going?" asked Malcolm. "You can't leave. Uncle said you can't run away. He'll be mad at me." To the lead MP, he said, "I go with them," while pointing to Bram.

"No sir, you come with us."

"It's alright, Malcolm. Your uncle won't be mad," yelled Bram. "Go back to the hospital."

As obnoxious as Malcolm was, Bram saw sadness envelop him. Like a small child being left alone by his parents. They were leaving him, and his uncle would blame him for losing them.

His struggle was short lived. With all his strength he was no match for the trained MPs.

"Mr. Bram, wait for me!"

The MPs got Malcom pointed in the right direction and arm in arm escorted him across the field and out the gate.

"This is a federal facility, sir, so please, do not come back or we'll have to lock you up and charge you with trespassing."

They closed the broken gate, locked it, and left Malcolm standing outside the entrance. He stood clutching the fence peering through the chain link with a sorrowful, bewildered expression on his face.

CHAPTER 8

"Boy o' boy, Mo, it's a lot bigger in here than it looked from the outside."

The door from the cockpit opened. A man wearing the same kind of uniform as the captain approached them.

"Hi, I'm Jack Anderson, the co-pilot," he said offering his hand. "I just want to check that you have everything you need." Then, with a glance at Mo, he said, "Boy, she sure is a big one. Guess the captain told you to ensure she isn't free to move around. How much does she weigh?"

"Around five tons, maybe more."

"Wow. Her moving from one place to another could make the plane shift."

"That's not good?" asked Bram.

"Right, not good at all. There's some heavy rope over there for you to tie her up, however that's done."

"So, you're going with us," stated Bram.

"Yeah. I'll help the captain get us to New York. Look, put her over there and be sure she's tied down good and tight." He pointed to an area a few feet away that had some heavy duty 'D' rings protruding from the floor. "Wouldn't be good to see her roaming about the plane, would it?" he repeated. "I'll check with you later just to be sure she's ready." He thought for a moment. "Are the ropes okay?"

"They're fine. A bit small but they'll do the trick," voiced Bram.

"How's that?"

"She could break most any rope put on her had she a mind to," offered Bram.

"Well, let's hope she's happy being here," said Jack a bit concerned.

"Jack, why are there Army vehicles on board? Mr. North would have no use for them."

"You're right, they're not his. He made a deal that if we can deliver them to a New York Army base, the Army would lower the price for us flying you guys. Gotta go."

"One more."

"One more what?"

"Question."

"Shoot."

"Why is an American Air Force base here in India?"

"We helped India win the war over the rebels."

"But they didn't."

"Well, I guess it was kind of a truce. Anyhow, we're wrapping up and going home. Oh! By the way, when we take off there will be a lot of noise until we get airborne. Once we're up, the noise will lessen, and the ride should be steady and quiet. Be sure you're strapped in when we start to move. Okay?"

"Okay," said Bram.

Jack ran his hand over the cabin walls, then stamped a foot on the well-worn floor. "By the looks of her she must have seen a lot of action."

"What do you mean?" said Bram.

"Nothing. Best I move along. Need to complete a checklist before we can leave, which should be in about half an hour. I'll check back with you before takeoff."

Jack smiled and disappeared into the cockpit. It gave Bram an odd feeling the way he had looked at the plane, but no matter, he assumed Jack knew his job. Bram fastened the four ropes around each of Mo's legs quite loose but tight enough to keep her in check. Apparently, someone had the foresight to put some hay bales in the plane for her. He broke open one and put a couple of sheaves near her and put some oats and barley in a container up front where she could reach them if she got hungry. Ten twenty-gallon jugs of water were lined up along the wall. Mo had settled into her new quarters. With the food and water within reach, she was content.

A car horn honked! What? Bram thought he was hearing things. Again, the horn. He turned around to see Malcolm sitting in the storage jeep. He didn't wave, his smile was gone and in its place was the Malcolm who had the same look when Bram tried to wipe the blood off his clothes. Bram was quite leery of approaching him. He knew he was roughed up earlier by the MPs and perhaps he was there to take revenge. How he managed to get on the base without being seen and climb into the tied down jeep concerned Bram but with the plane about to leave he had to find out what Malcolm wanted.

Bram cautiously went over to the jeep.

"Malcolm, what in the world are you doing here?"

"You're running away. I can't let you do that."

Bram noticed he was sweating. His Hawaiian shirt was soaked. Yet, it was a cool day. "Didn't Mr. North tell you he rented this plane to fly us home?"

"No, you're running, and I can't let you." Malcolm opened the door of the jeep and stepped out. His face was distorted, his eyes wandered independently. "He said. . . he said, I should do whatever I want to stop you."

"Malcolm, listen to me. Mr. North told me to fly in this plane. He knows."

"He didn't tell me. He didn't tell me," Malcolm repeated. "So now you have to come with me. We have to go."

Malcolm grabbed Bram's arm. His big fat chubby hand was like a vise. Bram realized he was dealing with a sick person. He felt maybe the trip to India, the responsibility of watching him and Modoc, and then being escorted off the field, along with his limited mental capacity may have been too much for him and he snapped. But right now, Bram had his hands full. He glanced back at Modoc. She was busy with her bale of hay and had no idea what was happening. He tried to call her, but the whine of the plane's engines coupled with the propellers revving up smothered any hope of her hearing his call. Bram looked around for something to fight off Malcolm, but everything had been battened down. As the ramp started to rise upward, Malcolm tightened his grip on Bram's arm.

"Hurry, we have to leave," said Malcolm.

Bram was not a small man and was strong and versatile, but struggle as he did, he couldn't break the grip Malcolm had on him. They got to the ramp as it was partly closed. Malcolm pulled Bram to the floor trying to squeeze through the opening before it closed. Bram saw they wouldn't make it. The steel ramp would crush them both. He grabbed a D-ring bolted to the floor used to secure cargo and held on with all his strength; he was just in time as the ramp slammed shut with a metallic bang.

Malcolm panicked, sweat poured from his body, his face glowed beet red, and his shirt was sopping wet. He got up and dragged Bram with him. Bram fought to stay upright trying to grab whatever came his way. If he managed to grab hold of something, Malcolm would beat his hand till he let go. There was no way he was going to stop him. Malcolm was possessed. The roar of the propellers revving drove him to become even more determined. He pulled Bram back along the cabin wall to a side door and opened it. The cool breeze hit them as the plane taxied down the runway. Malcolm looked out of the opening as the plane increased speed. The ground was ten feet down, and Bram knew Malcom was going to jump and pull him along!

"Malcom, stop! Don't do this. Let go!" Bram fought with all his strength, hitting Malcolm with everything he had. He had to get loose from the maniac's grip or he would be dragged out of the plane. Malcolm tightened his grip on Bram and jumped!

From behind them, two strong arms grabbed Bram and held him securely as Malcolm's grip slipped away and he fell onto the runway!

Jack had come for his final check before takeoff and saw what was happening.

They both lay on the floor exhausted.

Jack was out of breath. "Who the hell was that?"

"North' s nephew," panted Bram trying to catch his breath. "A real psycho."

"Why was he pulling you out the door? Both of you could have been killed."

"I know. Thank God you were here. I would have fallen out the door with him had you not come along. Thanks so much, Jack. That was too close."

"Sure, no problem. Happy to oblige." Jack smiled as he stood, dusting himself off. "That was the weirdest thing I've ever seen." He pulled the door closed.

"You think he made it? He must have hit pretty hard," said Bram.

"If the wheels didn't catch him, he probably made it. Maybe a lot of bruises. He was a pretty big guy."

"North told him not to let me leave," offered Bram.

"Why would he do that?"

"Long story for another time."

"Glad you're ok. What would Modoc have done without you?" laughed Jack.

"Let's not go there," Bram said.

"The captain's probably wondering where I'm at. Better get in your seat," he said, as he headed toward the cockpit. "See you later." He hesitated. "As soon as we make the turn onto the end of the runway, the captain will stand on the brakes and the engines will rev. Then he'll release the brakes and we'll head down the runway and lift off."

Bram took a deep breath, shook his head, got up, and left hoping all was well with Malcolm. He really bore him no ill will.

"How ya doing, Mosey?" asked Bram giving her leg a big hug.

Modoc stopped eating and gave a 'what was that for' look. She responded with a low grumble and rubbed her head against him, nearly knocking him over, then went back to eating. She seemed to be doing just fine. She, like Bram, had no idea what being in the air was all about. Bram noticed there were times when she would stop eating, holding her head up high as though she heard something, then trumpet which vibrated throughout the plane. A loud ratchet sound of the engine giving full power sounded for takeoff. Then another. Bram felt tinges of panic course through his body as reality set in. He had no idea how this monster of a plane could leave the ground but threw it off knowing he had no choice in the matter.

Bram held Mo's ear giving them both security as he looked out the window. He saw a quick flash of flames and smoke, then a popping noise from the engine as the propeller spun faster and faster causing the plane to vibrate as it stood still. He heard it being repeated with the other three engines. Modoc stopped eating, wrapping her trunk around Bram as he spoke to her, but the noise was too loud. Then the plane moved. The popping sounds stopped and Mo, seeing that all was okay, relaxed and went back to chewing a much too big chunk of hay.

Bram sat in the one chair available and buckled himself in as the plane moved faster down the runway. They were on their way. The realization of going back, probably back to a prison cell, leaving Modoc to the whims of some trainer who wouldn't know anything about Bram's teaching method, was all too much to think about. His main concern was Modoc losing her patience and hurting the trainer.

The plane interrupted those thoughts as it moved faster down the runway. The noise from the engines was deafening as it picked up speed and raced down the airstrip; trees and bushes whizzed by, then became smaller as the plane took to the air. Modoc stood quite uncertain as to what was happening. Bram saw the airport zipping by, then moments later they flew over farmlands, Stone Valley, and as they cleared the tent hospital, he thought he saw people waving as the plane gained altitude. Within minutes all went quiet. Only the steady hum of the engines was heard. Bram couldn't believe they were up with the clouds. Below he saw forest and a few farms. Modoc had stopped eating and was watching the clouds. Some were solid white, others grey and some in the distance were black. Good fun.

Bram wondered what she could be thinking. Surely these were not the same clouds she saw while looking up from the ground. One never knew. A heavy droning noise filled the air space inside the plane. Bram watched as Mo's eyes fluttered and closed for a brief down time. He knew elephants slept for short periods, then they were up and started eating again. Perhaps it was the hum of the engines, but it brought about his own drowsiness as he dozed off for the first rest he'd had in quite a while.

He had no idea how long he'd slept when he was awakened by a sudden jolt.

CHAPTER 9

Modoc finished her barley and was munching on the last mouthful when she felt the plane lurch. Then again. Her ears went straight out. She spread her legs to balance and coiled her trunk ready for the hidden enemy who did that. She had never been in a place that was strong enough to jolt her like that. The third lurch knocked her off balance. She landed against the side of the plane causing it to bulge out from the impact. Fortunately, her leg ropes prevented her from going any further or she would have pushed the cabin wall out. Bram woke and jumped out of his seat. Taking hold of Mo's ear, he ran his hand over her head to comfort her.

"Easy, girl. It's okay," he said, not knowing what had just happened.

One minute the plane was riding smoothly, the next it was jumping all over the place. Bram looked at the cabin wall where she had hit it. He knew if her ropes had broken it would have given way. What a horrible thought. God forbid.

"Come down, Mo, down."

He figured if she was down, she couldn't bump the wall and he wouldn't have to worry about her losing her balance, but she didn't want to. Coming down gave her no line of defense. She couldn't protect herself from a sphinx position. She would be defenseless.

"Modoc, come down!" Bram said with a much stronger voice. He felt her body resisting. The next jolt threw her against Bram knocking him across the floor. That scared her. Never had she seen him hit like that. Maybe she thought she had done it. Down she came, butt first then the front.

Jack came out of the cabin staggering, trying to keep his balance.

"Get yourself tied down, we're in for a rough one."

"What happened?" Bram yelled over the engine noise.

"We lost an engine, and another is about to go." He was in sheer panic. "We're going down, so hold on." He disappeared back into the cockpit and the door slammed shut.

Going down? Down where? How? Bram had never heard this kind of jargon. He was petrified. The plane started to fall and went into a steep dive.

Bram yelled at Mo, "Lay down, Mo, hurry! All the way."

Using the choon, he pulled her over, laying her in a flat position. He pushed the hay bales around her hoping they would help protect her. Bram was scared. More scared than he had ever been. He thought, what happens when the plane hits the ground? We will all be at God's Gate. Through the window, he saw smoke and fire billowing from an engine. The ground was whirling around coming closer as the plane seemed to be trying to level itself out.

For an instant, Bram saw the tip of a wing hit the dirt and skid; that sent everything spinning, spinning, spinning as the plane met the ground hard enough to lift Mo off the floor and for Bram to hit the ceiling. The jeep came loose and slammed into the cockpit wall just missing Modoc as it passed. Containers and equipment flew bouncing off the cabin walls. Mo panicked. She tried to get up but was jostled around, knocked from side to side. Some of her ropes broke; bales of hay were lifted off the floor and slammed into the wall. Bram felt himself being lifted, suspended in the air for a moment, then thrown against Modoc.

"Mosey! Mosey!" Then all went dark.

CHAPTER 10

Bram woke to smoke and fire. Everything was in disarray. Mo stood over him thumping her trunk against the floor, a sign of terror. A yellow liquid dripped from her trunk; streams of blood ran down her side, her eyes bulged out with fear. She let out an earth-shattering trumpet. She was terrified. Her body shook uncontrollably. Fire raged from several engines with smoke so thick it was hard to see let alone breathe. Bram's first thought was they had to get out of the plane. Quickly!

A glance showed Mo had broken all her ropes but one.

Bram needed her to break that last rope.

"Move up, Modoc! " Bram shouted. "Now, Mo, move!"

She shook and made sounds not heard before. "Move up, girl," he ordered again. She moved up till she came to the end of the rope and stopped. She had never of her own free will broke her restraint. Bram grabbed her ear.

"Move up, Mo, move up. Now pull, Mo, pull!"

That got her attention. She knew what pull meant from the logging camp. She lay into it, straining till the strands broke and she was free. Now to get out. The jeep lay on its side against the cabin door. Containers, broken hay bales, Army supplies, and debris lay scattered everywhere. The smoke was getting thicker. Then he remembered the captain and Jack.

He moved to the jeep and tried to push it over. It was stuck, wedged solid against the door. "Come, Mo, over here. Give it a push." Mo ran her trunk over the jeep.

She was shaking and disoriented. All she knew was Bram's voice and touch.

"Push, girl, push it! " She put her head against the jeep, grabbed a wheel with her trunk, then put her weight into it and pushed. The jeep gave way and rolled to one side. The cabin wall splintered, cracked, and gave way. The door broke open and inside were the captain and Jack, both unconscious.

Bram went to the captain and tried to lift him out when he came to.

"Captain, get up, please, hurry!" Bram grabbed his arm and helped him stand. "This way, I've got ya, hurry up."

Half-dazed but with Bram's help, he staggered out the broken door. Jack was slumped in his seat. Bram left the captain and went to Jack and tried to lift him up.

"Come on, Jack, we've got to get out of here." Blood dripped from his head, and he was unconscious. Bram grabbed Mo's ear.

"Over here, Mo, quick." Only Mo's head could fit in the cabin.

"Pick him up, Mo. Good girl. That's right."

In the circus, she used to pick up dancing girls, and she had picked up Malcom, so she knew what to do. She wrapped her trunk around him and lifted him out of his seat, then backed out, dragging him over the destroyed door. Once clear, Bram looked for a way out. They had loaded from the back of the plane which was now a crumbled pile of equipment and an overturned tank that made it impassable. The whole back of the plane was burning. Thick, black smoke filled the cabin making it impossible to see. Bram felt dizzy, coughing, choking. He knew if they didn't get out soon the smoke would do them in.

Mo had set Jack down and was standing over him shaking, in a complete state of shock. The captain was coming around, realizing what had happened. Bram noticed smoke being sucked out of a crack in the cabin wall.

"Mosey girl, over here."

She was defecating, urinating, and totally bewildered from the crash. The smoke was far thicker up around her head, so she could barely see him. But hearing Bram's voice she turned to him.

"Over here, that's it. Put your head down, Mo."

There were broken windows with sharp pieces of glass protruding. He ran his hands over her head gently pushing her down, moving sideways to adjust to the wall away from the windows. Bram felt her trembling. She couldn't see Bram, but she felt his hand and listened to what he wanted her to do.

"Head down, Mo. "

She put her head down and felt the wall in front of her. She was directly in line with the seam in the wall.

"Now, Mo, go for it. Push! Mosey, push!" At first, she just stood there in a daze, then feeling a nudge from Bram, she pushed. The seams started to crack open. "Again, Mo. Push! Hard!"

This time she used her tusks and gave it a big push. The cabin wall gave way and she burst out into the bright sunlight. Bram and the captain followed, half-dragging Jack out of the plane where they collapsed on the ground coughing and choking.

Mo staggered and inhaled great gulps of air; her body trembled as she struggled to keep her balance, but they had made it. All were safe.

CHAPTER 11

They tumbled out of the plane coughing and wheezing from the smoke, then laid there too exhausted to move. Bram lay at Modoc's feet trying to catch his breath. He stood and laid his head on her shoulder and talked soothingly, stroking her head and her trunk saying all the good things he knew she liked to hear.

Mo stood quivering, taking in huge gulps of air. Her trunk hung limp, body covered in ash and cuts with blood running freely down her side and head. A large wound showed on her upper cranium from where she had hit the wall, the place where the doctor had said was only cartilage and bone. Thank goodness for that. Occasionally she would stagger and catch herself.

"You did good, Mosey. Yes, you did. You are the best elephant in the whole world." She belly-rumbled and with effort, lifted her trunk to his shoulder, and drew him closer to her head till they touched. Her eyes roamed, looking. So, loving, caring.

Both the captain and Jack were coming around. Bruised and bloody, they got themselves up and surveyed the crash. The captain said, "Let's move away. It could explode."

The plane was giving its final death quivers. Small explosions were blowing the storage boxes clean through its hull. Jack went back into the still smoke-filled cabin, grabbed a fire extinguisher, and started to put out the remaining fires.

"Jack, what are you doing?" coughed the captain.

"Just putting out the fires," he said.

"Why? You think we're going to fly her out of here?"

Jack, realizing how impossible that was, sat down on the ground and let the extinguisher slip from his hand. "Yeah, sorry, I wasn't thinking. Just my instincts kicking in."

The captain got up and walked among the debris kicking a few things he remembered.

"What a mess," he exclaimed.

The surrounding area resembled a war-torn battle zone with debris scattered fifty yards in every direction. The bulk of the plane lay broken, the shell split in pieces like a scattered jigsaw puzzle. One engine had come loose from the wing, its propeller embedded in the ground. The right wing, still intact to the body, had dug a ditch into the ground and scraped a path for a hundred yards on its aborted landing.

"Captain, you are one terrific pilot. How you brought the plane down like you did was a miracle," said Bram having a flashback of when he hoped for a miracle to escape.

"Yeah, well, we almost didn't make it. We were just blessed." His voice was raspy from inhaling the smoke.

"Yes," said Bram thinking of Ja and his blessing. "What do you think caused it?"

The captain thought about it. "Had to be a malfunction in the system. One engine followed the other. Hate to say it, but it was probably faulty maintenance. They just missed something. The mechanics are used to working on jets. There is no checklist for these old timers."

Bram was concerned about Modoc. "Wish we had some water to give Mo," voiced Bram. "When I went for the extinguisher, I saw a crushed jar that still had some water in it. All the others were smashed along with a few thermoses of coffee," offered Jack.

"Just before the engines conked out, I saw a small river coursing through the upper side of the desert," said the captain.

"Really?"

"Yeah, had a few trees and what have you, on the banks. Kind of pretty. It's too far for us to travel to, maybe a couple hours walk, and beside I'll make sure the rescue plane will have enough water for all of us."

"She's totally dehydrated. Do you think the plane's fire extinguishers have any water in them?" asked Bram.

"No. They only carry chemicals," replied Jack. "Nitrogen and Carbon Dioxide. But wait a minute. I just thought of something." Taking a gulp of air, Jack disappeared back into the plane and emerged minutes later with a crate of Cokes. "There's a stack of these in the storage area. Will she drink Coke?"

"Sure, no problem. The kids in the circus were always giving her their Cokes. They liked to watch her hold the bottle with her mouth, raise her head, and drink."

"Let's get the crates out of the plane; the heat could make them explode."

The men disappeared back into the smoke-filled cabin and one by one carried the crates out of harm's way.

"They're all cans, no bottles," confirmed Jack.

"Hmm! Okay," said Bram. "Captain, if you guys open them and get them to me, I'll pour the Coke in her mouth. Just keep them coming."

Mo knew. She didn't hesitate for a minute. She had her trunk up and her mouth opened even before they got the first can open. She didn't stop her chirping from the time the first Coke hit her tongue, followed by a belly gurgle after the last can.

Jack raised his drink. "A toast."

The others joined him.

"To Modoc and her two-legged friend for saving our lives."

Cans were clunked, Modoc trumpeted for more.

"The sugar in the Coke will give her some added energy as well," said Bram. He stopped at the second crate. "That's enough for now. It will help to sustain her till she gets some water."

"When I reach them on the radio, I'll ask that that they bring some. So, is everybody alright?" asked the captain wiping some blood from a cut on his forehead."

Both Bram and Jack had cuts and gashes, some with blood still dribbling down their faces and arms. Their clothes were ripped and smeared with blood, but nothing was serious.

"We're fine, Cap. Right, Bram?" asked Jack.

"Yeah, nothing a hamburger and a cold beer wouldn't cure."

"And a hot bath," added Jack.

"How about Modoc?"

"Well, she's still in shock but she'll be okay."

"And just as the farmers' cuts were healing."

"Yeah. She has cuts and bruises everywhere and a case of diarrhea. The worst is this large gash on her forehead where she pushed the wall out," he said as he ran his finger over the wound.

He would remember to clean it out the first chance he got. Modoc's shivering had stopped but her trunk still hung loose. The tip lay on the ground, her body slouched. She was exhausted and still in shock.

"She'll be fine in time," said Bram.

The captain got up and went over to her. He wrapped his arms around her head. "I have never hugged an elephant before, but, Mo, you are not just an elephant because no other animal could have done what you did."

"She had someone helping, Captain," said Jack. "She had Bram."

"I know, but in the middle of all this, she didn't just go crazy and try to get herself out. Instead, she stayed, listening to Bram, helping others. No, I'm sorry but what she did was a human emotion. She has something inside her that thinks like us."

"I know what it is," voiced Jack.

"What's that?"

"She has an undying love for Bram. She would do anything for him."

"You two make a good pair, Bram. I don't know what to say. You guys saved our lives." The captain couldn't contain himself and gave Bram a hug. Bram, his face a bright red, was totally embarrassed.

"I'll give you mine later," laughed Jack.

"We are so lucky to have crash-landed here," said the captain, changing the subject.

"In a desert?" said Bram.

"Yeah, it's damn near flat. No hills. If there had been any, we wouldn't be standing here now."

"Do you have any idea where we're at?"

"We were flying in Northern India over the Sinar Desert."

"What?" said Bram. "You mean we're not in America?"

"Good Lord, that's still a long way off," offered the captain.

"But we were flying for a long time."

"Just two hours. We're in the north of India. It's a big country. We landed in a pretty desolate spot I might say."

"So now what?" asked Bram.

"Once I get through to the Army Transportation Emergency Office, they'll arrange to have a plane sent out. Shouldn't take them too long to get here. We'll have to clear a spot for them to land."

"But, Captain, there is nothing out there but flat sand," said Bram.

"Many years ago, when I was in training, a colleague of mine had to force land in a field just outside the city. He radioed in that he had found a flat area and was on his way down. He never made it."

"So, what happened?"

"Although the area from above looked smooth, it turned out to be full of gopher holes, not deep, but enough to drop a wheel into it. Wouldn't notice it from above. From the air it looked like a green field, perfect to bring his plane down."

"What about the pilot?"

"Pretty banged up but eventually pulled through. Since then, I check everything. Out here there are sink holes bigger the any gopher hole."

"How do you know that, Cap?"

"Any country as arid as this can have them. Best to check in the morning. Can drop the wheels of a plane instantly. They would be a pilot's biggest concern."

"I'll check first thing in the morning," said Jack.

Night had fallen hours earlier, so they decided to build a fire to warm themselves against the evening chill and change into some clothes they found that hadn't caught fire. Bram and Jack went into the plane and gathered seats, crates, and anything that would burn and dragged them out to start the fire burning. In a box with miscellaneous tools, Jack found a machete to chop the wood items into pieces.

"Guess I'll give a shout to the base now," said the captain as he headed for the plane.

Bram asked, "Can you see if that man who fell from the plane is alright?"

"Sure."

Minutes later the captain came out of the cockpit. "I couldn't get through to them. The radio is damaged but not enough to keep it from operating. Guess you'll have to wait to find out your friend's condition."

"He's not my friend," Bram said. "But he was just doing his job."

The captain thought for a minute. "I think it's the area we're in. I'll try later. On second thought, they couldn't land till morning anyhow. No landing lights here."

"They will need to get in touch with Mr. North. After all, it's his plane," said Jack.

Bram, on hearing that they were going to call North, experienced shivers down his spine. He had resigned himself to going back and being sent to jail. North would give Mo to another trainer to beat her into doing a performance. But hearing Jack say it brought back the reality that it was really going to happen. Then out of the blue came a thought. A new one. Escape! He had thought that the farmer incident would be his last chance to escape but now…just maybe.

Escape into the desert. Of course. Could a thought be a miracle? Why not. At the least it would be the messenger. His mind raced. He would load Modoc with just the essentials to get to the river the captain spoke of. Once there, he would stay until Modoc got her strength back. Then they would head for the mountains. Yes, maybe the desert escape was the miracle he had asked for. It posed many dangers, but Bram was willing to take the chance. Better than going back, he thought. He couldn't speak for Modoc, but he felt the choice he was making was one she would agree with. Bram stood looking long and hard toward the distant mountains. High and majestic, they looked farther than they had before. But they were his freedom. Could they make it? Only God knew. He would be sure Modoc got all her strength back before leaving. With the mountains would come forests and surely water, some wild foods, berries, and many eatable plants. He would know what to eat by watching Mo. She would know. He figured if they walked mainly at night, they could avoid the heat.

And, what about Modoc? In her condition she couldn't travel very far. If they reached the river, the captain said he saw greens on the bank, and with the river they would have water to drink and bathe in. He could cleanse all her wounds, and, above all, it would give her time to relax and get her strength back. It sounded close enough for them to make it. Going back to face North was not going to happen.

"No way," he said aloud.

"What?" said the captain.

"Nothing. I was just thinking out loud."

Bram knew he and Modoc had to leave before the rescue plane arrived.

"You know," said Jack. "This Mr. North guy is going to have kittens when he finds out his plane is totaled."

"Kittens?"

Jack laughed. "It's just an expression. It means he is going to be quite upset." He passed out blankets he found in the plane. "Nights in a desert can get pretty cold."

As the fire burned low, Bram waited till the men were asleep, then quietly got up and moved Modoc to the other side of the fire so as not to wake the men. He whispered to Mo, "Down, girl."

Once down, he dragged hay bales out of the plane and started to tie them to her side.

"What in the world are you doing?"

A voice from the dark jolted Bram. He turned around to see the captain standing in the shadows watching him load Modoc.

"We ... have to leave," said Bram, a bit choked up by the captain's appearance.

"Leave? You're joking, leave and go where?"

"Uh, toward the mountains," he said.

"Why would you do that? A plane is coming that will take us to the States."

"I know, but we can't go."

"Well, I can't let you go," said the captain. "You are my responsibility. I was told you might pull a stunt like this; and besides, why would you want to?"

"I just have to."

Bram felt he had betrayed them. But what to do?

"I don't understand. Why?" asked the captain.

"It's a long story, sir."

"There is nothing you could say that would allow you to leave."

Their talking woke Jack. "What's going on, guys?" he asked.

"Bram wants to leave," said the captain.

"What? You're kidding."

"Yeah, I can't let him go. I can't figure out why he would want to leave in the middle of the night and go out in that god forsaken desert."

"Hey, Bram, the Captain's right. Why would you?"

"It's a long story," repeated Bram, a bit shaken by being caught.

"You said you would tell me what happened at the mountain gorge," said the captain. "Is that part of it?"

"Yes."

"Well, you're not going anywhere, so you may as well tell us why."

"Yeah, it's not like we have anything else to do," said Jack.

"So out with it," said a much-irritated Captain.

"I have to start at when I lived in Germany."

They sat near the fire, each with a can of warm Coke, and for the next couple of hours Bram told of his life since leaving Germany.

CHAPTER 12

"My father, Josef, worked for the Wunderzircus in Germany. He was the head animal trainer in charge of all the animal acts. But his specialty was the elephants. There were three. Emma, Tina, and Krono in the act and he would perform with them twice a day.

"Father had his own elephant, a very large bull (male) by the name of Brutus. Because he was a bull, father brought him up with a lot of affection, the same training he taught me on how to raise Modoc. He knew if not controlled at an early-stage Brutus could become dangerous. Brutus was kept in our barn along with a few goats and sheep during the cold winter months. Father was training him in the hopes of using him in the circus someday. During an exceptionally cold winter, North asked to keep his elephants in our barn to keep warm. My father, feeling sorry for them, said alright."

"What about the other circus animals?" asked Jack.

"They were all cared for. The big cats would stay as they worked in the arena and their meat was stored in the freezer units, the bears were easy to care for in the winter and the chimps and other small animals stayed with their trainer. Their cages were in his trailer where he lived.

"So, you see, that really only left the elephants."

"Okay, go on with your story."

Bram continued. "Brutus was enamored with Emma so one night he broke his chains and found his way to Emma. Theirs was a love affair and two years later Modoc was born. North claimed the baby was his because he owned Emma, and my father claimed it was his because he owned Brutus. The battle raged on for some time until an agreement was reached. Father would agree to house all of North's animals during the cold winter months. He would feed, water and care for them if they got sick. For that, the baby was his. An expensive situation. When my father died, North claimed that Modoc was his. He felt since my father died the agreement was void. I told him that my father's wishes were now mine as stated in his will. To this day he feels that Modoc is his."

"Can't he get another elephant?"

"Yes, of course, but it's like my father never died. North carries on like he is still alive. He feels he must win even after death. I can't let that happen nor will I give up Modoc to suffer his brutal ways. He is mentally deranged and is still vindictive. And now that my father is gone, he simply wants to win."

"So that's the reason he came here," Jack said.

"Yeah, he wants Modoc back. He's a sick man, he is. Anyhow, when I was born, Emma gave birth at the same time my mom had me."

"So, you two were born on the same day," said the captain.

"Yes, practically the same hour. My father named the newborn, Modoc, after a famous elephant from the past. We grew up together. She's my best friend. When she was big enough, I used to ride her into the nearby forest. There was a field of wildflowers where we would play chasing birds, hares, whatever. I even met my first love while riding Modoc. Gertie, a Swedish girl of Nordic descent. I'll never forget the first time I saw her. She was radiant, picking flowers in a blue cotton dress which accentuated her blue eyes and long blond hair. She heard Modoc stomping along, turned, looked right at us, and smiled." He stopped for a while revisiting those days in his mind's eye.

His eyes welled up holding back a tear of remembrances. "Yeah, those were fun days."

"I can imagine," said Jack, smiling.

"During one of those freezing winters, I remember my father called me to his bedside.

"Yes, Papa. You 're not feeling well?"

"My son, I am tired and need to rest. You must now take my place and do the elephant act."

I was so young, but my father had taught me well, so I told him, "Yes, Papa, now don 't you worry. I can do it."

"Bram, my boy, Modoc is young and learning. She is a very special elephant. Promise me you will take care of her. She will need you to be by her side."

"I will, Father. I promise we will always be together." Papa passed away that winter night."

A tear fell from Bram's watery eyes. He took a deep breath.

"It sounds like your father was a caring man," said Jack.

"And a wonderful father," added Bram. "He is dearly missed. I never saw North after that.

"I kept Modoc with the other elephants, so I guess he thought she was his.

"When the circus closed its doors for the winter, other than keeping North' s elephants, the performers and most of the sideshow people used to come by, build a small fire inside, and sit around keeping warm telling stories. It was good fun.

"There was Appelle, the clown, Hercules, the strong man, Marigold, the torso lady, Lilith, the fat lady, String, the thin man who also doubled as the tall man, Mesmera, the snake lady and Serina, the acrobat. She used to hold onto Mo's tusks and let her spin around. It was so fast I was always worried she would come off. There was never a warmer, friendlier group of people. They all looked out for each other."

"I thought only male elephants had tusks," said Jack.

"That's true, but every so often, a female would come along carrying them. They were never very large. I often wondered why, I guess down the line her genes got crossed. But they come in handy sometimes."

"And a torso lady?" asked Jack. "How did she function? I assume she didn't have any appendages below her waist. I mean, well, it must have been difficult."

"She never complained. She had an Indian companion who took care of her needs. Her name was Moon Spirit."

"What an interesting life you have led," said the captain, putting some more chairs on the smoldering fire. "But so far you haven't given me a reason to go tramping off into the desert."

Bram continued. "Everything was going fine till Gobel, the circus owner, died and the circus was sold to Mr. North."

"This North guy is the one who hired us to take you to New York," said Jack.

"Yeah, that's him. When he took over the circus, he was going to send the animals by ship to New York to perform. That meant I would be separated from Modoc, never to see her again.

"That couldn't happen; I had to be on the ship. Even if it meant leaving all my friends and Gertie behind. I knew the other elephants would let another trainer handle them, but Mo was different. She had never let anybody work with her. She wouldn't allow it nor would I. So, I hitched a ride to the dock where they were loading supplies and equipment onto the ship. I spotted Mr. North. He was watching a giant crane lifting crates of cargo onto the ship while smoking a rather large cigar. Puffs of smoke filled the air. I could swear some was coming out his ears.

"I had never spoken to North since my father died. My father was the only person he would speak with. Most people were afraid to speak to him. He was known to fire you on the spot. In my case I was just a young person who worked the elephants with my father's costume.

"He didn't even recognize me. As soon as I could, I introduced myself.

"I said, 'Excuse me, Mr. North, may I speak with you?' He looked down at me like a snake about to eat a mouse. Scared me a bit."

"What could you possibly have to say to me?" he snarled.

"Well, Sir, I am your elephants' trainer now that my father passed away. Now I do the act.' I told him I was prepared to leave on the boat, take care of the elephants, and put on the performance."

"So, what did he say?" asked the captain.

"He asked me my name. So, I told him. 'Bram, Bram Gunterstein.' "

'So, you 're Josef's brat ' he said.

"His face took on a look of disgust, his lips sucked in, and a winkle appeared on his forehead. He took another drag on the cigar and blew the smoke in my face."

"I already have a trainer,'" he said and walked away.

"Well, you can imagine what that did to me. I wondered why he was like that. There was no one else who knew the act. I stood there not knowing what to do.

"Then a voice said, "He's prejudiced.'"

'He's what?'

'Prejudiced. It means he doesn't 't like people of certain religions. He didn't 't like you because you 're Jewish.'

"I looked around. 'Where are you?' I asked.

"This man dressed in a seaman's uniform stepped out of the dark from beside some crates. His name was Kelly. It turned out; he was one of the ship's crew helping to load the animals.

"'What's that got to do with working elephants?' I asked him.

'Nothing. There are just some people like that.'

"I couldn't believe how people could be that way. I was so angry I felt the blood rush to my face.

'Wait till he finds out Modoc is Jewish,' I told Kelly."

Both the captain and Jack broke up laughing.

"Anyhow, we became friends. He helped me get on the ship. I was a stowaway and had to be careful I wasn't caught."

"So, this Kelly was a good friend?" asked Jack.

"The best. Without him I don't think I would have been on board. I hid down in the hold, ate the fruits and vegetables they were feeding the elephants, and hid under Modoc's legs. Then I was caught by a ship's officer called Hands. When he grabbed me, I knew why they called him that. He picked me up with one hand. He was going to throw me overboard, or so he said, but instead, I ended up working in the kitchen."

"After a few days of working in the galley as Hands called it, a big storm was headed our way. Much bigger than seen before, according to the ship's captain. Shortly after the storm started, I ran to see if Modoc was ok. She wasn't. Water was pouring down the staircase flooding the hold and Mo, as well as the others, was already up to her knees in it. I unfastened the locks around her legs and the others so they could move.

"There was a large cannon that was being housed in the hold where the elephants were being kept. This was one big cannon. The kind you see in front of libraries or government buildings. It probably weighed as much as Modoc. It was securely fastened by a few chains, or so I thought. Each time a big wave came, the ship rocked, and the cannon would roll a bit, straining the chains that held it. I figured if that kept up it could break them and that would set the cannon free to roll out of its storage area."

"So, what can a cannon do?" asked the captain.

"Nothing if it's in a calm level place but with the ship rolling the cannon would be free to move if not chained up. I was afraid it would hit one of the elephants or the barrel would punch a hole in the side of the ship.

"As the storm got worse, the waves got bigger and rocked the ship from side to side in huge rolls. The elephants were having a rough time staying on their feet. Then, sure enough, a big wave hit really hard, the chains snapped, and that monster cannon roared at us, nearly hitting Emma. When the pitch of the wave reversed, it rolled back toward other fastened items and crushed them against the back wall.

"The elephants were panic stricken. They didn't know where to go to stay out of its way. When it rolled out again, it hit one of the pillars holding up the roof. I thought the roof was going to collapse. It was terrifying. The elephants and I had to dodge it not knowing just where it would go. Then, everything went quiet, and I suspected a bigger wave was coming. It felt like the ship was suspended on the top of a colossal wave and would come flying down sending the monster cannon on a path of destruction. It did just that.

"The ship gave a mighty lurch; the cannon came flying past the pillars and exploded against a section of the bulkhead wall. The cannon's barrel struck the ship's outer hull breaking it open and the sea poured into the hold. The power of the water coming through that hole picked me up and knocked the legs out from under the elephants."

"Good grief," said Jack. "Then what happened?"

"I saw Modoc fall as the water pulled me down, too. That cannon wasn't done yet, though. On the second roll, in a terrifying moment, it crashed against the hull again with tremendous force and broke open the other side of the ship and passed on through! A gigantic wall of water cascaded into the hold throwing me about, hitting walls, elephants, and the ceiling. It formed a massive riptide that whipped everything in its path and washed us out into the open sea."

"Whoa! Whoa! Bram, you mean to tell me you were washed out into the ocean?"

"Yep. Everything that was in that section of the hold ended up being washed out through the hole the cannon made, including the cannon."

"So where was Modoc all this time?"

"I didn't know. I was completely discombobulated."

"You what?"

"Why, is that wrong?"

"No, but where in the world did you hear that word?"

"A worker at the hospital said he heard it from an Army guy."

"Well," chuckled the captain. "Just sounds strange coming from you."

"Hmm. Well anyhow, when I surfaced, I called out to her. But with the storm, and people and animals crying out, it was impossible to hear anything. I looked everywhere for her, but she just vanished. I was trying to catch my breath all the time. Thank goodness I had learned to swim back home in Lake Cryer. I was thrown up to the surface where there were people all around screaming, yelling for help. It was awful. The ship sank right there in front of us! I saw some life rafts in the far distance but only for a flash, and then they were gone, out of sight. I thought of all the animals that must have drowned. I prayed that God's Gate was opened, and my animal friends were being let in.

"Some of the people were drowning, others hung on to each other. Those of us who could stay afloat locked hands in a big circle and kept each other from going under. It made our circle quite large. A few that couldn't swim were clinging to others, pulling them down. It was horrible. Our circle held tight, and we floated away into the dark of the night where all we could hear were the waves hitting our circle. All through the night and next morning we floated. I kept calling for Mo. Down deep I knew she was gone. Lost in the ocean. In the morning, I noticed the circle had gotten smaller. Some who were injured floated away too weak to hang on."

"Wow! That's incredible. I can't imagine being in such a horrible situation," said Jack.

"Way off in the ocean I heard the trumpet of an elephant. I didn't know which elephant it was till I saw her. It was Modoc! She was being carried by the current heading our way! I could see she would pass us up as she was too far away. I yelled to the group to form a line! 'Hurry! Hurry! Modoc! Modoc! Over here!'" I don't know if she heard me, but I saw her coming. She was caught in a fast current that was bringing her close but not close enough. She was going to pass us by. I had the people break the circle and stretch out in a long line with me at the end. We only had one chance to grab Mo. We stretched out as far as we could then she saw me and with incredible energy she lunged. Her trunk grabbed my hand and pulled me and the whole line of people to her where we all quickly formed a circle around her."

"Good Lord, man, that's amazing," said Jack.

"Well, it was so unreal. We gathered around her. She was like a floating island. Those who couldn't swim well scrambled up top. Others, too badly hurt, had drifted away. We formed a circle around her and held on. We were to stay that way for three days hoping a rescue boat would come.

"By the second day the circle had gotten smaller as more people slowly dropped away, too weak to hang on. All prayed to be rescued, but nobody came. We were about ready to give up when we heard a boat. It had heard the ship's SOS distress call before it went down and had come to rescue us. It was small but big enough for all the people to get aboard. Once everybody had climbed on board, the man running the boat yelled for me to get on, but Modoc was too big to get on the boat and I wasn't about to leave her. So, I floated away with her. I couldn't leave her alone."

"What?" cried the captain. "You could have climbed aboard. You chose to stay with her? You...you! Ah! Never mind. Go on."

"Yeah, well, by nightfall we were both about done in when a large tugboat who had heard the distress call from the first boat came. It was the kind used to put boats in the water that are stored on the dock. So, it had a crane that could pick up Mo. We tied leather slings around her so she wouldn't slip out of them. Both Mo and I collapsed on the deck. We had made it!"

"Bram, if I hadn't gotten to know you, I don't think I would have believed you. That is amazing," the captain said.

"Well, it happened. We were taken to a hospital where in the weeks that followed, we recuperated. I learned we were in India. North thought we had died so we were safe for the time being.

"I had the occasion to meet the Maharajah. We stayed at his palace where I was fortunate to meet the royal white elephant. In the months we were there, Modoc and I learned how the mahouts trained their elephants. It was quite strenuous but most rewarding. It was then we found out that North knew we were alive and was on his way. We left. Saying goodbye to the Maharajah was so difficult. He had become our friend. Without his help we would never have made it.

"We were hoping to find a lumber camp where we could put our newfound trade to work. I felt with the knowledge Mo and I learned at the palace, we could do the work of a mahout. It was during our time in the forest that I met an Indian girl by the name of Sian. She took us to her father's lumber camp where Modoc was given the chance to prove she was capable of being a mahout's elephant and I a mahout. That's where Sian and I fell in love."

"You had mentioned earlier that she was killed during the war," said the captain. "Sorry about that."

"Yes, she was." Bram quickly changed the subject. "I would prefer not to go there if you don't mind; it brings back horrible memories."

"No, of course, we understand."

"Her father, his name is Ja, gave Modoc and me a chance to prove our worth. Working the timber is a very hard and strenuous job for both the elephant and the mahout. We were put to the test of being mahouts, which we passed. I was so proud of Mo. The test was one that only a man and his elephant having trained for years was worthy of passing.

"Sian's father became my mentor. He and the mahouts taught me the ways of the Hindu beliefs. Living at the camp was a wonderful experience. We were not privy to the wrath of the outside world till a rebel leader and his soldiers came into the camp and threatened us all. They were part of the rebels that were at war with the Indian Army.

"When they heard that the Army was on their way, the leader forced us to outfit our elephants with their weapons and supplies to prepare to take the Dullirah passage, a hazardous trail up through the mountain pass. To use the mountain pass as an escape route was insane. An impossible route. Way too narrow, far too dangerous. I tried to tell him, but he wouldn't listen. We formed a line of thirty-one elephants, almost half a mile long, and made our way up the path. It was then that the Indian Army sent their planes. They shot indiscriminately, killing rebels but also elephants, mahouts, and my beloved Sian."

"Sorry, so sorry."

All was quiet for some time, the silence saying more than any words could.

Bram finally spoke. "Well, that's it, I ended up at one of the temporary hospitals with some injuries as did Modoc who was taken to a place called Valley of Stones named from the elephants that died there or were injured.

"North came and told me of the plane to take us back. His plan is to give Modoc to a new trainer and send me to jail. That's where we met."

"So full circle," said the captain. "Well, I'm under strict orders to get you and your elephant back safely, but after hearing what happened, I mean, good Lord that's an incredible story. It's almost unbelievable."

"It's all true," said Bram. "So, you see, I've got to go."

Jack was quite sympathetic. "We've got to help him, Cap."

"Of course, but by doing what?"

"Well, first, let him go. When the plane arrives, we won't tell them anything. You just left in the middle of the night, and we don't know what direction you went. We can help him load Mo with enough food and water, err, Cokes, to last a while and give him a map of the area."

"You have a map of the desert?" asked Bram.

"We have a large topographical map, so it won't show much. It shows the whole Northern Region, so the desert will be a very small part of it," said the captain.

"Let me go try the radio again, and I'll grab the map for you while there." Captain Tyler then disappeared into the ruins of the cockpit and found the map. Fortunately, it was under some equipment and hadn't burned at all. Unfolding it, they laid it on the ground, then put rocks on its corners to keep it flat. It showed the entire region of the Sinar Desert with the Himalayas across one end of its border. At the edge of the desert stretched a strip of forest. Bram tapped the spot. "That's where we'll go." He noticed pinpoints scattered throughout the map. "What are these?"

"The map shows them as wells. They're probably pretty primitive judging there are no towns near them," said the captain.

"At least it's good to know they're out there. What else?"

"The river you saw. This little scraggily line here must be the river. It runs quite a long way. When you leave here, just head toward the mountains. You can't miss it. You have to cross it to get to the mountains."

"If you make it to the forest, you should be ok."

"At least you'll have water, and I'm sure there is enough forest food, like berries, fruits, whatever grows there," said Jack.

"Have you ever been in a forest and found fruit?" asked the captain.

"Well, no, but don't worry, if food is there, Modoc will find it," said Bram.

"Once you're near the forest, you will be close to this dot on the map," continued Jack.

"It's marked as a village. How close?"

"Maybe twenty miles."

"That's close?"

"It's the closest in the whole area," answered Jack.

"What happens if you make it to this village and then after that?" worried the captain.

"Right now, I just need to get away from North. So, it's one step at a time, right?"

"Right."

"Look, guys, don't worry, we'll make it."

Jack handed Bram the map. "Keep it, it may become handy."

"What else?"

"We wish you God speed."

It was morning when Bram was packed and ready to go. Mo seemed back to her old self, save for the many skin abrasions. She had the last two bales of oat hay strapped to each side, the remaining four cases of Coke, two to a side strapped next to them and a small container of food that had been brought for the journey to the States.

"Isn't that too heavy for her?" asked Jack.

"Na, she could carry far more than that, and besides, she will be eating the oat hay so the load will get lighter."

"Here's a box of matches to light a fire," said Jack.

"A fire in the desert?" said the captain. "You're kidding."

"Never know. Just like here. It gets cold."

"You sure she's ok to make the trip?" said the concerned captain.

"If it wasn't for the river being there, I don't think I would try it. But with the river, she'll be able to bathe, clean all those wounds, and eat. So, I think she'll be fit enough. And you know, I was just thinking; after what she went through in the plane, I'm not so sure she would have been willing to get in another."

"You mean the one that's coming?"

"Yeah, or any plane."

"Never thought of that. You're probably right, and I don't blame her."

The captain went over to Modoc. "Bram, you and Mo saved our hides. We wouldn't have made it out without your help. We'll never forget that." He patted Mo's trunk and she gave a belly rumble. "I wish there was more we could do. By the way, what does that belly rumble mean?"

"It's her way of saying she likes you. She chirps a lot, too, like a bird but it means the same."

"Well, we like you too, Mo, and big thanks," said the captain patting Mo's head. "When the rescue people arrive, we'll tell them you left in the middle of the night, and we don't know which direction you went. Once you're gone, we'll mess-up your tracks."

"Another thing, Bram. You have to be careful out there," said Jack. "I understand there are nomads who raid the villages and travelers."

"The Air Force gives us a pamphlet for survival. It mentions the Sinar, and in case we are forced down to be prepared. It also mentions herds of wild elephants, but that shouldn't be a problem for you."

"Oh yeah. They're just as dangerous to me as they would be to you," said Bram.

"They don't know that Bram is the world's greatest elephant trainer," said the captain. He smiled. "All jokes aside. Apparently, there are some big herds out there so be careful. And they won't be as tame as Modoc here."

"How can there be elephants in the desert?"

"They're not. They're by the river. According to the map, the river widens out. That's where the forest is quite large. I guess that's where they live."

"Good to know. We'll stay away from that area. Don't worry. I'll be careful."

"Which reminds me," said Jack. "Before you go, how did I get out of my seat in the cockpit? I was unconscious."

"Mo picked you up and carried you out," answered Bram.

"I tell you I still just can't believe it. Every plane should have one. How did she know to do it? I mean, well, I still am amazed."

Bram told them about hauling and picking up the teak at the mill. "All the things she did, she learned at the camp or in the circus. She just needed me to tell her which one and what to do."

Suddenly they heard static coming from inside the cockpit.

"That's the radio. Someone heard my call." The captain went into the cockpit to answer it.

"Who would be calling this early in the morning?" joked Jack.

A few minutes later, the captain reemerged. "That was the base. They'll be sending a rescue plane out later this morning. I gave them our coordinates, as near as I could. I guess you should be moving on. They were still loading equipment. It's a 70-B standing by. It's a much bigger plane. They assume we still have the elephant."

"Won't they be surprised?"

"Yeah, I know. They'll call North to let him know. It's his plane and elephant."

"Yeah, of course."

The captain reached into his pocket and pulled out a card. "Bram, here's my number in the States. If you ever need anything, I'll be there for you."

"Ditto," said Jack.

"Ditto?" questioned Bram.

"Me too, Bram, me too."

So, with that, the men gave Bram a shoulder hug and Mo a pat.

"Savvy," said Bram.

"Savvy," said the captain, with a smile.

Wet eyes showed on all three men. A thumbs up from Jack.

"Leg up, Mo."

Bram settled himself on Mo's neck. A wave goodbye and a chirp from Mo as they then headed out into a desolate, unknown territory.

CHAPTER 13

"A report has just been received from a commercial airline pilot flying over the Indian Sinar Desert that he was able to discern smoke billowing from what appeared to be a downed airplane. Its tail was protruding from the wreckage that showed a section of the lift gate which is exclusive to the 376-Army transport planes. It is believed this is the same plane that was carrying an elephant from India to the U.S. Can you imagine! We will bring you updates as soon as they are available."

Jake rushed over to the circus trailer office. A short stocky, bald guy in his forties who had been with the circus for umpteen years. He was North's 'fall guy,' easy to blame, absorb anybody's guilt that came his way, yet sharp enough to keep away from his boss's claws.

"Hey, Boss, have you heard the news?"

"Damn you, Jake, I'm right in the middle of watching the World Series, so it better be good."

"You know what?" Jake stammered.

"What! Get it out, man. Speak!"

"Your plane just crashed. It's on the news. It went down in the desert."

"No shit! Any survivors?"

"Don't know, probably not. I'm checking with the Army. See if they know anything."   "Yeah. I left my nephew Malcolm there to watch them and see that they don't escape."

"Malcolm?"

"Okay. Now don't start. That's his name. He was probably on the plane with them."

"Yeah, but it's too early to know."

"Even if Malcolm wasn't on the plane, he's too dumb to figure out how to get back to New York. Ugh. I'm going to have to call my sister. Well, I hope he likes curry," North rambled. Jake wasn't fazed by how callous North was towards the idea of his nephew lost in India. If it didn't make him money, he didn't care about it.

"They're probably all dead," continued North. "A big plane like that just isn't going to make it down safely. Can we get any insurance off the bastard?"

"I take it you mean Bram. I doubt it. We never planned on this."

"How about the elephant? Aren't all the circus animals insured? I think a few of the important ones are."

"Oh, yeah—that's right. I remember you didn't want to spend the money and—"

"Shut up, idiot. Just go and check it out."

"Sure, Boss." Then Jake was out the door.

North picked a half-smoked butt from an ashtray full of cigarette butts. He lit it and sat by the TV.

<u>BREAKING NEWS BULLETIN</u>

"This is an up-to-date report on the US Army flight 275 from Nashi, India, to the U.S. It is believed to have been carrying an elephant when it crashed in the Sinar Desert in Northern India. The elephant was reported to have been owned by one Mr. North, owner of the WUNDERZIRCUS operating in Germany and touring in New York City. The reason it was carrying an elephant is unknown. It went down somewhere in the Sinar Desert in the northern region of India."

The report continued with other news North ignored until…

<u>UPDATE</u>

"This just in. A private plane flying in the Sinar Desert region this morning has seen the wreckage of what we believe to be the Army transport plane that crashed in the desert. The pilot, a John Katter, has altered his course and is now flying over the wreckage. Station KB 40 out of Jodhpur has connected us with the pilot."

A loud screeching static was heard, then silence . . .

"John? Hello, John, can you hear me?"

Crackling static.

"Roger, John here. Read you loud and clear. Go ahead."

"John, I understand you are flying over the crash site of an Army transport plane flight number 275?"

"Roger on that."

"Can you tell us what you see?"

More static.

"There is scattered wreckage strewn along a dirt path where the plane scraped the desert floor for several hundred yards. I can see the numbers 27 on one wing. The rest is broken off and the opposite wing is missing entirely. There is smoke billowing from inside the plane. The tail section appears to be on fire."

"John, do you see any signs of life?"

"Negative on that. The crash was quite severe. I don't see signs of survivors. Don 't believe anyone could have survived. Over."

"There are reports that the plane was carrying an elephant. Do you see any signs of it?"

"Negative. I'm running low on petrol, so will have to leave the site. Don 't want to join them down there."

A slight laugh was heard.

"Before you go, can you give us your location?"

"Well, I don 't have an instrument panel, so I'm flying by the seat of my pants. Ha! But as the crow flies, I'm about 80 miles northwest of the city of Jodhpur. Over and out."

"Thank you, John Katter. We now return you to our studio in New York City."

"Jake! Where are you?" North's voice bellowed.

Jake came rushing inside the office. He was holding a bunch of papers in his hands.

"You asked me to see if the elephant was insured."

"Later. Damn, that's just my luck. That kid probably caused it to crash. All these years of fighting with him over an elephant. Ach! And now they're both gone." He lit a cigarette. "No more fighting. Pity." Then a smile. "Actually, I kind of enjoyed it. I must say that kid had gumption. A real little go getter."

"He's not a kid any longer, Boss."

"Has it been that long? Well, just had a thought. Set up some P.R. that the circus is holding a tribute in honor of Modoc for dedication to the circus and her world-renowned performance. She was kind of famous. That should fill the seats."

"But she only performed in Germany, so how can she be world renowned?" Jake questioned.

"Ahk! Just do it! I'll figure some angle." The more he thought about it the more excited he became. "I can see the headlines now."

"FAMOUS ELEPHANT MODOC DIES IN PLANE CRASH"
"TRIBUTE TO BE HELD AT THE WUNDERZIRCUS"

"We'll reduce the entrance fee, just a little, and put donation boxes at the entrance showing we are giving the money to some animal charity. Ha! At least the public will think that. There are so many animal nuts out there; they will flock to give their respects. Also, put a big donation box, maybe two, at the exits. Put a sign that reads: TO THE ANIMAL ORPHANS OF THE WORLD.

"I should be able to pocket quite a bit of change there."

"Sure, Boss, I'll get right on it. How about the jeeps and tanks and all that equipment?"

"That's the Army's problem. We were just delivering them."

"You did insure the plane, right?" questioned North.

"Yeah. It was so out of shape you weren't sure it would make it."

"Well, I didn't think it would crash, maybe some down time for repairs but not a crash? But that should bring a bundle. I lucked out. Don't just stand there. Get on with it." North put his feet up on a chair and had a big grin spread across his face. "Finally got you, you little bastard," he said aloud.

Jake was just leaving the trailer when a TV 'Newshour' truck pulled up.

"Excuse me, sir, is Mr. North around?"

"Yeah, he's in the office. Why?"

"We're from the 'Newshour' show and would like to interview him regarding the lost elephant."

"I'm his assistant. Let me check and see if he's interested." Jake jumped up the trailer steps into the office. "Hey, Boss, there's a TV reporter here to see if you want to do an interview on the lost elephant."

"Interview me? Well, yes, of course." He went to the office mirror, straightened his tie and brushed cigarette ash from his jacket. "It's something I'm good at, and it's great P.R. for the circus." He lit another cigarette, then poised in his most elegant manner. He opened the door, put his hand on his hip, and stood at the top step. He cleared his throat to get attention from the reporter standing below him. "Gentleman, I'm Mr. North, can I be of service to you?"

"Yes, if you don't mind, we would like to talk to you about the lost elephant."

North walked down the steps with a swagger. "Yes, of course. Where would you like me to stand?" he asked. Across the office trailer was written Wunderzircus. He waddled over to the sign. "How about here?" he asked, posing in front of it. His hand never left his hip.

"Perfect," said the newscaster.

A bright floodlight was turned on as North cleared his throat again. A red light turned green on the camera and the interview began.

"Mr. North, you are owner of the Wunderzircus?"

"Yes, I am."

"It's our understanding that you owned an elephant that was being flown from India to the United States?"

"Yes, that is correct."

"It's been reported that the plane has crashed, and there are no survivors. Can you give us your thoughts at this time?"

"I am deeply saddened by the loss. The elephant, Modoc was her name, was dear, so dear to my heart. I brought her up since being a pup, er, baby elephant. She adored me, and I will miss her."

With that, he sniffled enough for an attendant to hand him a tissue. He blew his nose. The sound was quite like an elephant's snort.

"How about the trainer?" asked the reporter. "I understand he was flying in that plane as well."

"The dear boy. He was like a son to me. I adored him too. We'll miss them both. I hope the world will join me in a prayer that their death was not too scary."

"What?" The reporter stared at North askance.

"Er, what I mean is that they didn't suffer. A plane going down and nothing you can do about it. So sad, so sad."

The reporter couldn't wait to end the piece. "Yes, well, thanks for your comment. This is..."

North went on, "We are going to hold a tribute to Modoc's passing."

The reporter signaled his assistant to turn off the floodlight.

"In honor of this great elephant, I'm going to lower the admission so all can come. We are also giving most of the funds to 'Save the Wildlife Foundation.' I hope all will come and join us in celebrating Modoc's extraordinary life and, of course, that of her dedicated trainer as well. Both were such an essential part of our family."

The light shut off. "Hmmm. Thank you, Mr. North."

"N-o-r-t-h. And be sure to mention our tribute."

"You just did. Thank you, Mr. North," said the irate newscaster, "and now we return to our studio."

North returned to his trailer. "Was I great, Jake, huh?"

"Yes, Boss, you definitely made an impression."

"Yeah, I did. Okay. Get to work. Let's make some money. P.R., Jake, P.R.! Where is that elephant insurance report, I asked you for? Idiot! Must I do everything around here myself?"

CHAPTER 14

The morning sun rose over the crest of the faraway mountains. With it came the burning rays that took away the chill of the night. Bram had decided to walk rather than ride Mo. She was still recuperating from her terrifying ordeal in the plane. Most of the wounds were forming scabs, other than the ones on her forehead and trunk.

"Well, Mosey, we're sure not going back home. No worries there. Ha! I can just see old North's face when he hears about the crash. He'll have kittens!"

Bram often talked with Modoc when they were alone. Sometimes when he accentuated something, his voice became loud, or he would laugh uproariously, and she would join him with a chirp or squeak. Even a little hind leg dance. Bram felt elated. Even though the conditions were uncertain, he was invigorated by being free.

Bram didn't know much about the desert, but from his many travels, he knew there were many different kinds. Some with scrubs with 'tumbling' weeds chased by the wind, dust devils twirling hundreds of feet into the air, large cacti shaped like people during the day, or scary monsters by nighttime moonlight.

Then there was the desert of the dunes. Vast and silent, a mysterious place where dunes reached hundreds of feet into the sky. Those changed form as shaped by the wind.

Bram and Modoc were in the land of the cactus. Here, the cactus ruled. As far as the eye could see, they stood like an army. Some were ready for battle with thorny arms raised as though to slaughter the enemy. Those defeated lay on the ground torn and ripped by the sword held by the warriors above. Vultures perched on the shoulders of some, waiting to feast on anything that had fallen; others stood like wounded soldiers with arms dismembered or a head dislodged; all stalled in a time warp.

Bram's worry was Mo. The sun beat mercilessly against her as her large grey body absorbed the heat. Elephants don't sweat. He remembered her throwing mud or spraying water on her back during the hot days. Occasionally she raised her trunk and spewed an imaginary sprinkle of wet drops on her back.

Bram had draped the small cloth the nurse had given him over her back, but it didn't help much. He found a dried-up animal skin, hard and shriveled, lying near a cactus that he laid on Mo's back as well. The skull was attached to the skin and gave a grim picture of their situation. Lizards were everywhere basking on the hot rocks or doing pushups. Were he to touch the rock, he would be burned. How could they endure it, he wondered?

Bram watched the horizon searching for some signs of the river. Nothing. Everything looked the same. A desert fox sneaked past low to the ground, its crafty eyes looking, searching for its morning meal. The vultures circled above hoping the fox would make a kill so they could clean up the leftovers. The fox looked fit, its coat was shiny, and it walked with stealth. The vultures' feathers were smooth and strong, gliding the air currents with ease.

"How could those creatures survive in this inferno, Mo? Wish we had the same ability."

Mo was in no mood to listen. Her body ached from the sun's burning rays. She was parched. Her body needed water; without it she would shut down like a factory without electricity.

The more he walked, the more concerned Bram became. His thoughts wandered. What would happen if the captain was wrong? Hard to believe but maybe with all the confusion he misjudged. Nah! Not the captain. It will come, he told himself. He noticed Mo would occasionally stumble, still weak from her ordeal. The hours drifted by. Still no river. He stopped by a large cactus that was casting a shadow big enough for him to benefit from a smidgen of shade but not for Mo. He hurriedly broke open a dozen cans of Coke and one by one poured them into Modoc's mouth. Flies had gathered on her open head sores. He spread the blanket over her head letting some of it hang down over her trunk so when she walked her swaying kept the blanket moving and shooed the flies away. He took a few glugs of a Coke and remembered the captain saying they couldn't miss it. Just head for the mountains he had said.

The day had gone and with it the sun. Bram's worry increased. Had he missed it? Did the captain miscalculate? He looked forward to the night knowing they could get much further along without the scalding rays of the sun burning them at every step. The moon soon rose to light their way.

Bram knew little about the moon and its journey through the sky. After only a few hours it waned and disappeared below the horizon. He was surprised when it had such a short stay and then disappeared. A wall of total darkness descended. If they tried to walk, the sentinel cacti were there waiting to embed their two-inch thorns into their flesh. Quite eerie.

Bram felt Modoc's trunk feel its way to him and curl around his arm. It either gave her security or she felt the need to protect him.

It was time to rest. He sat with his back against Mo's leg. Bram listened to her long bubbly breathing. Time gets lost in a void when there is nothing to refer to. Was it minutes or hours before the sun began to rise again? It came like a fiery beast throwing its rays over the snow-covered peaks in the far distance. A new day had begun. The sun rose in a clear blue sky and shone like a beacon of fire aimed directly at them. There was no refuge. No place to get away from its scorching rays.

With the mountains still looming off in the far distance, they continued while dodging a cactus here or rounding a boulder there but hoping the river would show itself.

Six hours passed and there was still no sign of the river. His concern grew for whether the captain could have misjudged the distance or even its location, The mere thought seared Bram's mind. The captain saw it when the plane was about to crash.

Maybe? thought Bram.

Mo's fatigue was apparent. She swayed in her walk, unable to keep a steady gait.

The end of the day was approaching when Bram heard the quacking of ducks. Ducks! Ducks needed water. Yes! The breeze had turned cool and brought with it the refreshing smell of water. The river! Bram ran ahead. Just over two small hills, the river stretched left and right for miles in each direction.

"Oh! my God, thank you, thank you."

Not too wide, perhaps 100 yards, it was a smooth flowing, bubbling river. A narrow strip of trees and brush grew alongside it on each bank. A small flock of ducks took flight when Modoc appeared.

"Mosey, we made it! There it is. Have at it."

She trumpeted and shuffled over to the nearby bank. She stood for but a moment, shook her body like a big dog, threw her trunk in the air, blasted a big trumpet, then in she went, Cokes, hay bales and all. She crashed head down causing tumultuous splashing and trumpeting. Bram followed her in, dodging the thrashing feet, trying to take off her trappings. As her bandages floated free, she blew bubbles by gurgling in the water. Some poo floated by. She was in nirvana. Bram gathered all the supplies he could and hauled them to the shore leaving her to play on her own. He took to the grove that the captain called a forest, exploring the area as well as searching for anything edible. Probably from the air it looked like a forest but in truth it was more like an oasis with trees spread apart and little brush. There would be more than enough for Modoc to eat but for him it was a different matter. It took him quite a while to find a small assortment of fruits and berries. He called Modoc out of the river. She would tell him which were safe to eat. Rarely was there something she ate that didn't agree with him. She came out of the water, still rambunctious, and feeling good. Bram held out the food. The finger at the tip of her trunk touched each one. Some she rolled over, threw one in the bush, and quickly gobbled up the others.

"Okay, now we know," he said.

But a few berries would not sustain him. Back in the glade he cut some of the long vines that hung from the trees. When he was at Ja's timber village the mahouts taught him how to weave a simple fish trap. Once done, he placed it in the shallows by some large rocks near the shore. He would return later in the hopes of finding his dinner.

The desert chill signaled the day's end. Seeing as there would be no rain and the grove would give enough protection from the sun there was no need to build a shelter. Picking a spot on the shore, Bram started a small fire using the matches Jack gave him. The same ones the captain felt they wouldn't need. He smiled at the thought.

When the fire was burning bright Bram returned to his trap hoping to find a nice big fish. He was surprised to find a swarm of fish all crammed together. He chose one large one and turned the rest loose. It was good to know he would have no trouble having food in the days to come. He cooked on the open fire and added fruit and berries to his meal. What a delight.

"You don't know what you're missing, Mo," teased Bram, knowing she wouldn't eat a fish. She did manage to sneak some mangos from his plate. He did his namaste being thankful for all that had been given to him.

Mo found her own dinner by breaking off some huge branches of bamboo along with the leaves and branches of some small trees. Once sated, she was back in the river for an evening swim alongside Bram. As the burning orb of the sun disappeared over the horizon and darkness arrived, the sky filled with an exaltation of stars. Their brilliance cast a glow across the river causing the small waves to sparkle. The grove of palms caught up by the evening breeze sent them swaying. Shadows of imaginary things ran through the grove, as Bram and Modoc settled down by the fire. She lay on her side in the soft sand to ease the weight off her legs with Bram resting his head against hers. They played in the sand for a while as she made circles with the tip of her trunk while he drew faces with a twig till they both fell asleep. They slept that night free of care and worry. Tomorrow would be another day.

The drone of an airplane woke them. The Army plane! He quickly threw some tree branches over Modoc and kept her lying down as the plane flew over. They were lying close to the edge of the glade by a line of trees so there was no way they could be seen. He took a minute to imagine what would happen when the plane landed. A smile crossed his face. But that was days ago. Maybe they can't find it?

Two weeks passed since their arrival. Each morning found Bram doing the meditation taught to him by Ja. He took Modoc's medallion and his choon, both depicting the image of Ganesha, and propped them up on a mound of sand. He put Modoc in a sphinx position, bowed his head, and palmed his hands in the sign of the namaste.

"Dear Ganesha, Modoc and I have come to thank you for showing us the way to this beautiful place. Modoc's wounds are healing, we have food to eat, water to drink, and we will grow strong to continue our journey to the mountains. Watch over Sian and all the elephants that arrive at your golden gate." Once done, Bram put Modoc's medallion back around her neck and the choon in the folds of his Patiala (pants).

Bram took a few minutes to study the mountains. So grand, the colossal Himalayas stood snow-capped and majestic. They were not close. He pulled out the map Jack gave him. He had chosen a direction that would take them past one of the wells shown on the map. Bram knew that to find the well would be nearly imposable, but he had to try. He picked a certain peak that was in line with the proposed well. That's the one he would aim for.

Modoc found a floating tree and was having a ball pushing it around, letting out some loud trumpets. Big mistake. From somewhere out there another elephant answered! Oh, boy, trouble, thought Bram. Other elephants coming could mean big trouble. Jealousy, possession, fights. You name it.

He knew wild herds had been known to kill lone elephants. He remembered what Jack had said about the herd being dangerous. Whatever they decided for Mo didn't include Bram. His fate would be forgone. What to do? Bram had no idea where the elephant that answered Modoc's trumpet was, but it didn't sound far off. The one thing he knew was it would be coming, and he had to hide Modoc. His first thought was the grove, but the trees were sparse, the ground was more sand than earth, and their tracks would be easier seen. So that was out.

The herd didn't waste any time. Another trumpet sounded much closer. Bram quickly tapped Mo's trunk.

"Hold!" he said.

She quickly put her trunk in her mouth to keep her from trumpeting and she knew it well. She stood quietly, her eyes following Bram's every movement. Down the river Bram saw a line of elephants crossing over to head their way. He figured there were some twenty in the herd. He had to get away from the forest. That's where he figured they would come from. Should he leave? Just start walking towards the mountains. Bad thought. Modoc was not yet fit enough for that arduous journey. Again, the herd trumpet. He had to do something and fast.

"How do you hide a five-ton elephant?" he spoke aloud. His instinct told him to get into the river. "Move up, Mo."

Off they went into the river. Catching the current, he hung on to her as they drifted downstream. The river was too shallow to hide an elephant. But at the bend, the main river swung off favoring the more straightforward current and leaving all the debris to accumulate at the bend causing a swamp-like bog. Dead trees and downed logs, branches entangled in one another had accumulated there. Patches of reeds had sprung up from the mucky water leaving it a perfect haven to hide in. Bram headed for it. Pushing through the rubble he moved a few floating trees to get Mo in a position where it was hard to tell her from the dead trees. He put whole branches on her back and draped green moss from her ears.

"Now you leave it, Mosey, ya hear?"

A roll of her head showed she understood but the temptation to check it out was there. She couldn't take her eyes off it.

It wasn't long before the herd appeared. Sure enough, they came out of the grove trumpeting their arrival and walked directly into Bram's 'camp.' Bram took hold of Modoc's trunk, but by now she seemed to know she wasn't to trumpet. Seemingly upset that there was nobody home, one of the big bulls kicked sand over the cooking area while others caused a bit of a ruckus pulling down the trees Mo had eaten from and throwing the branches over their head. Another was carrying some of the brush on his back. All were trumpeting and some were pooping.

A couple of the punks (young ones) took to the water letting the river drift them downstream heading where Bram and Modoc hid. Bram, seeing them coming their way noticed the ridge of Mo's back was sticking above the waterline as was the crown of her head. He quickly piled cakes of mud on her head and back which she thought was good fun. A few belly grumbles could be heard from way down in the mud. Bram put some of the mud on his face which Modoc thought was hysterical. At least it seemed that way because she let out some farts causing huge bubbles to come to the surface and burst. Bram shot a look at her which made her sink her head a little lower in the water.

Mo laid her trunk snake-like across an old dead tree branch. Bram pressed on it and told her to 'stay.' She knew what it meant. Her head stayed still, but her eyes roved in all directions. Both Bram and Mo, covered in mud, stood waiting knowing the punks were headed directly to the bog.

On they came till one of them pushed right into the bog. The other one drifted into the bog not ten feet away from where they were hiding. Trees were picked up, some thrown, others crashed into the bog, some hitting Modoc across her back. She started to rise till Bram gave her a gentle reminder with the choon. Her eyes shifted to Bram who was looking at her, not moving. She had seen that look before. Best not to move. Were the punks adults they would have been found, but the young ones were too busy playing and left the bog as they found it. They drifted idly, then entered the mainstream and disappeared.

Finally, the herd, after kicking the sand into piles and gullies, pulling down trees, and pooping all over the place left and headed back down the same way they came while hooting and hollering all the way.

It reminded Bram of a group of troublemaking hoodlums.

"That was a close call, Mo. Hope they don't come back."

When to leave? Bram knew a lot depended on when Modoc was fit. Seeing her romp in the river told him that she was 'Ready when you are.' Bram knew it wasn't the walk that concerned him, it was the heat. Her sores were healing, her belly fat, and the gleam in her eye bright and clear. It was the end of the fourth week when Bram decided. The new moon was bright and clear. It was time to go.

Bram woke early. This would be the day they would leave.

"It's time to go, Mo. First thing tonight when the moon comes up. We'll spend the day preparing, so we can get you all loaded up by nightfall."

He scrubbed Modoc with some basil and coriander that grew in abundance around the base of many of the trees, bathed her and treated the wounds. Most were healed but the larger ones would leave scars. She was fit: her belly was fat, her sores looked good, and she was full of water.

Evening was fast approaching. He started to pack.

He had kept the last two hay bales away from Mo. Those were strapped one on either side. For the last few days Bram had been soaking large strips of tree bark in the river. A favorite among elephants, they would chew on them for hours and finally eat the softened remains. The bark, lying flat, would also keep the sun from burning her skin.

With water being his main concern, he used the machete Jack gave him to cut six, twelve-foot-long bamboos. Bram knew that inside all bamboo there are compartments at every joint. Taking a long hardwood branch he sharpened the tip, then using a rock pounded it into the bamboo breaking through all the compartments until only the last one was intact. He submerged the bamboo in the river filling all the compartments with water. Then, putting three to each side of Modoc, he arranged them, so the open ends were higher than the other preventing the water from spilling out.

He could fill the empty Coke cans, but that wouldn't help much, and most would spill. The couple of waterproof canvas bags given to him by the guys could carry some. He cut down Mo's favorite, a dozen long thin tree limbs that were full of leaves and strapped them to her back. He crushed as many berries and fruit as he could find, put them in some large leaves and tied them with vine. Finally, a few days back Bram had laid out a few dozen fish to dry in the sun. He sandwiched them between two thin layers of bark and tied them with vine. Those along with the berries he hung on the branches on her back. Bram looked Mo over. He had to laugh but couldn't let Mo see him. She could pick up his attitude and he didn't want to hurt her feelings. She looked like a grotesque tree monster from a different world. But what was important was it gave them both a chance to survive.

"I'm scared, Mo, but what else to do? We have to reach the mountains before we run out of water for you."

It was time to go. Bram knelt by the edge of the river clasping his hands together.

"Dear Ganesha, this is Bram and my elephant friend, Modoc. Sorry to bother you. I know you're busy. We must leave this wonderful place you have provided. We must go now, but I am worried. Your sun gives us heat in the winter and grows our food in the summer, but it has not been a good companion for us when in the desert. So please, if you could, come with us and maybe help us find water for Mosey, and if there is anything we can do for you, we are willing." He thanked him with a namaste.

"Okay, Mosey, let's do it."

They left at the first light of the moon.

CHAPTER 15

They had lost the moon. Low to the horizon, it had taken refuge behind the mountains plunging the desert into total darkness. Best to sit and wait, thought Bram.

Bram had lost track of time since he and Modoc left the river. The dunes had arrived; not a cactus was seen. Bram saw them as a dead world of mountainous graves for giants. No two alike, their tops cut like a razor's edge. Hotter than the land of the cactus, a desolate caldron where the sun was born. No birds flew in the sky, no animal left its tracks. The voice of silence was overwhelming.

They had been trekking at night to avoid the hot sun. To do so, they had depended on the moon to light their way. But now the moon was waning. What would he do when it was gone? He had planned on being at the mountain by then, but it seemed impossible now. Bram divided the nights between sleeping and walking. They usually slept for those last few hours, dreading the morning when the burning heat of the sun returned on schedule.

The mountains he had seen from the crash site seemed just as far away as when they started or was it a mirage? They rippled across the horizon, waves of disjointed illusions that had driven many men to their grave while praying what they saw was real.

Lakes appeared, towns, people, men on camels, disfigured in a kaleidoscope of unreal phantoms. Vivid illusions came and went to vanish in a cloud of sand. Unreal except to the mind.

Modoc was Bram's main worry. The hay bales had gone first, then the long tree branches, followed by the berries and finally bamboo that had held the water. When the water was finished, Bram gave the bamboo to her. He chopped it up as best he could, so she didn't use up her energy. With the water gone she was showing signs of dehydration. Her belly sagged, her skin was dry, and she was losing energy. Sometimes, she would let her trunk drag in the sand, too heavy to hold up. As the sliver of the moon reappeared, they stopped to rest. Bram took off the Coke bag hanging at her side. That was all that was left. He remembered there were two cans remaining. He reached in to get them and "Yowl!" he yelled, throwing the can over his head into the sand. The sun's hot burning rays had caught the last two cans in its clutches. Even after the sun had gone down, they retained their heat. He carefully picked up the can with a rag and popped open the tab. The Coke inside was just warm.

"There's only a few left, Mosey, so open your mouth, girl." Bram reached up to pour in the Coke. She turned away. It wasn't because it was warm. She blew hot air from her trunk scattering the sand and stood quiet. Her strength gone, her body dehydrated, her desire to live was gone.... It was then Bram felt that she knew, in her way, she was dying, and a warm Coke was not going to save her.

"Mosey? Come on, now. We can make it," he spoke aloud. His hand was shaking as he dropped the can in the sand. It was then that the realization came to Bram. Modoc was really dying.

"Good Lord, what have I done?" he thought.

Flashes of their past life came racing into Bram's mind. She was his life. No, this would not be acceptable. He spoke aloud.

"We will make it," he said convincingly. "We just need to find a well. Yes, a well." Bram's mind could not handle the thought that Mo was dying. "Let her go." He heard his inner voice. "No, never, I... l... can't. Move up, Mosey."

Bram could see her straining to move her foot. It was then he knew that she would never move another step, but he just couldn't accept that. He dropped to his knees, closed his eyes, and with his voice racked with pain spoke aloud:

"Dear God, please help her. She needs you. She can't speak to you because she doesn't know English. She is a wonderful elephant; we have grown up together." His voice choked up. "She has been a good girl. Never gives me any problem, so please, just show us the way to the well. I…I...can carry the water in the Coke bag and...and well, I could... " His voice wandered off with irrational thoughts. "You can see the well from high above where you are. Show us the way."

Bram was hallucinating. He imagined a stream of water coming from the well. It splashed over them drenching Modoc as she gulped it down. His mind became a kaleidoscope of imaginary things that led him near to delirium.

"Please, please... That is all that I ask."

He cried without tears. There was no moisture for the tears he shed. He opened his eyes to the hot desert sun. There was no stream, there was no help coming. The searing heat was taking its toll. Modoc started to shake. She tried to move up but her once strong, powerful legs could go no further. She stood listless. This would be the day she could die. Bram went to her and put his cheek to hers. They stood on the dune silhouetted against a flat blue sky. For a moment he saw her in all her glory. Tall, strong, vibrant, squeaking her delights at being alive. But in the blink of an eye reality returned, and his stomach clenched tight from the shear thought of losing her. He couldn't catch his breath. His body shivered in the hot sun.

'I, her best friend, have killed her?' he thought. 'Dear God. No.'

He sank to the sand clutching her leg and cried. His sobs were caught in the stillness. There was no breeze to carry them off and no echo; they remained locked in the silence of the desert.

"Mosey, I'm so sorry, girl," his voice rasping, dry. "I didn't realize how far it would be."

Mosey, not knowing what had come into her body causing her to feel weak, had accepted it. Something was happening to her. She sensed it was time to sleep as a warm glow enveloped her.

There were times in life when hope had run out and miracles didn't happen. Bram looked to the sky in hopes of there being a sign. He believed in such things. But not even a cloud appeared, only a stark, empty, never-changing blue void as was the desert, dry, and desolate showing nothing. The desert was like a huge graveyard bringing back memories of Stone Valley as he imagined headstones across the dunes. He shook his head not to go there.

Mo lifted her trunk and laid it over Bram's shoulder, managing a single chirp. Her legs were quivering and starting to give out. It was a struggle for her to stand. Bram ran his hand over her now parched skin.

"Come down, girl, you don't have to stand," he said, his voice dry and barely audible.

Modoc came down, slowly... Bram knew she would never be able to rise again. He crawled between her front legs to rest his head on her chest. It was good that animals didn't know death, or did they? Did they know of God's Gate?

Bram felt his own body giving way. He didn't know how to face death. Did you just relax and let it happen? Or did you try to think of all you had done, places you had been, your loved ones, mistakes that were made. Things you will miss. His mind went into a spinning vortex, his thoughts turned to Modoc, his enduring friend, and all they had been through, a whirlpool of remembering.

Then, Ja's words came into his mind. "If you are ever in need, go to Sian, she will find me and together..."

He had to find Sian. Where would she be? His mind took him whirling through time and space to where they had first met. It was at the lake. Under their tree. Yes, yes, she would be there. And so she was, fading in and out, pink, and beautiful, among blue satin clouds she smiled.

"Modoc needs you. Find Ja. Find Ja. Find Ja."

"I know, I know," she whispered.

Bram drifted off; Modoc's trunk lay across his lap. The heat of the day was no longer felt. A deep sleep had come.

CHAPTER 16

"Hey, hey, hey, what do we have here?"

A voice.

Bram woke in a daze. There were blurred faces close to his that came into focus to reveal a small group of young nomads standing around looking, pushing, touching, Modoc.

"Hey you, underneath. Come out! You're talking to yourself. You crazy or something?" Bram, totally bewildered by what was happening, crawled out from beneath Modoc.

Stumbling, he could barely stand.

"What's happening? Huh? You're out in this blazing hot desert sitting with a dying elephant," said the young nomad.

Bram was starting to come around. "Look my friends, she needs water, or she will die."

"So, what is that to us?"

"You are?"

"My name is Rakesh. I am the boss, and these are my men who I have trained to be with me. So, you can only talk with me."

Rakesh, the biggest of the group was an arrogant, cocky, full-of-himself young man. His 'men' were very young insecure boys afraid of Rakesh yet proud to be with him. Bram's thoughts were coming to him.

"Well, if you could help us and get her some water, she could earn you a lot of money."

The word "money" caught their attention.

"How?" Rakesh asked.

"When she gets well, she can give rides, haul heavy stuff, pull things; she is very valuable. She could do the work of ten men," he added.

"Yeah, maybe so, or... " Rakesh had something else in mind. "Yes, sure, okay, Mohammed, give her your water." Mohammed handed over a Coke bottle of water.

"No! No! No! She needs a lot of water," said Bram.

"Hmm. So where to get it? We'll have to go back to the well."

"The well, where is it?"

"Just there," he pointed. "Over that dune. We just came from there." He pointed to a dune not more than a half hour away.

The desert could be a deceiving place. They had passed it within a few meters. The water had been so close, but the dunes had hidden it quite easily. In the next hour, Rakesh had his 'men' fill old waterproof burlap bags they carried with them at the well and bring them back to Mo who gulped the liquid down bag after bag after bag till she started to splash it on her back to cool down. As she perked up, her eyes brightened, and her trunk lightened. She started to rise on her own.

"Hey, look, the big guy is getting up."

A short walk to the well was God's answer. She stood there spraying water on herself for the next half hour.

"Come, come, we cannot be here all day," said Rakesh.

"We need to get to the town and, uh, get work for her. Right, my men?" he said with a wink.

His 'men' nodded but said nothing. Were they indeed well trained, or afraid? What was with the wink? What deception did Rakesh have in mind?

Bram knew something was amiss but decided to best keep his wits about him. His strength was returning. He had never realized the power of water.

"So hey, thanks for the elephant, white person. Now we will take her."

"Take her?" said Bram.

"Yeah, we just saved her, so now she is ours."

"But I thought... "

"No, no. What? You thought we gave our services for free?" He laughed. "Hey, guys, let's go."

They tied a ridiculously small cord around Mo's neck.

"What's her name?" asked Rakesh.

"Modoc."

"Hmm, ok. Modoc, whatever, let's go."

She stood quietly, not moving. He tugged on the rope.

"Come on, Big Mama, let's go."

Still nothing happened.

"Okay, what's the code? You know, the word to get her to move."

"Me," said Bram. "She won't go with you without me."

"What? You mean we have to drag you along to get her to move?"

"Yep," Bram mimicked.

The group got together and talked.

"Then okay, let's go."

"Where?"

"To town."

"Is it far?" questioned Bram, thinking of Mo.

"Hey, my friend. Don't get pushy. We can leave you both out here to die, so let's get the job done. You said we can make money off her. The only place to do that is in town. Right? It's about an hour's walk."

That was good to hear, thought Bram. "Yes, yes," he said. "Of course. Let's go."

Best to go with them and worry about the rest later, thought Bram. Any place that would get them out of the sun and where he would have a chance to get help. Bram knew there was something this nomad was planning, but he had no way of knowing what.

"Move up, Mo."

She started to walk toward the group who scattered to get out of her way.

"Now we're talking. Hey, guys, we got ourselves an elephant."

CHAPTER 17

Bram was happy to see them moving in the direction of the mountain. He had no idea where this town was. He tried to remember the map but the only town it showed was in the opposite direction.

It was so good to see Modoc back to her old self. Although her belly and skin sagged the water had given her new energy. Surely there will be food for her at the village.

As the group moved out through the desert, Bram overheard them talking about Modoc. They were speaking in Hindi. They had no idea Bram spoke the language, so he heard enough to learn they had no intention of going to town. They were going to sell Modoc! He heard Rakesh telling one of his men, "Vinod will pay us good money for her."

What to do? To sell Modoc! What a scary thought. But there was nothing that could be done, at least for the moment. Best to get to where they were going and plan an escape. Maybe something would transpire where Bram could change Rakesh's mind.

Within the hour the sand dunes disappeared leaving the ground flat with sparse patches of shrubbery like where the plane had crashed. Just ahead was a burned-out section of a few houses that appeared to have been part of a now deserted small village. Off to one side was an old broken down well. Water dripped down its side and a small pond stored the runoff. Modoc didn't hesitate. She lowered her trunk into it and sucked up the precious liquid.

Bram saw a group of older nomads sitting cross-legged in the shade of one of the broken structures smoking bandage (marijuana). The smell told it all. These were not boys but rather tough, older seasoned men of the desert. These were true nomads.

As they approached, some of the men got up and greeted Rakesh. They looked at Bram with a smirk then turned away. No introduction. Rakesh and one of the nomads who seemed to be the boss walked away, leaving the group of older men to sit and smoke their pot. Bram stood with Mo knowing exactly what was going on yet not being able to do anything about it. After a short while, they returned. Rakesh told Bram, "This is your new boss. His name is Vinod. I have sold my elephant to him." Vinod looked at Bram with smugness and went back to his men.

Bram had to stay calm. "I thought you wanted to make good money from her working," he told Rakesh.

"Nah, that's not who I am. Vinod here will do much better." As they walked away, Bram saw Rakesh counting a good deal of money. He stopped, looked over his shoulder, and said, "I have done a good thing for you this day, huh, white man, which is not my nature. Did I not save her from dying? Huh? I must be careful I don't fall into the ways of you good people." He laughed. "So now I deserve to own her, and it is my right to sell her. If not for me she would be dead? Huh, huh?"

Bram thought, perhaps in Rakesh's uneducated mind, there was a spark of guilt. But he was quite right. However, to own her was not part of the deal. "Go well, Rakesh, God be with you," Bram said.

"Yeah sure," he hesitated as though to say something. "Ah!" he said and left.

Bram knew that now he would have to face Vinod. He had no idea who he was or what he had in mind but, by the man's attitude, he felt it would not be easy. Vinod walked over and stood looking at Modoc. Bram held her ear not sure what Vinod had in mind.

"Now you will teach me how to work the elephant. Huh?" He walked around her, patting here and there. "She is a mighty fine beast. Big and strong. Like me!" From under his Lungi (sarong), he took a long tree branch with a rusty bent nail protruding from the end.

"You see, I too am an elephant trainer Ah! But no, first you show me your way. If you refuse, we will have to use other means to control her."

"I would be happy to show you," said Bram looking at the crude stick in Vinod's hand.

"Now, first you need to pet her, feed her, and give her water—"

"What! You think I am her keeper? I, Vinod of the family Khatri Belarusian and the great Emperor Chakrabarti should do such a menial job. Ah!"

"But it is the only way. You need to show her your love for elephants and—"

"You crazy! It is only my wife that I love." He thought for a moment. "Sometimes...but an elephant, ha!"

What to do? Bram felt so helpless in a country he knew so little about with people of different thinking. This man was a renegade, a seasoned, tough nomad, the ones he had heard about, the kind who could cut your throat and walk away laughing.

"It will take time," said Bram.

"Ah! You cannot play with me like you did with Rakesh."

He went to Modoc who sensed that this man was not a friend. She uttered a low belly tremor and put herself in a protective mode with her trunk in a tight balled up position. Vinod took the hook and jabbed it into Mo's armpit.

"Come!" he commanded.

The nail bit into Modoc's flesh, spurting blood on Vinod's garb. With a quick move, she grabbed the stick from Vinod's hand and flung it far into the air. Then, belly rumbling, she stood her stance.

"Oh ho! We have a fighter here," he said. For a belt around his waist, he wore a whip.

Long and lethal he slid it off, and swung it around, and cracked it inches from Modoc's eyes. "Please, Mr. Vinod, sir, she will not understand your way. Tell me what you would have her do, and I will see to it that she does your bidding."

"Ah! I do not need you to do anything!" he ranted. "You had your chance and you showed me nothing! So now I will show you how we teach our animals to obey." His men gathered around laughing and talking among themselves.

"Please sir," Bram begged.

Mo felt the open wound with the tip of her trunk, feeling the blood seeping out. She smacked the ground with her trunk and emitted a low grumble as she put her ears forward.

"Please sir, don't hurt her," Bram pleaded.

"Ack! No? No? She must know I am her master."

With this, he called for his men to tie ropes around her legs.

"What are you doing?" Bram asked, scared of what he might be thinking.

Vinod didn't answer but instead cracked the whip close to Modoc's ear. Once her legs were tied, he stood in front of her, poised as a mighty master his ego wished him to be.

"Now I will teach you the quick way to obey. The way we teach camels." He spoke to Mo as if she understood him.

Modoc, startled by the sound of the crackling whip, threw her body into a defensive mode. Stiff legged, trunk balled up, tail raised, ears forward. She emitted a low continuous guttural sound. Again, the whip cracked; this time causing a painful six-inch slash across her back. A line of blood ran down her side. Enraged that someone would do that, she went into a craze, whipping around, straining at the ropes.

Again, the crack of the whip and a slice of her trunk opened, much deeper than the first. With a screaming trumpet, she broke the ropes, one after the other, her trunk swiping the air, she went for Vinod. He jumped back and cracked the whip again, cutting another deep gash, this time across her leg. That did it. He couldn't get away from her. His men scattered in all directions.

She charged directly at him, grabbed his arm, picked him up, swung him up high over her head, and threw him headfirst into a pile of stone housing debris. Bram had not even a moment to do anything. It had all happened so fast. Mo stood shaking from the ordeal. She wanted to go after him again.

"No, Modoc! Steady, girl, no more. Enough!"

The tip of her trunk touched the gash on her upper trunk. The blood ran freely. Vinod's men rushed over to Vinod pulling him out from the pile of broken building material and laid him on the ground. He was indeed badly hurt. How badly Bram didn't know. The men yelled to Bram, "Chale Jao, Chale Jao (Go! Go!)"

"Foot, Mo!"

She hoisted Bram up on her back and still shaken, took off at a run in the opposite direction they had come, toward the mountains heading away from the horror of what just happened. She ran and ran through the desert, around the brush, through the gullies, over swells of sand running from the man and the whip that hurt her. The blood from her cuts was caught in the wind and splattered over her chest and onto Bram spraying droplets on his face and clothes. Bram slowed Modoc down to an easy walk.

His thoughts turned to Vinod. It had all happened so quickly. He felt sorry for him but what he had done was wrong. Elephants were not like camels or any other animal. You didn't do that to an elephant, especially Modoc. You just didn't. Bram slid off Mo to examine her cuts from the whip. They were deep but the last was the deepest and a trickle of blood was still running from it. Mo found some leaves on a nearby bush and was smearing them into the wound. Nature's remedy. The wounds would cause her discomfort while they healed but he knew the memory of what happened would remain.

Bram had always talked to Modoc.

"Your wounds will heal, girl, but I know you will always remember what you had to do." Bram ran his hand around the cut. "He shouldn't have done that, Mo. You did what you had to, and it was alright." Modoc needed Bram's approval when she did something that was out of the ordinary. To her 'alright' brought on a sign of relief. So, when he said the word 'alright' she knew that what she had done was okay. But it also reminded Bram of her potential to harm, whether unintentional or not. She was an exceptionally strong elephant and wise to the ways of men.

Being with Bram had taught her things no other elephant would ever learn.

She was an emotional elephant. Things that happened in her life were taken quite personally. Her feelings were treated with the most intensity, bordering human emotions, and she could become very protective. But that worked both ways. When she felt wronged by somebody that same intense feeling came on strong. You just didn't want to get on the wrong side of her.

Bram found himself back out in the sweltering heat of an unforgiving sun. The vastness of the desert was deceiving. All ways were the same. He had heard Rakesh speak of a town not far from the deserted one, but he couldn't go back the way he came for fear of running into him. He had to continue in the direction of the mountains.

His main concern was Modoc and water. They had left the ruins at a run leaving the horror behind. Fortunately, Mo had her fill when they first arrived at the village, but it wouldn't take long before the heat of the desert depleted that. The thought of Mo's previous near-death experience recurring sent a shiver through him. He realized that were it to happen again the result could be disastrous.

Modoc's wounds were oozing puss and starting to fester, the large ones ran blood streams that coursed down her legs. She broke off the branch of a nearby bush and swatted at the hordes of flies that had gathered to feast on the open wounds. Bram knew if they weren't treated soon infection would set in.

From the time they had arrived at the deserted village Bram noticed the mountains didn't seem as far away as they had before. They loomed far bigger, and he could even see details of the cliffs and canyons. With new enthusiasm, he continued toward them. Bram knew Modoc had picked up the scent of the mountain. She raised her trunk high in the air, the tip wiggled snake-like, blew a burst of air, and without any hesitation, she moved toward the mountains.

With the mountains so close, Modoc's enthusiasm caused a change in gears and at a renewed pace passing up Bram. Ten minutes into the walk Modoc stopped. Bram was lagging quite a bit. As he caught up, Mo raised her foot anticipating he would climb aboard. It was times like this that Bram's love for her was overwhelming. Her caring for Bram was unknown in the books of man/animal relationships. Such a blessing. Bram hugged her. "You're a good girl, Mosey, so good." He climbed aboard as she renewed her pace. To avoid the scorching heat Bram pulled the water bag down over his head. The rhythmic jolt of Mo's walk put Bram into a kind of stupor, half awake, half dozing. The hours drifted by when Bram heard Modoc give a little throat gurgle. He awoke and pulled back the bag. The sand had disappeared and through his sleepy eyes, he saw the dunes had disappeared as well. The foothills of the forest were within reach. Modoc picked up her speed, her body swaying in a different motion.

Another hour and they reached the first line of trees. Bram felt the cool breeze that could only come from a forest. Feelings of bliss and gratitude swept over him. He stretched his hands high into the air.

"Thank you, thank you, God. And Modoc thanks you. You had me going there for a while, for whatever reason, but you got Rakesh there just in time."

They had made it. Bram could hear the wind swaying the branches. "How glorious it all is, Mosey," said Bram giving Modoc a big hug. She lifted him up and gently lowered him to the ground chirping all the while.

For the first time since leaving the river Bram felt alive, regenerated, ready to take on the future whatever it would be. The desert flies stopped at the forest's edge. They were not welcome here. Mo shook the sand and twigs off her body, letting the freshness of the forest heal her wounds.

They got in under the shade of the huge trees lining the edge of the forest. Mo broke off some branches she could reach and chewed leaves, twigs, and all. Her need for food was as strong as her desire for water. Bram also felt the stress of the last few days and was exhausted from it all.

He knew they had to find the water, but he found himself too exhausted to go on. He slumped down against a tree, "Just a quick rest, Mosey, then we'll find the water."

He settled down under the tree and closed his eyes. He was surprised that the horrors of the war didn't cram his mind but instead his thoughts were of home. His mom, father, God bless them, the circus and then, suddenly, Gertie appeared.

He awoke with a start. Gertie! Bram's first love. With Sian gone, should he feel guilty thinking about Gertie?

He was returning to his deep sleep when he felt a nudge. It was Modoc. She stood alongside him still crunching some of the branches she had pulled from the tree. Again, she gave him a good nudge.

"What now?" he said. Again, the nudge. "Mo, okay, okay, I'll get up. I know you're thirsty." He got up, stretched, and noticed she had stopped chewing and was looked out into the desert. She had seen something.

From another direction than they had come the heat waves were distorting a group of camels carrying riders heading directly towards him. Bram couldn't distinguish how many there were. Their bodies intermingled in a mirage with the camels, legs tangled, robes whipping, camel heads floating, colors mixed. On they came not at a run but rather a swift gait.

"Nomads!" said Bram.

CHAPTER 18

"They're not dead."

"What's not dead?"

"The guy Bram and his elephant. They're still alive,"
kind of," said Jake coming into Mr. North's trailer office.

"No shit!" he said, putting out the stump of his cigarette,
nearly burning his stained fingers before fumbling to open
another pack.

"Yup. Listen, it's on the tube."

Jake changed the channel and turned on the news
station.

<u>NEWS BREAK</u>

"According to 'The Hindu Courier,' the plane's engines caught
fire. Captain Tyler, a seasoned Air Force Captain and veteran of
the Vietnam War, brought the plane down in a crash landing in
the Sinar Desert. It is purported that the pilot and co-pilot,
Major Jack Anderson, walked away unscathed. The passenger,
one Bram Gunterstein, and his charge, an elephant named
Modoc, a star performer at the Wunderzircus, have

disappeared! Apparently, they walked away without serious injury. We were able to reach out to Captain Tyler earlier today for a first-hand account of the situation.

Reporter: "Captain Tyler, I am Tommy Gibbs at the IAA studios broadcasting from our facility in London. Can you hear me?"

Captain: "Yes, quite well."

Reporter: "Were you the pilot who was transporting an elephant from India to New York City, USA, when the plane caught fire and you miraculously brought it down without anybody sustaining any injuries?"

Captain: "Yes, we were very lucky."

Reporter: "I understand the trainer along with the elephant have disappeared. Can you tell us what led up to their disappearance?"

Captain: "I have no idea where they went. My co-pilot and I woke in the morning and found them gone."

Reporter: "And why would they leave knowing a plane was on the way to pick them up and bring them back?"

Captain: "Your guess is as good as mine. I have no idea. I do know that the Sinar Desert is huge and not the friendliest place to be in. It would also be an easy place to get lost in."

Reporter: "Why is that?"

Captain: "It's the sand dunes. Some are as high as a five-story building, others are small, yet they can be very deceiving. You can walk around one and, in a minute, get lost. My biggest concern is if they had enough water. That elephant can really drink!"

Reporter: "Wouldn't an elephant be easy to see?"

Captain: "Not really. If you fly too high, they'll appear as dots and it's extremely hard to see whether it's a human, a camel, or an elephant; from the air they're all the same, just small dots in the sand. If you fly too low, you don't cover much of the land. But let's hope they will be found."

Reporter: "Do you have any thought as to why they left?"

Captain: "I assume the young man thought it would be fun and wandered off."

The captain was surely living up to his word to Bram.

Reporter: "Thank you, Captain. Have a safe flight home."

The Narrator continued. "The local Indian government, combined with the U.S. Air Force, is planning on sending out a few planes to scout the area as well as a search party: but with the vastness of the desert, and the extreme heat, they're facing a difficult job. The chance of finding them is quite slim."

"We will bring you further information as it becomes available."

"Jake, turn that damn thing off. See, I told you," North bellowed, "that little bugger probably caused the crash!" He fumbled with an unopened pack of cigarettes. "Wait a minute." North stood, hands waving franticly, as his mind went into outer space. "I've got it! Yes! Kill the first story! Stop the P.R.! Reverse throttle."

"This is a much bigger story, Jake." North put his hands in the air and drew an imaginary picture. "Elephant Survives Crash. Why, we'll have a parade, a homecoming, maybe a band, if it's not too expensive, and a special circus day to welcome our hero home." He ranted on.

"He's not a hero," murmured Jake.

"This could be even better than what I told that thief when I found him. Find out where they are, we'll go there with a small camera crew. I can shoot the crashed plane, the injury, everything, including the trip back and then the celebration." He finally got the cigarette pack opened. "Can you see us coming down Wall Street with Modoc? Jake, set it up."

"Boss. India is a long way off. That's a big trip so why not wait for the authorities to find them . . . and what about the circus? Who's going to run it?"

"Well, okay, but the minute they find the brat, we go. As for the circus, I don't run the damn place anyway. I have enough managers and bosses to keep the place running till I get back. Anyway, all I do is make decisions. Sometimes not so good." His thoughts wandered. "And collect the money. But what the hell."

The truth was that the performers ran the circus. These were dedicated people who loved what they did. North's only position was to handle the money and be an unfair, ruthless, cheap, boss.

"But, Boss, why do you spend so much time trying to get an elephant and a young man back here? You've spent a fortune and they're still out there. You could have bought five elephants for the money this kid has cost you."

"Shut up, just you shut up! It's my money and nobody tells me what I can or cannot do with it. And besides, this kid, well, this guy, whatever, has been the only one to outsmart me. The only one! I need to make him pay for all the problems he's caused me. I can't let him win!"

Sitting on his office chair murmuring to himself, he lit another cigarette and damn near burned his shaking fingers. Taking a long draw, he went into a near seizure causing a coughing spell. North was addicted to nicotine. It didn't matter whether it came in cigarettes, cigars, or a pipe. Whatever was handy.

But his disdain for Bram was overwhelming. He couldn't handle anyone getting the best of him and not being able to get Bram and Modoc back to the circus had driven him into an irrational state.

"Damn kid," he muttered aloud.

CHAPTER 19

"Nomads! Not again," voiced Bram.

Modoc stood quietly watching them as they came. A steady trot, all in unison, dust billowing, the riders' wraps blowing in the breeze. Bram thought of going into the forest, running, and hiding but they were in no condition to attempt it. Best to wait. Hope for the best. As the riders got closer, Bram counted five camels. All draped in colorful cloth and tassels. Up top sat four nomads dressed alike in the drab standard thobe (a long dress like cloth), with a waistband wrap. All had ghutra (scarves) covering their heads and faces. They appeared to be the security guards for the one who rode in front, as they all carried long curved blades which they had drawn from their sheaths and laid on their laps.

The leader rode a white camel known to be ridden only by people of high esteem. He wore a bright blue kandora (long robe), his head and face were also covered with a ghutra so only his eyes were unveiled. Atop his head sat a turban that matched his kandora. A large red gem was set in the front, surely for all to see. This was a man of nobility. He sat high on his camel's hump which was outfitted with far more colorful blankets than the others; and hanging from his camel's halter were pairs of red and white tassels.

Bram's only thought was they were some of Vinod thugs coming to seek revenge. They could have easily followed Modoc's huge footprints in the sand. Who else would have ventured this far? He was about to find out.

"Modoc, looks like we've got trouble."

Mo stood stiff legged. Her head jutted forward; trunk balled. She'd just had an encounter with another stranger. After what she had gone through it was understandable. She would be prepared not to let it happen again.

As they approached, Modoc uttered a deep reverberating belly rumble. She was not happy with them. "Easy, girl, easy," Bram said, patting her leg.

They reined up quite close to Bram with their camels bawling and kicking up a cloud of dust.

Bram stood his ground and tightened his grip on the choon. He had no defense but knew Modoc stood at the ready. He was surprised when the headman greeted him with his hand over his heart.

"Namaste," he said with a small head bow.

Bram bowed, answering back with his palms together, "Namaste."

The head man nodded for one of his men to lower his camel. Once down, he dismounted and stood close looking at Bram, then Modoc. Bram noticed he carried a dagger in his waistband. Two of his men dismounted and stood behind him with their hands resting on their knives.

"So," said Bram, "You're here to seek revenge, are you? Your boss shouldn't have done that to Mo. We could have worked something out. We will not go down without a fight." Bram took his choon from his wrap and put his hand on Mo's leg.

"So come, come." His voice quivered in fear.

The leader looked down at Bram with a puzzled expression, then threw his head back and let out an uproarious laugh.

His men joined him in a chorus of laughter.

Bram was in shock.

"Why would you think we are here to assault you?" the headman asked. Laughter still trickled from his grin. He appeared surprised at such an accusation.

"Since we have been in the Sinar, we have suffered at the hands of ruthless men. The desert has not been kind to us."

"My, my. You can relax. You need not worry as I am a person not capable of such things. Besides, I am one of you," he exclaimed, pulling down his scarf to reveal a bearded, mustached white man!

"You are white!" exclaimed an astonished Bram.

"Yes, since birth," he joked. A line Bram remembered using.

"But, but…" stuttered Bram. "How? I mean here in the middle of the desert to find another white man, well, it just seemed… "

"Yes, but is it no different than I finding you, another white person, here as well? I am on my way to my villa, but when I saw an elephant here in the Sinar, well, I just had to see if it was a mirage. So, I am just as surprised to find you here."

"You live here?"

"Yes, well, not here but close by. I was shopping and picking up my mail at a nearby town. It's only a three-hour ride from here."

"Is it past an old uninhabited town?" asked Bram.

"Why yes, you know of it?"

Bram smiled. "Just word of mouth," he said with a grin.

Bram was enamored with this man. It was apparent he was well-to-do and would have no need to rob them.

"And your name, sir?"

"Ahmed," he said. "There is quite a bit more to my name, best for you to use Ahmed. And yours is?"

"Yes, of course, my name is Bram."

Bram heard Mo give her 'you're not paying attention to me,' grumble. She was a bit uneasy with strangers and Bram was afraid she might do something rash. Best to introduce her.

"Modoc, girl, come here."

She blew some dust, scratched one leg against the other, and slowly ambled over.

"This is Modoc. It's okay, girl, you can relax. This man is now our friend, I guess," he said, still not sure of his friendliness. Modoc reached her trunk to Ahmed and gave him the elephant way of checking a person out by touching him in different places. "Modoc is my friend and partner in life, so you can feel comfortable with her."

"You speak to this elephant as though he understands."

"He is she and yes, she does."

"Well, pleased to meet you both," Ahmed said as he shook Modoc's out-stretched trunk.

Content that he was okay, she clicked and moved on to resume her chomping on anything green. The forest was a paradise for her. It had been a long time since she ate decent food, so she was ready to sample all the greenery in the forest. Her search for clumps of dried-up weed was over.

Ahmed looked Bram over with a keen eye. "You are a disguised American, are you not?" he said.

"Well, German actually and if you mean my bad Hindi, yes, I guess so," he stammered. "Is it that obvious?"

"Hmm. You spoke but one word in Hindi. No, it is your mannerism. But tell me, what brings you and your elephant friend across some of the hottest parts of the Sinar Desert? There are no tame ones around you see, they are all wild, so we have no use for them here."

"I didn't bring her here to work. We have come due to things happening that we were unable to control. One man, one unbelievable person who has no sense of morals, has caused us to be here. But that's a long, long story. For now, all I care about is water for Modoc. She needs some and quickly. We were going into the forest to find it when I saw you coming."

"Yes, yes, of course." He beckoned to one of his men. "Ahdir li Alma (bring me the water)," he said.

One of his men unloaded a large canvas waterbag from one of the camels and with the help of another carried it over. Bram had the man set it down in front of Mo who stuck her trunk in it and within a minute sucked it dry.

"Thanks so much. She almost perished out there." Bram nodded toward the desert.

"Yes, well, but now you have got my interest. I think your story is one I would enjoy hearing."

"Why? Am I not a stranger to you?" said Bram.

"I have not seen a visitor from the outside in many a moon. Especially one who is white, has traveled, and would not

bore me as do the locals. They are difficult to find nowadays."
He smiled. "And I hope your story includes this individual you
spoke of. Whoever forced you into the desert with an elephant
must be a truly evil man."

Bram was impressed with the man's impeccable and
friendly manner. He felt he could trust him with his secret
adventure. But he was in no mood to retell his story after having
detailed it to the captain and Jack. He decided it was best to
change the subject for now.

"You must be a man of great wealth," said Bram, looking
at his garb.

"Why would you say that?"

"By the clothes you wear, the camels you own, and the
men you employ."

"Those are material things. My wealth is in my
appreciation of life."

"Then you are a poet or a philosopher?"

He laughed. "Well, I guess you could say that. Maybe
both. In truth I am the Tsar of Agustina, a small town in the
country of Serbia. A country far, far, from here."

"I would have taken you for a man of India. Perhaps it's
the way you are dressed. In India the way you dress signifies
your status."

"My position here has never been questioned. But I am
no longer wealthy. I have put all I possess in my belongings."

"I'm impressed. Your story must be as long as mine," said
Bram.

"Maybe." He thought for a moment. "But it is yours that
fascinates me. Perhaps one that should be told with a brew."

"Someday," said Bram, knowing that would be a long
way off.

"Come," said Ahmed.

They went to a shaded tree area where one of the
nomads spread a blanket of many colors on the ground. They
sat crossed-legged. Ahmed waved his hand to one of his men
who promptly slid down the side of his camel, tearing some
heavy tarps aside to reveal a metal chest. This he carried and
put in the center of the blanket. Again, Ahmed waved his hand,
the man opened the chest, and out came two chilled glasses, one
of which he handed to Bram followed by two bottles of ice-cold

beers. A wooden bowl of mixed fruit and biscuits accompanied the beer.

Bram was in shock. "How is that possible, where? How?"

"I'm sure you are wondering where we get the ice in such a hot desert."

"Yes, it's unbelievable."

"Not really. The mountains give us fresh snow most of the year. There is a valley close by that is sheltered from the rays of the sun. The snow never melts there but remains until it turns to ice. The rest is obvious. The metal container keeps it cold. So," he raised his glass, "as you say, cheers."

They clinked glasses and drank the most delicious 'cold beer' Bram ever had.

"Now, your story?" said Ahmed.

"You're serious? We are absolute strangers to one another. We have just met and... "

"Had a beer together," offered Ahmed.

"Yes, shared a beer together. Now you want to hear the story of my life."

"To date."

"To date. Now?"

"My curiosity overwhelms me. To find a white man and an elephant in the Sinar Desert would whet anyone's interest. Besides, keeping it to yourself gives it little value; to tell me gives it a purpose."

"Well, okay, if that's what you want. I see no reason not to tell it. Hope you don't get bored. But I haven't heard your story yet."

"But, of course, you will, in time."

"Whatever," said Bram. "It all began . . ."

And through to the end, Bram elaborated on all that had befallen him up to that moment. For some reason telling it again was difficult. It only brought back his anguish at the man who was responsible for it. In that time, four empty bottles lay in front of each of them.

"My friend, you have suffered a lot," said Ahmed. "Your life has been a circle of mishaps. But what is amazing to me is you and your elephant have survived to come through it strong and full of vigor." He thought for a moment. "Please, you must be my guest and stay at my villa till you can right yourself on a very bumpy road."

Bram was in shock. "Well, we have come a long way, and are hungry and tired. My friend here is exhausted from her trek over land she's not familiar with. Yes, of course, we will be delighted to accompany you. Thank you.

"But now your story," said Bram.

"Ah. But it is not nearly as interesting as yours. You see, I was born in Russia to a wealthy family. During the war my parents were killed and—"

"Sorry."

"Yes, well, I inherited a good deal of money, land, and other assets. Due to political problems, I left with ample funds to start my life over. I ended up here."

"Why here?" Bram asked. "A man of your position would have his choice to be wherever he wants."

"It was by accident that I found this place. I am a travel buff, so when an offer came to go on a camel Shikari in India, I couldn't say no."

"A what?"

"A Shikari. It's what the Africans call a safari. We had twenty camels and had set out from Acabar, a small town north of here just on the outskirts of the desert, to cross the Sinar stopping at a few water holes along the way. We traveled for about ten days setting up tent camps at different water holes. I was intrigued by the beauty of the mountain range and when I saw the forest, I decided to head for it. Our nomad guides had never been there before and thought it might be a good place to see some of the more elusive animals like antelope, wild boar and maybe even the leopards that come down from the mountains."

"I am a great lover of animals too," added Bram.

"Yes, I can see that," he said, looking at Modoc. "We took a trail through this very same forest and as we traveled, it became thicker, almost impenetrable. It was then that we saw the sanctuary. A haunting place, it was hidden far back in the forest surrounded by giant trees. It stood on a slight earthen rise overgrown with a century of vegetation. Thick climbing vines like snakes had entered the house through windows, broken doors. Whole walls were covered in ivy. Some had flowers; others stayed drab. The basement floor had decayed, and rats, snakes, and vermin scampered as I walked through. Tree roots had broken the foundation and one of four minarets high on the roof had fallen. The overgrowth was so thick it was difficult to distinguish the front of the house from the back.

"The house showed an Indian design with a Persian influence. There were some old, rotted rug wall hangings depicting Persian artistry."

"How do you know that?"

"My study at the university."

"What you are telling me sounds like a mystical place," said Bram.

"Yes, well, strange as it was, I felt warmth coming from it. But there's more. I walked around the structure and there, not more than fifty feet away, I was amazed to find what we now call the Varuna Falls. Towering some ten feet in the air was a molten rock precipice and cascading from above a wall of water fell into a pool below. It was an awesome experience finding it so close to the house.

"I noticed a section of the rock wall surrounding the property had been broken down. I believed the elephants did it to come for the water.

"I'm sure the Falls came first, then the house. The original owners probably built the house close to it. The forest people speak of a time when the Goddess Varuna was in the forest and saw that the animals were in need of water."

"Who are these forest people?"

"They're aborigine people, small, quite shy, rarely seen. You can hear them playing music on unusual instruments. No one knows where they came from. Some say they came with the forest."

"So, you were saying?"

"Yes, well, she created the Falls with her hands. They said he who drinks from it, will stay forever young."

"That's the story of the 'Fountain of Youth' fable."

"Yes, I know."

"So do you believe it?"

"I go out each morning and drink from the pool, and I do look a bit young for my age," he laughed. "But, due to the water, the grass and plants around the area grow faster and stay far brighter than any others in the area."

"Why did the people leave?" asked Bram.

"We were to learn a war, a small one, had broken out and the rebels who came were a fanatical sect who wreaked havoc throughout the area. It was enough to have the people leave for fear of losing their lives. Oddly, the rebels never took the sanctuary over. They were more interested in revenge, and it wasn't long before the government caught up with them and put a halt to their savagery."

"The people who lived here never came back?"

"No, they were told it was haunted and the fear kept them away. That was more than a hundred years ago. Since then, it sat idle. Few people knew about it. Mostly old timers who came by occasionally. Strange, but in all those years, no one had ever shown an interest in it."

"Maybe it was waiting for you." Bram grinned.

"Perhaps, it's too far for most, too desolate for others, just perfect for me. It has taken us years to restore it to its original look. I bought the land from the government. They didn't even know the house was here. We call it Shangari."

"It sounds very mystical."

"More spiritual perhaps? For us who live there it conjured up a place of peace, warmth, and tranquility. It came from the goddess Durga, 'Mother of All.' But you will soon judge it on your own."

"So that's where you live?"

"Yes, but it is more, it is my sanctuary. You will see."

At a flick of his hands, the nomads had the blanket, bottles, and chest secure on the side of a camel and within moments Bram and Ahmed had both mounted up. With a 'move up' from Bram and a 'challo' (Go) from Ahmed, they moved into a medieval forest on a trail of soft multicolored loam made from the falling leaves of each season. They rode in silence alongside each other where the trail allowed, listening to the sounds of the forest.

"Why do I feel I have known you before?" asked Bram, curious about their new relationship.

"Do you believe in auras?" asked Ahmed.

"Yes, I have been taught how to recognize them," said Bram.

"Then you believe each of us has an invisible band around us that tells if another person is good, bad, trustworthily, or not? Perhaps it's called by another name like 'instinct.'"

"How about a 'gut' feeling?" offered Bram.

"Yes, they are all related."

"Perhaps revealing our life stories has helped," said Ahmed. "Maybe, because we have now become friends in a short while."

"It is a wonderful feeling to have a friend," added Bram. He thought for a moment. "But don't people have to prove their friendship to become friends?"

"In time, Bram, in time. But yes, I think we are surely a good match."

"I can see you have become a true Indian and have adapted their way of life," said Bram.

"When you live in a foreign country for many years, one must adapt or life will not be pleasant," said Ahmed. "But now, it's getting late, and we still have a distance to go." He urged his camel a bit faster. Modoc lengthened her stride as well. The pace was invigorating. At the far end of the forest a herd of elephants was passing through, breaking branches, trumpeting, going somewhere only they knew.

Ahmed raised his hand. "Best we wait here. I'm not sure what would happen if they got wind of Modoc."

Bram jumped down and tapped Mo's trunk. "Hold," he said. "Put it in your pocket, Mo." She put her trunk in her mouth and held on. The herd passed and, only after they were out of sight, did he give her the okay to relax.

"Good girl, Mosey!"

"Remarkable," exclaimed Ahmed on seeing what Modoc had been trained to do. As they moved deeper into the forest, Ahmed stopped at a small trail that led into a primeval thicket where even the sun could not penetrate.

"Bram, this trail will take you to our lake. It is one of the most beautiful I have ever seen. We have yet to name it. Perhaps it's waiting for you to do the honor."

"That sounds inviting. Mosey and I will christen it once we swim in its waters." As they continued, Bram couldn't help noticing the beauty of the forest. "This forest is alive."

"Alive?"

"Yes, I can feel it. There is an energy here that is very strong. There is nothing like the smell of a forest, the cool fresh air. It reminds me of the scent of the teak forest and the lumber camp."

Deer stood in the thicket unafraid, watching as they passed, flocks of colorful birds singing their song flew overhead.

With food in abundance and streams of icy cold water it was a land of plenty. It was all good. Mo seemed to be enjoying the walk. She was in a playful mood tweaking the camel's tail every so often or sampling some of the bushes.

As they moved deeper into the forest, the trail weaved its way through. Thick brush covered the landscape attended by giant trees that stretched into a canopy far above and shaded the forest below. In the distance, Bram heard the beat of a drum, the chanting of children. He looked at Ahmed.

"They are the forest people. Remember, not seen, only heard."

The trail widened as they approached a stone wall covered with immense clinging vines higher than Modoc's back. The sweet odor of jasmine was in the air.

"We're home," said Ahmed.

CHAPTER 20

A bearded elderly man wearing a loincloth sat cross-legged at the gate playing on the wooden drum they had heard. He stopped, gave a namaste, bowed, and disappeared in the bush.

"It is to welcome us back safely from our journey," said Ahmed.

Two huge wooden gates with flat metal hinges and bolts lashed together with camel leather thongs gave it an impenetrable look. They were opened by two men wearing lungis (sarongs) and white turbans. As they entered a beautiful garden of giant elephant-ear plants, Bram observed myriad jasmine flowers and pathways made from the bark of redwood trees.

Once inside, Ahmed, assisted by his men, dismounted while Bram slid down Modoc's side.

"Welcome to Shangari, Bram. I have a kraal for Modoc that once housed a young bull elephant. It had been injured and we kept it for a while rather than let it die. I hope Modoc doesn't mind till we build something more to her liking."

"Thank you so much."

"I will have a bale of oat hay put in the kraal and the trough filled with water."

"I'm sure it will be just fine," said Bram, leading her to the kraal. Bram put her in the enclosure and shut the gate. She pushed it open when he turned his back. "Mo, quit playing around." He closed the gate, and she pushed it open again. "Modoc! Stop already."

He put her back in.

"Here, try this," laughed Ahmed, handing Bram a huge lock hanging nearby.

"Mo, be good. I'll see you later."

A click of the padlock, a quick pat, followed by her chirp, then Bram joined Ahmed to head down a path.

The evening darkness had set in. Two men approached carrying flaming torches to help light the way. One followed, the other led. Bram followed Ahmed down a winding pathway. Through the light from the torches Bram hesitated for a moment as he caught glimpses of a majestic garden of flowers, rock waterfalls, and trees with knotted vines growing on them.

Ahmed, looking over his shoulder, saw Bram's interest.

"Tomorrow," he said, as they moved on.

There appeared out of the darkness, lit by the blazing torches, two huge doors. Eight feet high made of what appeared to be teak wood carved in a Hindi style. The doors were opened by two small Indian boys who greeted Bram and Ahmed in the Hindi fashion.

"Namaste," one said.

"Namaste," repeated the other, hands cupped together.

Bram acknowledged their greetings as did Ahmed as they entered a large high ceiling room lit by dozens of candles. Indian and Arab rugs covered most of the buffed hardwood floor. Statues of bronze Hindu deities etched in gold and silver enhanced the room along with matching furniture in color and design. Colorful tapestries hung from the ceiling depicting war, famine, and love all in brilliant color and design. Ahmed had refurbished the house in a mixture of Hindi, Pakistani and American style.

The flickering candles gave it all a surrealistic feeling. Barefooted men and women wearing loose fitting white harem pants tied at the ankles and matching blouses and shirts were walking in and out of adjoining rooms, some carrying food, others bedding materials and kitchenware. Bram was taken aback by the lavishness of it all. A petite Indian woman approached Ahmed.

"Bram, this is Mirer, who will show you to your room and care for your needs. Maybe a quick shower and then I'll see you for dinner. It's down that way," he said pointing towards a corridor.

Mirer was a house girl who 'palmed' Bram a welcome and took him to his room whose décor reflected the same look as the main living room. She laid out clothing for him, closed the drapes, set the bed, tidied up where necessary and bid Bram a good evening. It was all too much, thought Bram.

The shower was pure ecstasy. The muck and grime gave way to the steaming hot water revealing sores, cuts, and bruises that had been hidden. Stubborn scabs refused to give way till a scrub brush broke their hold, opening the red raw flesh. It made him think of Mo's injuries, far worse than his.

Bram arrived fresh and clean wearing the Indian clothes laid out for him: a kurta (knee length shirt) and a pair of jodhpurs (baggy pants) complete with a pair of (chappals) sandals. He was greeted in the dining room by one of the house helpers with a glass of sparkling wine. The torches, rugs, and Indian furnishings gave the rooms a warmth that one could find comforting without being overwhelmed.

The dining room was as inviting as the main room. A long-polished oak table ran down the middle of the room and in the center sat a large bronze sculpture of a reclining Buddha. Bram ran his hand over the glossy finish.

"It's like giving it a second life," said a voice. It was Ahmed. He had arrived. On his arm was an attractive Indian woman perhaps in her 30s, her long black hair tied in a ponytail.

"Bram, I would like you to meet my wife, Latika. Honey, this is Bram."

"Yes, of course," she said, offering her hand. "You are the young man with the elephant."

"Yes, ma'am." He took her hand, not knowing whether to kiss it or shake it. He chose the latter. "She's called Modoc."

"I understand you and uh, Modoc, have had quite a journey."

"Yes, ma'am. We have."

"Well, you can consider this your new home for now, and Modoc is welcome as well."

A man approached wearing a pilot's flight jacket and matching apparel.

"And this good-looking man is Coogan McGuire, our pilot," said Ahmed.

Coogan was of a mixed breed Indian and Caucasian. He was the epitome of what every pilot should look like. Tall, well-built, a smile as wide as his mustache, and a small, pointed goatee. To finish his immaculate style, he wore a black turban. Bram thought he might salute rather than shake hands.

"Yes, well, so good to meet you. Do you fly?" he asked seriously.

Only when my wings are attached, Bram wanted to say. "No, just once."

"Well, come by, I can give you a turn around the forest."

"Now, how could that happen, your plane only flies one person," interrupted Ahmed.

"Hmm," he hummed, trying to get out of it. "I've handled large packages from the towns, and they fit."

"You're thinking Bram here is a package, do you?" Coogan was trying to worm his way out of it. Ahmed gave a big hardy laugh. "Gotcha on this one. Just pulling your leg."

Coogan said a bit flustered, "Yes, well there you have it. Time for a drink or two," he said walking toward the bar.

"Nice fellow, always protects what his plane can do," said Ahmed.

"What kind of plane is it?"

"A single engine piper cub. It holds the pilot and a few packages. When he isn't polishing his plane, he makes runs into nearby towns picking up supplies and the mail."

Bram was to find out he took his flying quite seriously. One would think he flew a jet fighter, but he was proud of his small plane. A nice guy.

An elderly Hindu walked over. He was dressed in a white thawb (long tunic) with matching pants and wore a white turban. "Dinner is prepared, Sahib."

The dinner was fresh fruit and vegetables from their farm and slices of chicken smothered in a creamy raspberry sauce. A delicious meal that left one totally sated. A drink after dinner, small talk, and Bram headed for the bedroom exhausted in a good way. He was worried that perhaps the pain of remembering the tragedy on the mountain would take away a night of tranquil sleep. But it had been a long day, what with the horrors of the deserted village, the heat of the desert, and finally the meeting of Ahmed, then ending up in a wonderful place gave way to a night of peaceful, sound sleep. His last thought was of Gertie.

Morning came with the ringing of the breakfast bell.

"They ring it one hour before breakfast is served," Ahmed had told Bram at dinner the previous night.

Bram had a quick shower, then donned a set of his new Indian clothes set out for him. Loose fitting garb suited for the hot Indian weather. It allowed the hot air to circulate and keep the body cool. But before breakfast he had to see Mosey. He took a walk out in the garden and, not knowing which way to go, he called her name. A few chirps told him her location.

"Morning, Mo. Hope you had a good sleep," he said, stroking her head.

Up went her trunk around his neck and smack! An elephant rendition of a kiss!

Bram noticed a huge pile of grass and brush in the corner of her pen. "I see you already had your breakfast this morning. Someone is taking good care of you."

Her chirping was enough for him to know that she was content in her new surroundings.

"I see you found your way." It was Ahmed.

"Morning, Ahmed. Yes, I was just seeing if Mosey is okay"

"I told the guard to put in a forest breakfast. All kinds of greens. Is that alright?"

"Yes, of course, she loves it. Thank you."

"Would you like a morning stroll after breakfast?" he asked.

"By all means. I'm anxious to see it all," said Bram. "But I need to treat Modoc's injuries."

"Of course, I see it will be a long process. Let's enjoy our breakfast, then I will gather a few of my people to help."

And so it was. After a lavish breakfast, they met with three gardeners who brought an array of medical supplies. They swarmed over Mo's entire body washing, picking, scrubbing, and treating her injuries. She was in her glory being preened over from head to tail. Once done a huge basket of fruit was brought out to her. She couldn't stop chirping and belly rumbling as she stuffed her mouth with all her favorite foods.

An hour later found them walking through the estate's gardens, around the waterways, admiring the many miniature temples and statues of the numerous deities.

Four minarets rose, one from each corner of the house. Slender and graceful, they spiraled up to a majestic pinnacle. When Bram first saw the area, he was taken aback by not only its overall beauty but for the abundance of its ancient trees.

Explained Ahmed, "Some have been here for more than a hundred years. There are giant sequoias, baobab, the tree that God planted upside down, the banyan with its many arms was a forest in itself, the mighty teak, the hard mahogany, all have their place in the sanctuary.

"When most people buy a place, they change it to their liking. My choice was to leave the trees as they were. If there was a need to build, I would build around them."

"So, you have," Bram said, noticing many paths, ponds, and statues set randomly, neither aligned nor symmetrical with other trees in the area.

There were trees growing in the middle of the garden, in the path coming in, a few grew in the house with holes cut in the roof. Circular troughs were built around the base of each tree to catch water when it rained.

"The trees come first," Bram said.

"Indeed, they do," confirmed Ahmed.

Bram was most anxious to see the Varuna waterfalls. Ahmed led the way down a small shiny black stone pathway that branched out and circled the base of the Falls. Some ten feet high and perhaps twenty feet across, the water came from deep within the earth and gushed up a rocky mountain of jagged molten rock to then cascade down to the pond below. At the base of the Falls grew a mini forest with trees and bushes, but all of miniature stature.

"Ahmed, this is spectacular. Never have I seen anything as beautiful as this." Then, something caught his eye.

"Why is the forest miniature? This is amazing."

"I think it must be something in the water," suggested Ahmed.

"So, if we drink it, we'll become small?" teased Bram.

Ahmad laughed. "No, no but it is strange. There are things in nature that take on the need of their surroundings. Maybe that's the case here. When you look at the pond and forest up close, your vision will adjust, and the forest will appear full size. You could easily imagine tiny people walking through the undergrowth."

Bram got down low, so he was directly in line with the forest. Sure enough, he felt he could walk on the narrow trail through the forest.

"Yes, you're right," he said, gazing at the forest. "I would have expected to see birds flying over, fish leaping in the pool, deer springing out of the woods."

It was truly a phenomenon. It gave one a sense of well-being.

Some of Ahmed's people were there blessing the water and giving thanks to the God Varuna. "They treat it as a place of worship," said Ahmed.

"The entire compound is built on a 5% grade," Ahmed continued. "It's all based on gravity flow. Water that comes from the Falls travels through this channel," he said pointing to an open waterway, "where it divides into four canals. One goes to the garden, another to the nursery and a larger one to the cultivated farming fields. The overflow makes its way through another canal that travels through a hole in the wall into a huge trough that supplies water to the wild animals, especially the elephants."

"It's an ingenious method and all from the Falls," said Bram.

"There's more. The water has properties that become fluorescent and emits a soft green light. It's beautiful at night. There is an antibody that kills any bacteria that flows through it."

"So, it's got to be the purest of all waters."

"Yes, that's what keeps us so healthy."

"It's truly a phenomenon of nature," said Bram. "Do you believe?"

"What?"

"That the Goddess Varuna drank from it and perhaps that's what gives the Falls its ability to give health and vitality to all who drink from it?"

Ahmed thought for a moment. "I have learned to not disbelieve anything."

"Were the outside world to hear of it, the estate would be ruined by the rush to get the water," said Bram.

"Fortunately, we are far too remote for that to happen," said Ahmed. "Other than a few old timers, no one knows it exists."

"But if I am the first to have come from the outside, have I not broken the secret?" asked Bram. "I feel bad that maybe I have stirred the calm waters. That I have altered your way."

"No, my friend, you have enhanced it. Were you of a different nature, I would not have brought you here. You are what Shangari is all about."

"You believe I was meant to be here?"

"I do. Perhaps it's my spiritual thinking, but you were meant to be here," said Ahmed. "No matter what hardships you suffered, you have now found your calling. So be happy."

"I am, we are," Bram said, thinking of Mo. "But, Ahmed, what about all your staff. Don't they ever ask to leave? Don't you worry that they would tell others of its existence?"

Ahmed thought for a moment. "Bram, each and every one are friends of my wife and me. In all these years, not one has revealed our location. And if they do, then it's God will. We live on their love for Shangari."

"Now I understand why you call it a sanctuary."

Ahmed beckoned to a young man. "Bram, this is Sanjoe. He will be at your constant call to help you with all your needs. He speaks better English than you do Hindi," he laughed.

"It's a pleasure, Mr. Bram." He bowed his namaste."

"Same here, Sanjoe, nice to meet you."

Sanjoe was a strong, lean, boy, perhaps 14, 15 at the most. He wore a knee-high Kurta (shirt) over a pair of Western jeans. Of Indian descent, his features were as most of the young men of Calcutta. Brown, near black skin. Pitch black hair that ran down the back of his neck, thick black eyebrows, a perfect smile that featured the whitest of teeth, and dark eyes that revealed his honesty. A gentle man, eager to prove himself.

And so, in the weeks that followed, Bram walked with Sanjoe learning each and every facet of the operation.

"Mr. Bram, why do you want to learn about the estate?" asked Sanjoe. "You spend every day since you came here studying every aspect of it."

"I don't want to be a burden to Ahmed, Sanjoe. If I learn, I can be a benefit to him and assist in running the estate."

What Bram didn't tell Sanjoe was that working at Sangari gave him a peace of mind that he had not experienced in so long a time. It was a closure of all the horror that had happened to him.

The garden, its plants, the smell of the ginger and lavender were as an aphrodisiac. It also filled his mind with thoughts of Gertie.

CHAPTER 21

Since his dream of Gertie, Bram's nights belonged to her. He prepared himself that once he lay in bed, he allowed his mind to drift back to his home in Germany. There he'd find Gertie and stroll in the flower fields and ride Modoc to Cryer Lake where they swam together in its cool waters. He always kissed her before the dream ended. It was all so real. He felt he was intruding in her life without getting her consent. But since seeing her picture in his dream, she had never left him. He realized his love for her had only lain dormant, but now it had awakened. But would she still want him? Maybe her love for him had gone to another. He had to know. He got up early, sat at his desk, and wrote her a letter:

Dear Gertie,

Since I left the circus, my life has been a chaotic journey that has taken me through some of the most difficult times one could experience. I cannot return to the circus as North will put me in jail and Modoc will be subjected to a trainer who will beat her into submission. I was pulled away from you during those trying times when I was running from the wrath of North, but now it's time for us to come together. My life has done a turnaround and we, Mo and I, have found a paradise and are living well. Since arriving here, I have had you on my mind each day and night. I want you in my life. Nothing in my life is fulfilled without you being in it. I love you so much and am asking for you to join me. You are far away and how to get you here will take some doing. If you have another life, I can only wish you happiness. But if not, please come and together let's share a life in a place where dreams are made. Will you come? I've never stopped loving you. Please be careful. If North were to find this letter, my life would never be the same. Mo says hello.

     Love,
     Bram

Bram needed to find a way to send the letter to Gertie. He was prepared to walk the desert if necessary. Surely Ahmed would know a way as he probably has business in the outside world. He caught up with Ahmed while he and the others planted crops for the season.

"Well, the only way is to use Coogan," Ahmed said. "He flies into the few small towns around the Sinar picking up things needed for the estate. He would know the best place to get it mailed."

"Where can I find him?"

"He keeps the plane on the runway just on the other side of the crop area. He rarely leaves it."

Bram found the runway, a small dirt strip so short it seemed not long enough to get the plane off the ground. Ahead he saw Coogan working on his plane.

"What's up, Bram?"

"Need a favor. I have a letter that's extremely important, well, important to me, that needs to be sent to Germany. Is it possible?"

"Well, I fly once a week from Shangari to Goajai. It's a small town about a half-hour run from here. They have a post office, if that's what you call a box outside of the Namaste restaurant. I can sure get it there, but from then on, your guess is as good as mine."

"If you could, I would really appreciate it."

"Sure, no problem. I fly out again tomorrow. I'll drop it off then."

"Thanks so much."

Next morning Bram watched the plane soar over the compound, dip its wings to say, 'see ya,' and disappear over the desert.

For the next month, Bram worked in the fields as he agonized. He met the plane each time it arrived back from Coogan's runs, hoping a letter from Gertie had come. Nothing. When it got into the second month, Bram started to give up hope. Waiting could be so exhausting. Every time he heard Coogan's plane, his anticipation turned to hope, then to prayer. Would it be there and if so, would she come?

It was early Sunday morning before breakfast. Coogan had decided to stay overnight in town and was just arriving. As usual, he dipped his wings knowing Bram would be waiting for him. Bram met the plane as he taxied up to his parking spot, shut down the engine, and stepped out.

"Well! well! Anything? Anything at all?"

His face was grim as he shook his head no until… he pulled out a letter from his inside pocket. Now he had a grin on his face. It was a letter from Gertie.

"You... you! Ah! Give it here!"

Bram took the letter, gave Coogan a shoulder hug, and left. Where to go to open it? Did it matter? Well, yes. If she said no, he didn't want anybody to see a grown man weep. On the other hand, if she said yes, he would probably alert the house that a madman was on the loose. He chose his room. It was quiet, warm, and friendly. The envelope was marked with lots of different markers, wrinkled, and worn. It must have gone through many hands, he thought. He sat on the bed, gently opening the envelope, and visualizing Gertie placing the letter inside. He read:

My dear Bram,

Oh! How I have waited these years to hear from you. There were times when I gave up hope, not knowing if you had been injured or even died. I heard from your mentor, Ja. You must have given him my contact number in case something happened. He sure seems like a nice man. He was kind enough to inform me that you were alive and well. He told me of your girlfriend Sian's passing. I wasn't aware, but I understand. It must have been so tragic what with the airplanes and all. My heart bleeds for you. I can only imagine how much you must have cared for her.

Mom passed away a year ago. She wasn't the same after Papa's death. Never got over it. I say hi to our friends when I see them in town.

They always ask about you. It's been hard to tell them it has been a while since I heard from you, but now they will be happy that you and Mo are alright.

Dear Bram, of course I would want to come to you, to be with you for the rest of my life, but I fear your love for Sian still lingers in your soul. Although I understand your love for her, I would worry if you could separate us, let her go, and welcome me into your life. Please think about it, my love, and remember I am Gertie, your first love who has and will always love and adore you. Her hand from the other world needs to let you go.

I hope this letter reaches you and you are well. I will await your letter; but whatever your decision, be sure you can truly live with it. My love for you is and will always be forever.

Yours, Gertie.

Bram didn't know whether to scream or cry. He had said his goodbye to Sian at her grave. She would understand. Nor would he, could he, ever forget her. That night he sat down and wrote:

Gertie my love,

How wonderful to get your letter! I have read it five times! Maybe more! I sure understand your concern about Sian. I know God has His hand on her shoulder. She was a good person, and we will always be connected through our memories. I know she would want me to be happy. That's what love is, wanting the other to be happy. Sian is now gone, and I have moved on knowing her life in God's house will be one of peace and contentment.

So, Gertie, please come. Let us be together as one and move into our circle of life. I have given you directions on how to get to this little town of Goajai. It will not be easy as it is far from where you live, but with your tenacity you will find your way. A pilot named Coogan McGuire will check often for your arrival. Bring little, your needs will be met here. I can't wait to see you and hold you in my arms once again.

Till then,
Love, Bram

At dinner that night, Bram told Ahmed and Latika about Gertie coming.

"I hope you don't mind. I should have asked you first," said Bram a bit embarrassed.

"Bram, you have become a member of our home. We know that anyone you choose to bring here would be a very special person," said Ahmed.

"How wonderful for you," said Latika. "We will look forward to her arrival."

"I remember your story mentioning her," said Ahmed.

"How exciting! We'll need to have a celebration on her arrival," said Latika.

But when she'd arrive, no one knew. Bram looked depressed at the thought.

"How will she get here?" questioned Ahmed.

"Coogan said he can arrange for some form of transportation, maybe a camel, donkey, who knows, anyway, somehow he would get her here," Bram said.

It was amazing how time can change when waiting for someone. Normally, the time between morning and evening passed as it should, not hurried but just right. But when waiting for someone, especially if it's important, days can seem like weeks. So, it was waiting for Gertie. One evening after dinner, Ahmed took Bram's arm.

"Come with me," he said.

They went outside and stood in the garden of the Varuna Falls. It was the night of a full moon. As they approached, the green glow from the water cast an eerie presence on all it embraced.

"Look at the Falls," said Ahmed.

Bram did as he was told.

"What do you see?"

"The Falls... the rock. ...the... oh yes! Good Lord, the shadow."

The moon had thrown a strong dark shadow of the Falls against the ground. A section of the Falls jutting out from the main rock cast a perfect image of the Buddha!

"That's frightening. When did you notice it?"

"A month after the house was finished. Latika won't come out here under a full moon."

"I can surely understand why. That is one of the most chilling things I have ever seen."

"It is also reverent."

"Maybe it's just an accident?"

"You really think so?"

It was early morning when Bram awoke feeling that Mo needed him. It was nothing new to him. Happened all the time. Whenever a certain kind of spark flashed through his mind, he just knew that she needed him. Most of the time they were minor things like out of food, water basin overturned, lonely, just stuff. But he always responded to it. He got up, put on his loincloth, and headed out to her pen.

As he approached, he saw Modoc pacing up and down while hearing a lot of shuffling noises coupled with elephants outside of the wall blowing through their trunks. Ahmed came over.

"I heard the noise, so I thought I would come and check it out. But it's nothing to worry about," he said. "It's the resident herd. They come all the time. Mostly for water or just being nosy.

"They are a mixture of size and age. From newborn to quite old. How they ever got here no one knew. A group of elephants could never cross the desert without proper food and a lot of water. Nor could they scale the snow-covered peaks that surrounded the back of the forest. When we first came here, there were only eight in the herd. Since then, they have increased to twenty."

Bram stood and listened. They were just outside the wall blowing dust in the air carrying on quite a commotion. Some were reaching their trunks up over the fence; apparently sensing Modoc' s presence. They knew she was there.

"They're trying to communicate with her. It must be a shock to them having never seen another elephant other than their own group."

"Hmmm. Of course. Hope they become friends," said Ahmed.

There was a lot of clicking, belly rumbling, and trumpeting going on from both sides. She was answering back so all seemed quite nice and friendly.

"But they can have a bad side sometimes," said Ahmed.

"Like when the young males challenge one of the big guys?"

"That creates quite a ruckus."

"I can imagine."

Built into the wall every six feet were small rectangular turrets used for looking out at the forest. Bram went to one and got a close-up view of the herd until one of them stuck his trunk against the turret. It was too small for even the tip of his trunk to get into. Bram put the back of his hand up so the elephant could touch and smell his friendliness. He blew a gust of hot air against the hand and then put the tip of his trunk in his mouth sensing Bram's presence. Doing this, he could know if Bram was friend or foe.

When he backed off, Bram saw that it was a huge bull. An immense animal with tusks eight feet long, he was far bigger than any of the other elephants, big enough to lay his tusks on the top of the wall.

"That's Bandulla, the herd's Monarch," said Ahmed. "He has been their protector and is the sire, the father if you will, to much of the herd. Adult males usually only come to a herd for breeding and then, once satisfied, leave to live a solitary life. It's just the way they are. But not Bandulla. This is his home and family."

As the herd moved on, Modoc's anxiety stopped, and she resumed munching on the hay. It had been Bram's first encounter with the herd, but surely was not to be his last. As they left, he saw the matriarchal female. Almost the size of Mo, she was nudging the others to move along. The largest and oldest female in a herd was the leader. Being the boss, she probably felt the need to mother them.

Next morning found Ahmed, Bram, and some workers hard at work building Modoc her new home. Twice the size of the other one, it had some new features. A large itching post built at the height best suited for Mo to rub, a shower area with a wooden floor so it didn't get muddy and above, the shower itself high enough so Mo, being playful, couldn't reach it with her trunk, and pull it down. There was a giant button on a wooden backboard that when pushed (with her head or butt) she could turn the water on and off. And finally, a large vat that held separate types of food, barley, alfalfa, and grain all grown at the farm. Bram had a wooden sign hung on the gate. It read: MODOC, THE GREATEST ELEPHANT, LIVES HERE.

CHAPTER 22

It had been nearly two months since Bram sent Gertie his letter. Had she received it? Maybe she never got the mail. So many questions unanswered. Coogan's plane was gone but due back before dark. Bram walked to the small runway and sat to wait for its arrival. How many times had he done that? Dozens.

He heard the familiar drone of Coogan's plane. There never was another, only his. He shaded his eyes looking up to see it coming around for a landing.

"Please, dear God, let there be news!" he said aloud.

The plane came in, touched the dirt runway, and taxied up to its parking spot. The door opened and Coogan got out carrying some mail.

"Any news?" asked Bram.

"No, I'm afraid not," said Coogan. "Just a bunch of packages in the back you can help me with."

Totally dejected, Bram opened the door. A few packages came slipping down with a girl all wrapped up in them. It was Gertie. She literally fell into his arms.

"Bram! Bram!" she screamed.

He couldn't talk. Tears of joy streamed down his face. He picked her up. She had ribbons, tissue paper and string all over her. They kissed. Oh, did they kiss! He swung her around and around. He opened his mouth to speak but only a squeaky sound came out. He laughed. She laughed. Gertie had come.

"So, is this the one you been waiting for?" said Coogan, playing dumb.

Gertie grabbed Coogan and gave him a hug. "You brought me back to my man," she said. "Thank you."

"Well, I, just, yeah, okay, guess I did," he said blushing.

Hand in hand, they walked towards the gates so wrapped up in each other it would have been hard to tell whose arms belonged to whom! They stopped every few feet to kiss.

"MO! Gertie's home!" he yelled.

The guard threw open the main gate and in they went. Modoc went ballistic. Trumpeting, pooping, and dancing. Bram opened the kraal gate and Gertie ran in and jumped on Mo's trunk.

"Mosey! Mosey! I missed you so much."

Mo was having kittens. Dancing, swirling around. They had known each other since they were children.

"Come on, I want to introduce you to the people who have changed my life."

"Okay Mo, I'll see you later," hugged Gertie.

Mo wrapped her trunk around Gertie's body, face, wherever she could grab. She didn't want her to go. It took a few minutes for Bram to convince Mo but even then, she held her till the last minute when Gertie could wiggle free.

"I'll come back; I promise."

Bram had to lock the pen to contain Mo. She stretched her trunk over the gate as far as she could and blasted a trumpet so loud! Mo really loved Gertie. Both Ahmed and Latika heard the commotion and came running to learn what was happening.

"Gertie's here! She just came in," said a very proud Bram.

Gertie, a few ribbons still trailing from her, was riding high. She didn't wait for an introduction but leaped into both of their arms. Bram's introduction got lost in the moment.

"Gertie, this is Ahmed and his wife, Latika. And this is Gertie, the love of my life." Gertie never heard the introduction;

she was already in their embrace. Tears streamed down her cheeks.

"Why are you crying, child?" asked Ahmed.

"Cause I'm so happy," she said.

But Gertie wasn't the only one in tears. Everybody had tears running down their cheeks. When they realized it, they all broke up crying and laughing. Gertie was so full of love, she brought a togetherness that was overwhelming.

"So nice to finally meet you. I thought Bram would have a heart attack waiting for you. He loves you so much," sniffed Latika.

Gertie blushed and grasped Bram's hand a little tighter.

"Now, Bram, show Gertie where she can freshen up. Maybe a shower," said Latika. "That plane ride must have been horrible."

"With all those boxes, you must have felt, to say the least, boxed in," added Ahmed.

He smiled knowing his joke was corny. It just wasn't his style.

"Ahmed! Really," said Latika, a quaint smile on her face. "Now you just settle in; we will prepare a special dinner in your honor, my dear," she said. Then looking at Bram, she asked, "How does eight o'clock sound?"

"Fine by me."

Everybody went their way. Bram passed Ahmed and with a smile whispered, "Boxed in, really?"

The dinner was superb. A seven-course meal for this very special occasion. They all spoke at once.

"What was it like living in Germany? Is it cold there?"

"Can get very cold." She shivered.

"Sprechen Sie Deutsch." (Do you speak German)?" asked Ahmed,

"Yes, but I don't use it much. Not since I left home. Prefer English anyhow."

Gertie smiled. "Modoc chirps in German when she gets upset," she joked.

Ahmed stood and tapped his glass. The others joined him holding champagne flutes in their hands.

"To Gertie, our newfound daughter. Welcome to Shangari."

CHAPTER 23

"Good morning, my love."

A kiss on her cheek. Gertie awoke from her dream with Bram and Modoc in the flower fields in Germany. He sat at the edge of her bed, laid a purple flower on her pillow, and handed her a glass of orange juice.

"Wake up! Wake up!" he tickled. She laughed and scrambled herself under the sheets.

"Breakfast awaits!" he said.

A hand appeared from beneath the sheets.

"Mm. Yes. Come back to bed," she purred.

Her hand found his face, his lips. She slid her naked body out from under the sheets and pulled his lips to hers. They were so much in love. He was thrilled to kiss those lips, touch those places of his desire. Her kiss awakened his hunger to return to the warmth of her sensuous body, but his temptation waned as he thought of his hosts waiting for them at the breakfast table.

"My love, Ahmed and his wife will be waiting for us to join them for breakfast."

She stretched her lean body to rid it of all the morning cricks.

"Yes, of course. A quick bath and I'll be ready," she said, jumping out of bed, then rushing to the bathroom.

Indian clothes had been laid out for her to wear. A bit baggy for her slim boyish body. A brushing of her long blond hair and they were off hand in hand.

"Good morning, you two, have a good sleep, did you?" asked Ahmed.

Ahmed and Lakita sat at a table on the veranda overlooking the forest below and the mountains above.

"It was marvelous," said Gertie revealing a smile only for Bram.

"Please, sit here where you can see the view," offered Latika.

"Bram is going to show me your beautiful sanctuary today," said Gertie as she filled her plate with poached eggs, sautéed potatoes, and a mix of vegetables. "I'm anxious to see it all." One of the housekeepers helped fill her cup with fresh ground coffee. A dessert of cottage cheese topped with 'fresh off the tree' peaches completed the breakfast.

"Where did all these delicacies come from?" asked Gertie.

"Whenever I returned to Europe for business, I'd arrange with the farmers to prepare the seeds, cuttings, and whatever else was needed to replant again. Over the years we have established a fairly large garden. But you will see it today," said Ahmed.

"I'll sure you will enjoy it. And especially the Varuna Falls," said Latika. "It's so mysterious in a beautiful way. There is something about it that will hold you spellbound."

"I can't wait! It sounds so ominous."

"I also plan on showing Gertie the lake," said Bram.

"You mean the one we have never named?" offered Ahmed.

"You have a lake you have never named?" asked a surprised Gertie.

"Yes, can you imagine?"

"How strange. How come?"

"I really don't know why. We come up with names, but they never seem to stick," said Ahmed.

Latika added, "Yes, it's true. They're either forgotten or another one takes its place."

"It's like they're just not meant to be."

"It's the lake. It's waiting for the right name."

"Don't say that, Ahmed, it scares me, like it was alive."

"Well, maybe today is the lucky day," said Gertie. "We'll come up with a name the lake will like and christen it, so it's not forgotten," she laughed.

"Bram, have you seen it?" asked Gertie.

"No. Never. I guess I've been waiting to share it with you," he said, smiling.

"Well, you both will have quite a busy day."

"What about Mosey?" asked Gertie.

"She can come with us to the lake," said Bram.

Latika nodded to a server who was holding a sisal-weaved basket. "I had food packed for you knowing you'd never make it back in time for lunch." Latika smiled as she handed it to Bram.

Hugs, kisses on the cheeks, and they were gone.

The sanctuary was quiet save for the melodious songs of the warblers, joined by the wood thrush and the guinea fowls as they scratched their way along the walkways. The faraway music of the forest people filled the air.

They sat by the pools, not wanting to lose the beauty of the moment and listened to the soft murmurs of the water trickling over the rocks. The delicate scent of lilac filled the air to mingle with the sweet aroma of jasmine. A marriage of two essences joined as one.

It was not a time for words. While Gertie took in the beauty of the garden, Bram could only feast his eyes on her smile, the twinkle in her eye, the tightening of her hand on his. This was the girl he loved but who was also in love with him.

They strolled down the path to the orchard, picked the purple berries from the thorny boysenberry bush, while being careful not to prick their fingers, plucked an orange here an apple there. Some were put in the lunch basket.

"For Mosey," said Gertie. She removed a slice of bread from one of the lunch sandwiches to feed the swans drifting silently in the small inlet pond.

They played inside the banyan tree lost in its limbs of so many arms, then took a moment to kiss and to laugh at nothing in particular.

The splashing of water signaled their approach to the Falls. A giant Sequoia blocked their view till the Falls appeared majestic in all its splendor and filled the air with its mystery of existence.

Gertie stood in awe, watching the water cascade down into a rock pool, feeling the rock formations, dipping her hand in its sparkling clear water, and causing a small riptide. A shiver coursed through her body.

"Bram, it's so beautiful." It was then that she noticed the miniature forest. "Why is the forest around the pool so small?"

"No one knows. It has all the characteristics of a full-size forest only in miniature. Even the trees are perfect in every detail, just tiny. Ahmed showed me if you look long and steady at it you will be taken there to walk among the trees."

Gertie stood motionless gazing at the forest. For that instant she was transported into the forest standing at the shore of the pond. The Falls, full-sized, loomed above her head.

"Ooh, Bram!"

He caught her as she fell. "You okay?

"Yes, I just got dizzy."

"That was amazing!"

"I was there," she pointed. "Just there. It's all so mystical."

"There is something else I need to tell you about it." He noticed she was still a bit shaky. "Best we sit for a while." They sat on a nearby log bench, and he told her of its other mysteries. "When night falls, you can see an ominous green glow of light that comes from the water. Its glare turns everything it touches into this light green color, and that's not all—" he said.

He told her of the Buddha when the moon was full.

"That's awesome, and a little scary," she said. "Do you think it's supernatural?"

"More on the spiritual side. Let's just say it is very bizarre."

They heard Mosey chirping her delight, as they approached her pen. Surely, she must have anticipated their walk in the forest. She danced all over the pen, gently pushing at her locked gate. Gates unlocked, a smooch for Gertie, a quick drink of water, a scratching of that spot that couldn't be reached, the big gates were opened, and away they went into the forest.

As they walked, the woods seemed surreal. Beams of sunlight found their way through the dense canopy far above and brought a rainbow of vivid colors not seen before. The birds in the bushes didn't fly away as they approached nor did the deer in the meadow run into the thicket.

Mosey was having her moments picking and choosing which twig to break, which bush to nibble. What a delight when she found her favorite berry bush. The first berry was plucked, gently put in her mouth, swirled around, and savored before it was swallowed. Only then, did she plow ahead in stripping the bush clean before she moved on.

The forest had a way of making them smile, quickening their steps, and filling their hearts with an appreciation of all natural things.

Bram took the path leading to the lake. He knew they were approaching it when the air turned crisp and cool, and the scent of water filled the air. Shorebirds swooped and dove at not being familiar with strangers. They left the woods behind and climbed a grassy knoll that rose as they walked. Then, nestled in a protective valley was the lake with its shore snuggled into the nooks and crannies of the foothills surrounding it. Each fjord, every inlet, and every isle seemed to beckon to them as did its waters, still as glass, not a ripple stirring the surface. Small islands seemed to float free in silent serenity. Far off in the distance stood the mighty snowcapped Himalayan Mountains. Their foothills had crept down close to the lake. With them came the waterfalls spilling their ice-cold water into a fast-flowing river that fed the lake.

"Bram, oh! My God. It's breathtaking. It reminds me of Cryer Lake."

Gertie took the basket hanging from Modoc's neck and, after spreading a sari, laid out the lunch. A large wedge of cheese, two sandwiches, one missing a slice of bread, fresh fruit, and a jug of wine. Plus, of course, the fruit Gertie had picked for Mo. Afterward, it was so tempting to go for a swim—but with the darkness approaching, they had to leave.

"Another time," said Bram.

"Bram, how are we ever to think of a name for such a magnificent lake?"

"I know, Love, but you can't force it. It will have to come to you. We'll be back," said Bram speaking to the lake. "To give you a name."

They had decided to ride Modoc on the way back when Modoc stopped and stared into the forest. Bram followed her look and there, standing on of a rock bluff, was Bandulla, the huge bull from the herd. He stood still like an unreal entity. What a magnificent elephant he was. His two tusks were of equal size, his body strong and muscular. His eyes were on Modoc, hers on him. Were Gertie and Bram not there, Bram was sure he would have come to meet her. A second look and he was gone. The dark of the night had closed in.

"He's probably gone looking for another to give his amore to," Gertie laughed. "Males can be so promiscuous."

"Some, not all," Bram said, with a look that implied 'not me'.

They were within sight of the compound and were about to signal the guard to open the gate when they heard the low guttural sound that only elephants make. As they approached the wall, there, straight ahead, stood the herd spread out in the forest. They had come up on them unaware and most had stopped their munching and stood motionless looking at the new arrivals. What to do? There was no other entrance to the compound, only the one on the other side of the herd.

Modoc stood as they were, not moving a muscle. She pushed her ears forward and slowly lifted her trunk straight out picking up any hostile scent from the group. Coming through the middle of the group was Big Mama, the matriarch of the herd. Pushing her way through, she stood in the front facing Mo. She looked angry. They were being blocked from getting to the water trough behind Modoc. She had probably brought the herd this same route many times before and thought she had the right of way. But now an elephant never before seen was in her way.

"Bad spot to be in, Gertie."

Bram looked to each side then front and back for a way out, but nothing looked appealing enough to risk making a wrong move. The herd was spread out and had them, unintentionally, pretty much surrounded. Modoc moved a few steps forward as if to continue their walk. Her trunk vibrated a steady rumble, and her eyes were riveted on Big Mama. Mo had the advantage. Tusks.

Although short, they were still a set of lethal weapons that Mo knew how to use. Mama had none but it didn't seem to change her mind. She wanted to come through and Mo was in her way. The herd stood quiet till some of them started to move as if to separate and let them through. Big Mama would have none of that. She stood her ground not letting them pass.

"Backup, Mo, back, back," Bram said.

Mo started to do just that when they heard a threshing behind them. A group of elephants had gone earlier to the water trough and were coming back. The herd was scattered and were all around them. Bram felt it was not their intention to surround them in a hostile manner but rather it was their natural way of proceeding to the water and they were in the way. On the other hand, Big Mama wasn't about to give them any room to move. She was protecting the herd. She smacked the tip of her trunk on the ground thumping in rapid secession. Her body was trembling with anticipation.

There was nothing as terrifying as being in the vicinity of a big, mad elephant that was going to charge and not knowing a way out of the predicament. But they had Mo. Mo was protecting them as Big Mama was protecting her herd. It was a standoff. Both elephants took a defiant posture. They each emitted an incessant rumble. Mama picked up some dirt and, swinging her trunk, threw it up in the air. She was furious that Modoc wasn't backing down; she wasn't used to an elephant not retreating from her.

Bram felt Mo's muscles tighten. Sensing a physical confrontation between the two, he quickly dismounted and told Gertie in a low voice, "Slide down, now."

"Why?" she started.

"Just do it—Big Mama's about to charge and Mo isn't going to move."

Gertie did as instructed and slid into Bram's waiting arms. He grabbed her hand and quickly took her behind Modoc, the safest place to be. Bram knew Mo was not intimidated by Big Mama. She threw some dirt in the air and shook her head in defiance. Then it happened. With an earth-shattering trumpet-like roar, Mama charged!

She came, flying at Modoc, trunk balled up, ears straight out, head low to the ground. Mo dropped her head ready to meet the charge head on. It was horrifying to see an enraged elephant charging; but a few yards from contact Mama stopped. It was a mock charge. A warning. Elephants do that. It's meant to scare away any intruders, but it did not scare Mo. She had experienced far worse in her life, and she wasn't about to let this big girl get to her. Again, Mama charged and again Mo stood her ground. Another mock charge.

Mo never backed up, only balled her trunk like a boxer ready to deliver a punch. The tension between Mama and Mo was building. Something had to give. Bram knew that one of those charges would be real. He knew Mo was ready for her, but a full charge could be a deadly one for either of them. When they did battle, their immense size and weight could cause internal injuries, a broken rib cage, even a tearing of important organs any of which could cause death. Many an elephant died from such an encounter or suffered serious injury. Bram felt Modoc had no intention of hurting Mama unless she had to. Mama, on the other hand, was protecting her herd and would not back down, especially in front of the whole herd.

Just as Mama was ready to do her worst, from out of the evening shadow stepped Bandulla. He had apparently been standing off watching the confrontation. He didn't seem perturbed at all as he wandered into the 'arena.' His presence was enough to cause both elephants to stop their aggression. He seemed unimpressed with the goings on and stopped dead center between them. He blew some dirt on his back followed by a belly rumble far deeper than either of the combatants could emit. With that, the herd came alive, a few trumpeted, others finished the food they had forgotten was still in their mouth. The threat of war was over. Mama reluctantly led the herd into the forest around the 'intruder' to the water trough and in passing gave an intense look at Mo.

Bandulla stood for a while, then, as he turned to go, he swung his trunk against Modoc, touching, sensing, running it over her as he left.

The guard opened the gate as Modoc and the couple came through.

"You guys, okay?" asked Ahmed, having seen what was happening through one of the small windows in the wall.

"Now that was scary," shivered Gertie.

"Living in the forest, you never know what's just around the corner," said Ahmed. A moment of silence passed before everybody burst into laughter realizing what he had just said.

"Sorry about that, I didn't mean... Well, literally speaking of course."

"Sure, Ahmed, we understand," said Bram, holding back his laughter.

The dinner bell rang.

CHAPTER 24

In the following weeks, the staff kept reporting seeing Bandulla around the compound.

"He was by the farm just the other day," said one.

"1 saw him on the path," said another.

"He was at the gate pulling on the handle," offered the gate guard.

"It's Modoc he's after," said Bram.

"You think so?" questioned Ahmed.

"Yes, ever since he saw her holding off Big Mama, it was love at first sight."

"Well, he'll have to get her parents' approval to allow her to date. She's still quite young," joked Gertie.

The dialogue was bouncing back and forth for days kidding about Mo's love affair.

"I don't think it's wise for them to get together," said Bram. "It's dangerous."

"Only if she wasn't interested in him, but I don't think that's a problem," said Gertie. "She belly rumbles every time he's near. You know, my love, Mo's a big girl, she can take care of herself, and besides, Bandulla seems to be a gentle bull. So, what's your problem?"

"Well, I just think . . . I don't know, it just doesn't seem right," worried Bram.

Gertie saw the concern on his face. She knew he loved Mo as a father loves his daughter.

"Bram, my love, you know, you and Modoc have been together since childhood. It's normal for you to feel this way. You sound like a jealous father. Let her be. It's her life."

The following morning Bram was busy helping some of the men repair the wall. Some of the young elephants had been playing near the wall and knocked some of the stones loose. Unexpectedly, one of the gate guards came running over. He was quite upset.

"Excuse me, Mr. Bram, sir."

"Yes, what is it?"

"Modoc, she is gone. Somebody opened her kraal gate, and she is gone."

Sure enough, when Bram went to check, he saw that the main gate stood open as well. Bram knew if Modoc was let out of her pen, she knew how to open the hasp on the main gate.

"Where is the other guard?" asked Bram.

The guard shrugged his shoulders and looked quite sheepish. Some of the workers had gathered and Bram noticed some were holding back, with grins on their faces.

Later when asked about the gate being open, the guard professed his innocence. "I had taken my break and when I came back, it was open. And then I saw the two of them heading into the forest."

"The two of them?"

"Yes, sir, she was with Bandulla."

Nobody would accept the responsibility for opening the pen. Any one of them could have been the culprit. They all wanted Mo to have a suitor and well, whatever...

"He is a big man, Sahib," smiled a worker.

"Sorry, honey, your little girl ran away from home." Gertie laughed. "I hope she took her night bag."

Everyone got into the humor of teasing Bram that he could be a father-in-law.

As the days dragged by, Bram became frantic. She had never stayed away from home so long, and he worried. "Think she's alright?"

"Don't worry, when she's ready, she'll come back."

"Hope she'll be alright," he worried.

The gate was left open, just a touch, for the next few weeks. The guard sat back out of sight each night to be sure nothing came in that wasn't wanted. It was the end of the second week around midnight when the guard heard the familiar squeak. It was Modoc coming home. The guard opened the gate for her to pass in. Bandulla stood watch in the shadows. He grumbled his goodbye as she went through the gate before he moved into the forest. The guard ran to tell Bram.

"She's home, Sahib! Modoc is home. Bandulla brought her back."

"Where is he?"

"Gone back into the forest."

The word got out that Modoc was home. Everybody jammed into her new home welcoming her back. Some of the staff brought goodies for her. Most just wanted to know she was okay.

Modoc ate it up. She loved attention, and she was being, hugged, petted, and given goodies. What more could she ask for?

"Do you think she's pregnant?" asked Gertie.

"Well, there is no way of knowing. At least for now."

"Just think, our little girl could be a mother."

"Now, stop that. We won't know for a long time."

"How long?"

"Close to two years."

"What?"

"That's right, elephants have a gestation period of eighteen to twenty-two months. That's if she is pregnant."

"Maybe she'll have twins?"

"Gertie! "

"Time will tell."

"Yes, it will."

Since his escapade with Modoc, Bandulla was seen quite often around the estate. Due to his gentle nature, he'd become 'safe' to be around. He never showed aggression toward the staff or anyone else. People could come and go about their work and not be concerned about his whereabouts. He wasn't allowed in the garden as his love for plants and flowers would have been devastating, but the farmhands would pile all the old or extra vegetables in a place the workers had designated as 'his' place just outside the fence. The herd never bothered it when Bandulla was around. That was his food! He was still a bull elephant capable of doing damage to whomever and whatever he desired. He was not touchable. But he had a good heart. He could walk by people, but he would never touch them with his trunk. There was a wall of separation, wild vs civilized, that needed to be broken. In time, in time.

CHAPTER 25

"How about you going up to the lake and getting us some dinner?" asked Ahmed. He handed Bram a fishing pole, a bag of bait, and a bag that read 'Good Luck'.

"That's a great idea! I'll take Modoc, maybe she can help."

Bram was going to ask Gertie to go along but she was busy with Latika, so off he went with Mo wondering if he could do it. There were no guarantees of catching a fish after all. But why not, he thought. Sounds like fun. Maybe not for the fish, but he'd give it a go.

They arrived early in the morning. The lake was still sleeping. Not a ripple, nor a sound was heard. The stillness was breathtaking. A mommy goose, her head arched around and nested in the feathers on her back, drifted motionlessly. Her goslings, Bram counted eight, slept comfortably on her back cozy and warm.

Bram stood for a while taking in the beauty of the moment, while Modoc was doing her rocking, back and forth, anxious to get into the water. He took off his Lungi, rolled it up and put it under a nearby rock. The bait bag went in the Good Luck bag which he tied around Modoc's neck. With one hand holding the fishing pole, he "legged up" Mo and scrambled up her back.

"Okay, Mosey, move up. Let's go catch ourselves a fish." Bram figured the big fish would be out into the middle of the lake. No reason, he just did. Modoc moved out into the lake drifting lazily till she heard, "This ought to do it, Mo. We can drop anchor here."

When Modoc heard 'drop anchor' she was ready to play the water game they used to play in Cryer Lake. She stopped, dropped her head and trunk low in the water, took a deep breath and blew a trail of bubbles that drifted across the water. Good fun. But Bram's head was in another place. To catch a fish.

He put a few grubs on the hook, giving them a blessing for giving their lives, and tossed the line in the water. Then he sat there and waited…and waited. Mo had stopped her game and, as time wore on, fell into a slumber. Nothing. All was quiet. Something was wrong. Then a thought came to Bram. Of course, he thought. They don't know I'm here.

"Mo girl, swish the water. Like when we play. You know, swish, swish." He leaned down and swished the water with his hand. Mo, thinking it was another game, whipped the water with her trunk—hard. Then, getting into it, she raised her trunk high in the air and came down hitting the water with a resounding splash that caused a huge explosion of water and sent a small tidal wave across the lake to the shore at breakneck speed.

Surely it was enough to awaken every fish in the lake.

He had a bite. Something was disturbing the hook. The line tightened, zig zagged back and forth, then whizzed out from the reel zooming across the lake nearly taking the pole out of Bram's hand. He pulled back, hard, and there, out in the middle of the lake, a huge fish jumped clean out of the water! Wow! He reeled and reeled, pulling in the line, worried it was going to break. When the fish was close it swam under Mo's belly. That did it! She went berserk.

Thrashing the water with her trunk, she tried to beat the fish away. The fish came again, swimming between her leg and tangled the line around her feet. Mo panicked, thrusting her feet trying to get away from it. Then the inevitable happened. The fish touched her! Mo pooped, trumpeted, and tried to get away from it. Afraid he was about to lose it Bram handed the pole to Mo.

"Hold, girl, hold!"

Mo clamped her jaws on the pole, her eyes bugged out looking at the water trying to figure out where that 'thing' went. Bram jumped into the water and dove underneath her belly.

There was the fish all tangled in the line. It was big! He tried to grab it but each time it managed to wiggle free. He came up for air, got the fish bag, dove down again, and after a struggle pulled the bag over the fish's head. It was too big for the bag, but it was enough to subdue it.

Bram surfaced and tried to climb up on Mo's back. No way. She wasn't about to have that thing on her back! He had an idea. Bram settled back into Mo's chest floating the bag in front of him.

"Move up, Mo. Move up."

And move she did, like a speed boat she headed for shore. Once they arrived at the shore Mo was ready to go home. But Mo still wasn't about to let Bram drape the 'Good Luck' bag with the fish in it around her neck. No way! Bram laid the fish on the ground in front of her to show her it was dead. For the next half hour, she circled it, finally touching it with the tip of her trunk to convince herself it was dead.

On the way back, Bram recalled catching the fish. It had been a surprisingly traumatic experience.

"I guess this one fish will be enough for dinner," he said, talking to himself. "Boy, it sure takes a lot of work just to get one fish," he murmured.

Bram was proud of his accomplishment but wondered how many fishermen had to fight the fish underwater.

On arriving back at Shangari, he summoned a couple of the workers to help carry the fish into the kitchen and heave it up on the table.

"Good lord, Sahib!" yelled the cook. She ran out calling for Ahmed who nearly fell over when he saw the size of it.

"Hope it's enough for dinner," said Bram.

Ahmed was speechless. "I didn't know there were fish that big in the lake! Yes, well of course, I'm sure it will be," he said trying to stay calm. "What did you do to catch such a huge fish?!"

Bram thought for a moment. "Next time you go fishing, just take an elephant."

CHAPTER 26

"Let's go to the lake," said Bram.

"Now? Why now? You just got back," Gertie said.

"It's a beautiful day and well, let's go.

"But I'm right in the middle of sorting the laundry and...
"

"I know. But let's go."

"Okay, let me just finish these."

"Later, let's go."

"Boy, you're sure insistent. Do you want to get Mosey on the way?"

"Yes, she knows."

"Knows what?"

"That we're going to the lake."

"How?" Now she was worried.

"What's wrong? You alright?"

"Uh huh, I'm fine."

Gertie grabbed a blanket from the back of the sofa, a fresh baked loaf of bread and a chunk of Feta cheese from the fridge. Bram snuck a bottle of wine into the bag on their way out through the kitchen.

Standing at the gate was Modoc, being fed some tidbit by the gate guard. Bram gave the basket to Modoc. "Hold," he said. They both got a 'leg up,' and a namaste was given to the guard as they moved down the trail.

Gertie sat tight against Bram with her arms wrapped around his waist.

"We're so lucky, Bram."

"I know, I have you."

"No, silly, I mean being at Shangari and all, and Ahmed and Latika are so wonderful. They have taken us in as their children."

"And they as our parents."

The day was sunny and warm, birds were in the air darting here and there either being coy with their mate or catching insects. Gertie was curious as to why Bram was so anxious to go to the lake.

"You're going to try and catch another fish? That was sure a big one."

"I think it will be a while before I go fishing again. It didn't come easy."

They arrived at the lake. It was tranquil as always except for a pair of loons skimming the water across the far end where the reeds hid their eggs. Bram caught Gertie as she slid off Mo. They stood for a moment, taking in the fresh air that blew across the lake, catching Gertie's golden hair and scattering it in all directions. It was Bram's hand that smoothed it back in place.

Mo made her way down to the shore to pick at the moss growing along its edge while Gertie found the thickest patch of grass on which to spread the blanket and view the lake. She opened the food containers and laid out the few items they brought. Bram found some small rocks to put at the corners of the blanket to keep it from blowing in the breeze.

"What's this?" said Gertie, holding the wine bottle. "I didn't see you put this in."

Bram's smile was all she got as he unwrapped the cap, popped the cork and offered her the first taste. They drank from the bottle, bit off pieces of cheese together, lips touching, giggling at the sensuousness of it all. Within a moment, they were drinking from each other's mouths, sharing the cheese the same way. They were so much in love, soul mates from the start. Both were naked in but a minute and together they showed each other their love. Each thinking of the other's needs before their own.

"So, this is what you brought me here for," said Gertie with a smile.

"No," he said.

"No?" she answered. She sat up. A look of surprise crossed her face. "What then?" she asked.

He eased up to her ear. "Come with me," he whispered, taking her hand. He led the way to Modoc who was standing at the shore. She grabbed for her clothes. He pulled them away.

"But my wrap?"

"No, as you are. Leg, Mo." She lifted them both together as they scrambled up on her back. "Move up, Mosey." They felt the water creep up their bodies as Mo entered the lake. Gertie sat in front; Bram held her in his arms bringing her close till their bodies were as one.

Mo moved quietly out into the middle of the lake seeming to be aware of the intense moment. Her curled trunk made a wake same as the geese did.

"Just here, girl."

Mo stopped paddling and let her legs hang loose. Her body floated without effort. Dead silence. The lake's smooth vastness had a quieting effect that could put one into a daze. A strange feeling of floating above the water.

Bram gently picked Gertie up in his arms as they slipped into the water. For a moment their bare bodies glistened in the sun's fading light till they disappeared beneath the water, down, down into the abyss. There he let her go, floating free to see her in all her natural beauty. Her body moved effortlessly, undulating, her hair swirling like a halo catching beams of sunlight. They came together, coupled but for a moment, keeping the energy before they came up under Mo. Grabbing her tusks, they swung up and nestled down against her chest tucked in between her legs. It was their place. A cave, a hollow, the silence of the water echoed in their chamber. Neither spoke, the moment was eternal. Until Bram turned to her. He cupped her face in his hands looking, exploring.

"Bram, what?"

"Gertie my love, we will be together always, to care for and love one another."

"Yes, my love, always."

He pressed her to him as he inhaled her fragrance and whispered; "Will you marry me? Will you be my wife?"

Wet and trembling, she stared into Bram's eyes as a flood of tears washed down her face.

She started to cry. "Oh! My God! Yes, my love, yes, I will marry you!"

A giggle erupted, followed by laughter, then crying as a burst of pure joy came forth. All her young life Gertie dreamed of being Bram's wife. There was nothing more. All that life had to offer was here in this man among men.

"Yes, yes," she said again, her body heaving, trembling.

Her tears were swept away as Bram found her body inviting him to be one with her. He entered, there to feel the ecstasy of their love, to linger, then to withdraw, spent, thrilled, to lie in each other's arms. Their blessing was sealed.

"So, this is what we came here for," she teased.

Back on shore they finished the bottle of wine with a toast to love. They got dressed and decided to walk back. Mo followed, in a playful mood, she was doing her jig, snorting dirt in the air, tooting her crazy trumpet.

"Why is she in such a good mood?"

"I don't know," answered Bram.

"You think she knows what's happening?"

"I don't see how. Although she does get vibes when I am happy or sad. I guess she just feels my mood."

"We're going to get married! Mosey!" yelled Gertie into Mo's ear. Mo shook her head flapping her ears. "You think she understood?"

"Maybe. After all, she was our witness."

"What a wonderful day this has been," she said bringing her hands up into a namaste.

Bram froze. He just stared at her.

"What's wrong?"

"That's it, that's it! The lake!" yelled Bram. "We'll call it Lake Namaste. Yes, what do you think?"

"It's a beautiful name. Is it religious?"

"It's spiritual; it's Hindu for 'I bow to you.' It's a sign of respect. Respect is only given to someone or thing that earns it. The lake is all that life is about. Peaceful, beautiful, tranquil. It's God's perfect creation."

"You've heard it so many times. Why did it come to you just now?"

"I guess the time had come. That's the way it should be." Thinking of Ahmed, he said, "And this one will stick." He laughed.

"We'll call her Nan for short," said Gertie, smiling.

"Who said it was a girl?" Bram said, with a smirk of his own.

CHAPTER 27

"So, what do you think?"

"I think he will do it."

"But it is a bit unusual. Is what you're telling me true? I mean years ago it really happened?"

"Yep. It was the only way. I mean, who else would do it?"

"Right.

"Well, I'm ready if you are. Let's do it."

Bram and Gertie walked into Ahmed's office, just off the main dining room. He was busy working on the farm's records. "Hi guys, what's up?"

"If you're busy?"

"No, no, just the usual paperwork."

"Can we go have a drink out on the patio?"

"Oh! Boy, this must be serious." Ahmed laughed.

They settled down on the outside patio overlooking the forest while a server brought their drinks.

"So, what do you have in mind? It must be important to have drinks this early in the morning."

Bram cleared his throat. "Ahmed, ever since we met, you and Latika have treated us as your children. You have opened your hearts to us and for that we are eternally grateful."

"Well, yes, we care for you both as our very own, you have come into our lives, and we are so thankful for that. Why, you have made our lives a joy each and every day."

Gertie replied, "We feel the same. We love you guys and well, because of that, Bram has something to ask you."

"Well, yes, ah... " Gertie saw Bram was hesitant to ask. She pushed on his leg coupled with an affirming move of her head.

He blurted out, "And ah..." stammering. Bram just couldn't get it out.

"Bram? Ah! Ahmed, we want to get married," blurted Gertie.

"Good Lord, that's wonderful," said Ahmed. "What a wonderful surprise! We can arrange it for you to go into Jaipur and... "

"I'm afraid that would be too dangerous. North might be looking for us to make such a move," said Bram.

"But Jaipur is so big. I would think by now this North fellow would figure you're dead."

"Unfortunately, not. Coogan brings us news that the Army thinks otherwise and is still looking for us. If North thinks there is a chance of finding me," Bram hesitated, "believe me, he is ruthless. He will go to any means to find me unless it's proven I am dead. Until he knows for sure, he will not stop looking for us."

"Well, my goodness, we have to find a place where he couldn't find you."

"Well, there's more."

"Okay, I'm listening."

Gertie broke in, "We want you to marry us."

"What? You want what?"

"Well, it's like this," said Bram. "There is no place or minister anywhere near here and to go into a big city would be too dangerous. Some call it 'common law' whatever, but we want you to marry us."

"Bram, my friend, how can I marry you? It would be a great honor for me to do so, but I am not a minster or priest or any kind of a clergyman."

"Well, actually, you are. I went into your library and found some interesting information. We read from one of your books that in bygone times, in the small villages and towns, there was no designated person to marry couples, so the most important man of the village or town, whatever, would legally perform the ceremony. He just had to read from 'The Book of Marriage,' swear to uphold the laws, and it was done. As long as he was the top guy, a person the people respected, the man the people could turn to at a time of need, it was allowed.

"You're that man, Ahmed. Gertie and I would be honored to have you do it."

The room was silent. Ahmed stood and looked out the window for some time. Bram gripped Gertie's hand, both knowing that Ahmed's decision was so important to their future. Finally, Ahmed walked over and put his arms around them.

"You are my son and daughter. If someday in the future you will exchange your vows in front of a real minster, then if that is your wish, yes, I would be happy to perform your ceremony here at Shangari."

CHAPTER 28

So, it was on a sunny afternoon in the garden by Varuna Falls, Bram and Gertie were to be married.

Gertie was in a panic. What to wear? She only had the few clothes she brought with her. "Not to worry, my dear." Latika took Gertie by the hand. "Come with me."

She took her into her lavish bedroom and flung open the closet to reveal an assortment of beautiful clothes. Gertie had never seen such an array of beautiful saris. She ran her finger by them, looking, touching them: cashmere, velvet, gossamer, silk, all enclosed in see-through bags. At the far end, set aside from all the others and protected by a gold trimmed see-through bag, was the most beautiful of saris.

"Here my love, this is what you will wear at your wedding."

Unzipping the bag, Latika took out a sky-blue sari with crimson and gold lace interwoven with silver threads. A pair of red satin shoes was to match.

"Oh! Latika, it's gorgeous!" Gertie held it in front of her and looked in the full-length mirror.

"It is my wedding dress. You and I are about the same size. But most important, you are my daughter and who should wear it but you. Now, come here and sit on the bed."

Gertie sat wondering what Latika had in mind as she went to her dresser drawer and lifted out a large silver jewel box and handed it to Gertie.

"Here, this is something every young bride should wear at her wedding," she said.

Gertie's eyes sparkled with anticipation as she slowly opened the box. A flash of light burst from the box and sprinkled the room with its sparkling radiance to reveal the most beautiful diamond tiara.

"Latika, it's the most beautiful tiara in the whole world! I don't know what to say."

She ran her hands over it, feeling the diamonds, seeing them send their sparkle radiating across the room.

"How fortunate that it can be wore again by the daughter I thought I would never have."

They hugged till their tears fell.

Bram and Ahmed were just finishing their Fini beer, Ahmed's favorite brew brought in from Goa.

"Come my boy, it's time to see what you will wear to your wedding."

Off they went to his bedroom. Ahmed noticed Bram was surprised that they each had their own. "It is our custom to be together only when desire calls."

Bram knew he could never sleep alone knowing Gertie was in her own room. To sleep in each other's arms, to awaken, cuddle in her warmth. No, he would stay with his own customs.

Ahmed's bedroom was as Bram expected. Thick, carved teak bedframe, tables of oak, tapestries depicting nature and its wildlife. Huge leaf plants and fern palms were in every corner. A large window opened onto a closed-in garden and pond. It was as if Ahmed had brought a piece of the 'out of doors' inside.

They parted strands of hanging beads separating the walk-in closet from the bedroom. Once inside, Bram feasted his eyes on rows upon rows of clothes, Kurta, sherwani, ghagha, payama, all made with the finest material.

"Your choice," said Ahmed.

Bram was speechless. 'Father, never have I seen such fine garments."

He walked down the row of Kurta, Nehru, Sherwani, some pleated, some woven. Most were satin or silk. One in particular caught Bram's eye. He took it from the closet and held it for the light to shine on it. It was a gold embroidered brocade silk Sherwani, with a pronounced high collar. Long in length, high collared, stitched in brocade blue and gold silk thread with payama (pants) to match.

"Good choice," commented Ahmed.

A turban matching the Sherwani in color, material, and design was chosen. Ahmed went to his dressing table and opened a large jewel box to an array of gems, necklaces, and bracelets to dazzle the eye. Ahmed's finger stopped at a large teardrop-shaped blood red crystal brooch. He held the gem to the turban.

"Ah! Yes, this will do just fine."

"Ahmed," Bram said, admiring the stone. "This is fit for a king."

"I know," said Ahmed with a serendipitous smile, "I know."

Exhausted from the day's activities of picking out their wardrobes and then going over the ceremony with Ahmed, they laid in bed thinking what tomorrow may bring. Gertie cuddled up to Bram.

"What's wrong?" she asked.

"What do you mean?"

"I can tell. What's wrong?"

"It's the wedding," he continued. "Are we getting married as Hindus or Germans? We have to make a decision."

"Is there a difference?" she asked, totally unaware of the ritualistic ceremony that takes place in a Hindu wedding.

"Yes, a huge difference. We are living in a Hindu environment. All our friends are Hindu, our clothes, this room, everything is Indian. And Indians are Hindu. We live as Hindu, yet we are Christians German born."

"But, Bram, although I am Christian and proud of it, I love the life we are living. Everything is so...so colorful."

"So, you want a Hindu wedding?"

She thought for a bit. "I would feel guilty."

Bram thought for a bit. "Honey, there is only one answer. We will create our own wedding."

"What?"

"Sure, people do it. Things have changed. Years ago, we wouldn't be lying here in each other's arms before the wedding."

Gertie flushed a bright red.

"Sorry, honey, but that's the way it is. Our love for each other is the same before the wedding as it is after. The wedding doesn't change our love for each other, it only celebrates it. It's saying we are now one." Gertie sat up. Bram noticed a worried look across her face. "So what kind of a wedding do you see it as?"

"The way I see it?"

"Yes."

"Well, the overall beauty a Hindu wedding offers should be the theme. The vows and ceremony will be Christian."

"You think that will work?"

"Yes, I am sure of it—agreed?"

"Agreed."

Early the next morning they parted, Gertie to meet with her women friends waiting to paint traditional Indian designs on Gertie's hands and feet. Latika explained, "It's called 'Mehndi' which means 'blessing' and carries with it the prayers for good health and good spirits for the journey through life. It is a joyous time and good fun for all."

Bram saw that it would be as much a Hindu wedding as possible. From every corner of the compound came the staff bringing blankets, ornaments, and bright colored cloth of red and gold, the color of a wedding. The garden where the wedding was to be performed and the main dining area seemed to splash colors everywhere.

Bram was told the chief of the forest people with some of his followers were standing shyly at the gate.

"What does he want?" he asked the gate man.

"He wants to help."

"What can he do?"

"They want to bring you flowers from the forest."

"Flowers, of course, yes, tell him to bring as many as they can. What is his name?" asked Bram.

With a smile the guard answered, "Vishnu."

"His name is a god's name?"

"He says he was given the name in a dream because he takes care of the forest. He says you can call him Vishy. That is what his wife calls him."

"Okay," said Bram holding back a grin. "Tell Vishy to bring the flowers."

The little people left, beaming with eagerness to be part of the wedding.

It was just before noon that the guard summoned Ahmed. Vishy had returned.

Waiting at the gate was the whole tribe of forest people, perhaps twenty men, women and their children all wearing big smiles and each carrying bundles upon bundles of flowers: carnations, roses, dahlias, lilies, tulips. They had brought the gifts of the forest to the wedding and with the essence that goes with them. They were so proud of their offering. Bram was overwhelmed.

Bram beckoned them to follow him into the house, a place few of them had ever been. He gestured for them to go with the woman of the house who opened the bundles and showed them how to make nice arrangements. Then, off they went, putting them wherever they felt the need. Doors, gateways, arches and terraces, tables, and windows, with special attention to the wedding altar. Before they left, Bram made sure they understood they were going to come to the wedding and to stay for the celebration.

"They have asked if they may bring their music," said a woman being their interpreter.

Bram was thrilled with the offer. "Yes, of course, tell them we welcome it."

Coogan was to be the best man, Sanjoe the head usher, and Mirer the flower girl. They and some of the staff arranged the seating, brought in the statues that could be carried, and helped to build the altar. Large potted plants were placed all around.

Latika, although the 'mother' of the bride, would play a duplicate role as the maid of honor.

And not to be forgotten, Modoc was painted by the staff's children. Rather than draw childish characters, they went the more professional route and used their Indian tradition. Her eyes were treated as human with eyelashes turned blue and large under exaggerated purple eyebrows. The length of her trunk was colored in red and gold, the traditional colors of an Indian wedding. Around her neck hung a black and white bowtie they had cut from old sisal material and Ja's necklace was encircled with jungle flowers. Her ankles carried bands of small silver bells that jangled when she moved, and across her body were written the sacred words of the deities.

Rows of Indian statues were lined up on each side of the aisle leading to the altar. The altar was set up close to the Varuna Falls. A platform was erected and covered in the Indian and oriental rugs from the living room. At the top of the altar, the wooden arches were wrapped with jungle vines.

And so, on a Sunday afternoon to the sounds of jungle music came a couple, so happy, so excited to be married to one another. A couple who was so much in love. Waiting at the altar was dear Bram, all smiles and more emotional than most and showing tears on his cheeks. A bit jittery standing with him was the 'minister' Ahmed, in full Indian attire, glowing with pride knowing he would soon unite his daughter and son in marriage. Latika stood on one side of him, Coogan the other. Modoc stood by Bram waiting for someone to tell her what to do. Seated on both sides of the aisle were the entire staff and their children. The shy forest people had come huddled together. Afraid to move, they had put their chairs together in a circle.

As the music of the forest began, Gertie appeared at the head of the walkway. For a moment she stood glowing, a goddess of love in all her adornment. She looked radiant in her beautiful sari; the sparkling tiara nestled in her mass of golden hair. She was truly a vision.

Bram, always the emotional one, tried to keep it all in but couldn't and the tears flowed. Gertie walked down the aisle; her eyes fixed on the man she would be spending her life with. She joined him at the altar and reached for his hand to steady her nerves. Ahmed began reading from the Book of Marriage.

"To love each other through all eternity, to care for each other, to put the needs for each other before thy own, to hold each other's hand at the time of mourning."

The rings. They had arrived just in time from Ja. Each was made of gold with matched engravings in the tiniest of script that said 'Pyaar Hamesha' (Forever Love).

It was Modoc's cue. Bram gave her a nudge. She had been keeping them in her mouth so as wet as they were, she offered them to Bram.

The minister spoke. "May these rings bind you both in God's love." Bram put the wet ring on Gertie's finger, then she on his. The minister continued, "Do you take Bram Gunterstein for your husband?"

Gertie answered, "Yes, I do."

"And do you, Bram, take Gertie Keller for your wife?" Bram sobbed, "I do, I do."

"Then from this moment on, you are husband and wife."

They kissed a long tender kiss.

The staff stood and applauded; Modoc trumpeted.

Bram and Gertie were married.

CHAPTER 29

The dining room bustled with activity. Everyone was there. The house staff, farm workers, gardeners, security, everybody. All brought their families, wives or girlfriends, and children. Modoc was placed just outside the door so she could hear what was happening. The long oak table sat as many as it could hold. Others found room at smaller tables situated around the room. Ahmed sat at the head of the table with Latika at his side. At the other end of the table sat Bram with his now wife, Gertie. Coogan was there, as was Sanjoe.

Due to there being so many people, the food was put in large ceramic bowls and set on the table for the guests to help themselves. Laid out in a festive presentation were biryani (rice), butter chicken paneer, tandoori meats, samosas, chaat, daal makhni (lentil), and dosa (pancake). Decorated lids covered the food, keeping it hot till it was time to eat. This also gave the kitchen staff time to enjoy the evening.

The bar was unmanned. Large two-liter-bottles of red, white, rose, sweet and sparkling wines were lined up along with all the more familiar hard liquor: whiskey, scotch and bourbon.

Various bottles of beer were heaped in huge buckets of ice. At the other end of the bar was a variety of juices: orange, apple, grape, and mango. All for the taking.

Sitting on cushions in the corner of the room were the same group of forest people who had played their forest music at the wedding. Although these people were rarely seen, only heard, since Bram's arrival at the sanctuary, the gaiety he and Gertie had brought lured some of them out of the bush into a world unknown to them. They couldn't speak the language, but they came with offerings of smiles, jungle food, and art they had crafted. Each brought an instrument that captured the very essence of the animals and the nature of the forest.

At the sound of the dinner bell, food lids were raised, seats filled, and a din of voices was heard. Their thoughts; the wedding, Mo's anticipated baby, ideas, wishes, suggestions, a bit of nostalgia, and most happy, happy laughter. But as the room quieted, the forest people's music came to life and the melody of the forest brought warmth to the room.

The chatter went on for some time, but as dinner ended and dessert had been enjoyed, some of the kitchen staff rose and headed for the bar to return with bottles of champagne that were placed along the table. Corks were popped, bottles opened, glasses filled. No one drank as they anticipated a toast.

Ahmed stood, glass in hand. The room went quiet, and the music became barely audible in the background.

"My dear, dear friends, first I wish you all a namaste." He pressed his palms together with a slight bow as the room followed suit. "We have gathered here tonight for a very special occasion—to celebrate the marriage of Bram and Gertie. I first met Bram and Modoc after they had spent weeks crossing the Sinar desert on foot, suffering the scorching rays of the sun, ravaged by renegades, nearly dying of thirst, and plagued by a relentless sun. Bram is a man of outstanding courage, Modoc, an elephant of unheard-of fortitude.

"Dear Gertie had spent her life in Germany working on the family farm as well as with the circus hoping that one day Bram, the love of her life, would return. Her dreams came true when they reunited. She came to him by Parcel Post, jumbled about with packages and mail." Laughter rang out. Most knew how Coogan had brought her in the plane.

"And so it was that God has gifted us with these two vibrant people who now have come into our lives, bringing their love and joy to us in our sanctuary. They have filled our lives with a sunshine that brightens each and every day and we are blessed to share this glorious moment with them. So…on this very special day, we congratulate Bram and Gertie on their marriage, and celebrate their love for one another."

"Here! Here!"

Glasses tinkled as Bram and Gertie stood to accept the ovation. There were few dry eyes from the women in the audience.

Ahmed continued. "Because you have both become members of our family, we would be honored to have you as our own by making it official. We have obtained adoption papers. With your signatures we become your legal parents—and you, our children. That is, if you will have us?"

Bram and Gertie were in shock. How wonderful.

"Yes! Yes! We do!" they said in unison.

They ran to Ahmed and Latika smothering them with hugs and kisses. Papers were signed. Bram waved them in the air for all to see. The room burst into a round of applause as their glasses were raised.

"To our new Family," toasted Ahmed.

"Here, here! Bravo!"

The room was aglow with cheers and good wishes. Bram noticed there were three documents. "But there are three documents here?"

He looked at the paper and in the space for signature was written 'Modoc Gunterstein,' daughter of the Tsar Ahmed and Latika of Agustian.

"Do you think she will sign it?" laughed Latika.

"Maybe if she had a pen," said someone.

"Cheers! Right on!"

"In her absence I will do the honor," said Bram, signing her name on the document.

The whole room exploded in applause, people standing, whistling, feet stamping. By now, the drinks were starting to have their effect on a few of the guests. Whistling and foot stamping were added to the festivities.

Bram tapped his fork on the wine glass. "As this is an evening of celebration, Gertie and I would like to celebrate the naming of our lake."

"Huh! You what?"

Some laughed.

"Surely there are those of you who know it, perhaps have even been there?"

Throughout the room many heads nodded.

"And for those who have seen it, you know it's beautiful and serene, and all come away with a feeling of peace and contentment. Most people just refer to it as 'The Lake,'" said Bram, "but everything needs a name. Without a name, it cannot be rewarded, be recognized. Only with a name can you achieve recognition."

"You speak as though it was alive," said one of the staff.

"If you've sat on the beach and listened to the waves lap the shore or swam down to its depth to see its garden of life and the fish that live there, you would know what I speak of. So tonight, we bestow upon it the title 'Lake Namaste.'"

A round of applause.

"So, you have found a name for it, have you?" asked Ahmed. "A well-suited one as well."

"This name will not be forgotten," said Gertie. "But now, another celebration."

Bram continued. "Tonight is truly a time to celebrate. Becoming a member of this family is a wonderful honor. In the world as we know it, love stands out to be the most important single entity that life can offer. It brings with it the joy and happiness we all long for.

"There have been times in my life where my water pouch was empty, my blood ran thin, my heart skipped a beat, and I thought the end was near."

Bram raised his hands to hush the guests. "But there was one whose tenacity for life gave me the strength to go on, see it through. She has been there for me my whole life. We have journeyed far. Tonight, in our joyful celebration is someone I have shared my life with, one who has given me the love and hope I needed in time of despair. So, to end this wonderful evening, I wanted to give you all something very special." Bram got up on a chair and in a barker's voice cried, "Ladies and

Gentlemen, I give you the greatest elephant that ever lived, the famous Modoc!"

A loud trumpet was heard, the big doors burst opened, and out came Modoc wearing a pink tutu, a necklace of flowers, her eyelashes still painted red, her wedding attire still intact. A turntable started to play the music from her circus act as she went into her famous performance. High stepping, whirling around, up on hind legs she did the whole act ending with a bow and trumpeting.

Good Lord, the house came down. Hugs, tears, drinks spilled, a standing ovation. Modoc couldn't stop trumpeting and swinging her trunk in all directions. The place went berserk; the room became a crazy wild place chanting, "Modoc! Modoc! Modoc!"

The evening wore on till morning with those in love dancing the night away. Bram and Gertie snuck away to celebrate in their own way in the quiet of their room.

Modoc finished the wedding cake!

CHAPTER 30

NEWS BULLETIN

"The Indian government has announced today that after extensive search operations covering a 500 square mile search area for the missing elephant and its trainer, it is now assumed they have perished in the desert. Therefore, all search teams and air rescue will be called off. The governor will make a statement regarding the tragedy on the 8:00 o'clock news. Mr. North, owner of the Wunderzircus where the elephant preformed, has announced there will be a tribute given to them at the showground this coming weekend."

"Yeah! Now, that's a good bit of P.R.," said Jake.

"Well, that's it! No more looking for them. At least I will collect a lot of money from the insurance and the tribute."

North sat back in his chair. He opened the box of Corona cigars, felt for the best one, rolled it with his fat fingertips, lit it, and chewed the end.

"Jake! Where are you?"

"Right here, Mr. North."

"Jake, my boy, have a cigar. Let's celebrate the kid, er man, who won't be bothering me anymore."

"But, Boss, I don't smoke."

"Well, fake it," said North handing him a cigar. North took a long drag on his stogie. "Yeah, ya know, Jake, in the long run, I guess I won after all. I kinda feel sorry for the elephant. She drew a lot of people to see her."

"Well, go buy another. They're all the same. Hire some bozo to train one."

"Meanwhile, let's get ready for our tribute. Keep it sad. Tell that guy who plays the organ to play funeral music. A few signs at the entrance should say something like, 'Contribution will go to the MODOC foundation for saving the elephants in Japan.'"

"Where? There are no elephants in Japan."

"Whatever. Maybe you can get an elephant from the zoo to perform. We could say its Modoc's brother or something."

"Sure, Boss," said Jake disgusted. He knew that would be impossible. He was going to remind him they had their own elephant but why bother.

He thought, ever since North bought the circus from Gobel, it had gone downhill. The performers hadn't been paid their salary for some time. Only their devotion to circus life kept it going.

North, on the other hand, was a rich man, but greedy. He looked at everything with a devious mind. 'How to profit' was always on his mind. Those around him suffered. He would drive his Mercedes convertible onto the circus grounds and park it in the most auspicious place for all to see.

North sat back in his leather office chair smoking his Cuban cigar. He put his feet up on the desk. A smirk and a sigh of contentment crossed his face. He had won, or so he thought.

CHAPTER 31

One Sunday morning while everybody was having breakfast, a guard rushed in.

"Mr. Ahmed, please sir, come quickly!"

"What's the matter?"

"Please, just come."

He ran out the door, Bram, Gertie and Latika right behind him. A body lay at the compound gate covered in blood, a huge gash across his chest. Ahmed knelt down trying to figure out what happened. The body was of a young Indian man wearing a pair of sisal churidars, (pants) sisal shoes, and a rag for a headband.

"Is he dead?"

"Yeah, I'm afraid so."

"Who is he?" asked Bram.

"I don't know. He is not one of our people," said Ahmed.

"Who in the world would have done this?" voiced Gertie.

Bram looked at the wound. "You mean what did this and whatever it was had to be quite large." The man's entire chest was caved in, and a long deep gash was centered in it. "Whatever did it must have been quite strong to rip him open like this," voiced Bram.

"Maybe a tiger," said Ahmed. "Hmm."

"No, I don't think so. There aren't any claw marks. This is a much bigger wound. Either a person with a large weapon or," he hesitated, "an elephant."

Ahmed had his guards wrap the body in a canvas sheet and put it in a shaded place and cover it with ice from the mountain.

"It will keep him from deteriorating," Ahmed said. "Coogan, you'll have to fly the body into the police station in Goajai. Get a couple of men to help you empty the plane to make room for it and you'll need to keep it on ice. Use the big chunks because they won't melt as fast. Should be all right till you get there. I'll give you a written statement as to what we have seen. Give it to the chief officer."

"I'm on it," Coogan said.

Within the hour Coogan had filled the gas tank, revved the engine and, with the body loaded, was on his way with written details from Ahmed as to what had occurred.

"Why send the body? Couldn't we just bury him here?" asked Bram.

"They have some strange laws out here. They need to identify the body and see that there was no foul play. It's really just a ploy. They don't have the facilities or the money to make the trip."

"What will they do?" asked Bram.

"Probably not much. Things of this nature just get pushed aside. They'll send a report to the main office in Delhi, and it will be filed in some drawer. Unless a witness was to appear, which isn't likely, it will never see the light of day."

"Poor chap, must have been a horrific experience."

One of the nursery men was standing next to Ahmed waiting to speak. He seemed quite shaken. "Mr. Ahmed sir, I saw a man."

"What? When did you see him? Where?"

"Just now, sir, when I heard of the dead man, God accept him, I was on the way here when he appeared at the far end of the orchard."

"Was he alone?"

'I saw no one else."

"Thank you, my friend. Keep your eyes open in case more come."

"Well, I think we've got a problem. Never have there been strangers who have come to the estate."

"You think they're here to rob us?"

"Why else would they come?" offered Latika.

"Spread the word. Tell the workers to keep on the lookout if others come," said Ahmed.

"Yes, this I will do." And he was off.

"Maybe it was just one who was curious," said Bram.

"We can only hope so."

The next day the herd came to drink when Bram spotted something while watching them with Ahmed. A young bull's tusks were streaked with dry blood. Across his chest a stream of coagulated blood had run its course from a two-foot-long slash. The gash was to the bone and was undoubtedly from a machete.

"That's your killer," said Bram. "And it surely explains why the man was killed."

"How do you figure?"

"Whoever got that close to inflict such a wound as that would never survive. Once an elephant is provoked, there is no way you're going to get away. Either this happened during the man's last moment, maybe being picked up by the bull and he was frantically slicing the air with his blade or," Bram thought for a bit, "or he was a poacher, maybe thought the bull was secure in a trap and he was trying to finish the job. Just guessing. Either way it was a horrible way to go."

"You think poachers are to blame?"

"Who else?"

"But we have never suffered a poacher. Tomorrow we'll scan the forest and see if there are any traps. If so, that will confirm they are, indeed, here," said Ahmed.

"What about the bull's injury?" inquired a nearby worker.

"Not much we can do. But not to worry. I'm sure he will heal," said Ahmed. "In the years I have lived here I've seen many animals with injury treat themselves."

"How?" asked the worker.

"Wash and treat," Bram chimed in.

"Just like we do?" the worker continued his line of questioning.

"Right," confirmed Bram.

"How?" the worker asked again.

"He'll probably wash it off in the lake, then there are certain healing plants in the forest he will put on it. He appears to be strong," Ahmed surmised.

"Look! He's already over by the trough spraying water on it," Bram pointed out.

Early morning found Bram, Ahmed, with a dozen of the staff, spread out in the forest to search for traps. Sure enough, many were found. Some of them were the horrible kind like a steel jaw full of razor-sharp teeth that would snap shut when an animal like deer and antelope stepped on it, others were more humane. The animal would enter the trap and the door would close behind him. They were more for smaller animals like mongooses, monkeys, and jackals. Some were found dead; others were lucky and still alive in the box traps and were turned out.

"Well, seeing all these traps, it's clear how the man died," said Bram. "It's pretty obvious he was trying to trap an elephant and it didn't work. Whatever happened, the bull did him in."

"Bottom line, poachers have come into the forest."

"How do we deal with them?"

"Aren't there some big animal reserves around that have rangers who could come and handle the situation?"

"I don't think so. They're hundreds of miles from here. If they were closer, they would help. But they would never come this far."

"How about the local police?"

"Nah, they're not about to search for them in the forest, but if we catch them, they'll come and pick them up. Even then we would have to pay them something for their help."

"You're kidding."

"That's how it is."

"So how do we go about catching them?"

"Tonight, after dinner let's get together and talk about it."

That night Bram and Ahmed, along with Coogan, Sanjoe and many of the staff and workers gathered on the patio to work out a plan. Gertie, Latika and some of the women joined in.

"Why not have your security guards go after them?" suggested Coogan.

"We only have a few and our forest is more like a jungle, it's so thick with foliage. If they saw them, they would scatter and hide in the underbrush. Then, it would be impossible to find them.

"Or our people could be ambushed and killed."

"No, we need to get them out in the open."

A worker from the nursery came in.

"Mr. Ahmed, Sir, you told me to spread the word if anybody sees a stranger and yes, we saw that there were two over by the wall."

"When?"

"Just now."

"So, they are really exploring the premises."

"These men came to poach the animals till they saw the house. I think they will go for both. But which one first?" Bram voiced the question they all thought.

"They're poachers first. That's what they know best. I think robbing the house may be an unknown to them," Coogan added.

"Ah! Never have we ever had this happen. It is much more serious than we thought," voiced Ahmed.

"So, what do you suggest?"

Ahmed was deep in thought. "We have no choice," he said. "We cannot be idle and wait for them to come and raid the house. If we must do battle, it is best to do it away from the house. We will have a much better chance of getting them when they are all together . . . you know, the one thing that will draw them out is if they think an elephant is caught in their trap. They would do anything for ivory. They have set their traps and will want to see what they've caught. Let's find one of their elephant traps."

"And to do that?"

Ahmed thought for a moment. "We could use Modoc as bait."

"What? No way. Too dangerous," said Bram.

"I would do nothing to endanger Modoc. But I was just thinking if there was some way for the poachers to think she was in one of their traps," said Ahmed.

"You mean rig it so there is no danger to her?"

"Yes, if we could find an elephant trap, trip it so it doesn't work, and then put Modoc near it… something like that," he said.

"I saw one of their elephant traps when we were looking," said one of the staff. "It's not far from the house. They have put four huge vicious looking steel traps under some foliage up by those giant oaks. The traps were all chained to the oaks about eight feet apart so if one doesn't get an elephant, the others will. There were signs that they put food in the middle to entice them."

"Did you disarm it?"

"Oh, yes, Mr. Ahmed, Sir. They are very strong. It took three of us, but I am happy to say it won't work."

"That sounds like what we are looking for. That way when they come, we could grab them."

"And there is no way they could hurt Modoc?" asked Bram.

"No, there is no way," he repeated.

"How does that sound, Bram? Is there anything else that would concern you?"

"Guns! How do we know they don't have them?" said Bram.

"Well," said Ahmed, "If they had them, they would have taken down an elephant from the herd. It would have been much easier than setting a trap and hoping an elephant comes by."

"And, too, one of their men would not have been killed."

"Makes sense," said Bram.

"Where do you think they are?"

"Probably up around the ice valley hiding out somewhere in the thicket. The runoff from the valley turned it into a swamp. It a perfect place to hide," said Coogan.

"So, this is how it would go down. We put Modoc in the middle of the traps as 'bait.' Bram would get her to rattle the chains like she was trapped and have her trumpet. When the men appear, we will grab them. What do you all think?" explained Ahmed.

They all chimed in. "Sounds good to me."

"Let's do it!"

"Bram?"

"Yeah, as long as Modoc is safe."

All agreed.

"There is one more thing. If we were to fail, Shangari would be next. They would come here and wreak havoc. All that we have worked for would be taken. Our lives would be at stake."

"Don't even go there," voiced Coogan.

"Won't happen," said a voice from the staff.

"Never," said another.

"We may not be trained fighters, but we have the will to win."

"But we don't know how many of them there are."

"Let's hope we have enough staff to take them down."

"We'll have only one shot at this. There won't be another."

Ahmed added, "I will talk to the staff. We'll get only able-bodied men willing to take the risk.

"Namaste," said Ahmed.

"Namaste," said all.

"Okay. Then, see you in the morning."

Gertie had a hot coffee ready for Bram as he awoke. He dressed quickly, sipped the coffee, and held Gertie for a minute, her head nestled against his neck. He felt the tears on his neck.

"Don't worry, honey, it will be fine," he reassured her. "It's time to go. I'll pick up Modoc on the way."

They kissed and the door closed.

Modoc was awake and waiting for Bram when he arrived. She knew something was stirring. Early morning everybody had gathered at the gate eager for the hunt. The staff cared for the forest, especially the animals, as though it were their own and were ready to fight for it. But now their home, their work, their livelihood was in jeopardy.

Ahmed spoke. "Thank you all for coming. As you know, we have been invaded by poachers. People who have been known to not only kill animals but humans as well. They are ruthless and barbaric and will do whatever it takes to achieve their goals. If given the chance, they will move to raid our home and steal what is not theirs. We cannot allow them to disrupt our lives. So we must prepare ourselves. We are fifteen strong. Where they have their fighting skill, we have something more powerful, our love and devotion for one another, our home, and our will to fight for what is right. That is more powerful than their knives."

A unanimous uproar confirmed all were on board.

"If there is anyone who has second thoughts and prefers not to join us, we will understand."

None spoke.

Machetes were handed out. Blades had been checked for sharpness.

"I have laid out all the knives, garden and field tools that can be used as weapons. Take whatever suits your fancy. We must reach the site before the sun's up when poachers come to see if they were lucky and caught some animals during the night."

"Ok! Let's do it!" several said.

Gertie and Latika had followed their men out. The other women followed.

Ahmed spoke to the women. "I hate to anticipate what might happen, but you should prepare our medical facility and equipment. Perhaps set up a few more beds in the infirmary. It's just a precaution, but a necessary one."

The women were there, each in their own way, to give their men a kiss, a hug, a blessing.

"By careful."

"Love you."

"God be with you."

Dawn broke to what appeared would be a misty day. The fog rolled in making it hard to distinguish anything five feet in front of them as the group entered the forest. It was unusually calm save for the far-off mournful cry of the loons at Lake Namaste. The men positioned themselves around the oaks that surrounded the trap. Using their machetes, they dug shallow pits to lie in and covered themselves with forest foliage so as not to be seen. Then they waited. Others took to the trees. They kept the obvious approach paths clear.

Bram showed Mo the chain. Heavy and long, he picked it up to show her what to do.

"Pick it up, Mo."

It didn't take anything but a moment for her to understand. She had picked up many things when asked to.

The key word was to tell her to play. Bram saved that for last. He knew what she would do. Bram put Modoc in the middle of the traps and had her 'stay,' then he scattered some oat hay and fruit for her to eat so she wouldn't get bored and wander off. Now to find a place to hide. It had to be close enough to signal Mosey. Any thick bush would do, but he didn't want to be in the path of the approaching poachers. He noticed the traps had been put under one of the large oaks and would be a good place to hide.

Scrambling up the backside he found the elbow of a large branch that arched out over the trap site and hid among the thick foliage. He hadn't felt good about being too far away from Modoc.

Here he could view the whole area and still be close enough to Modoc.

Ahmed gave the signal that all was ready on his side. Bram gave Mo the cue to rattle the chains.

"Pick it up, Mo, good girl." She looked around trying to see where Bram was. "Go ahead. Pick it up." Once she saw him up in the tree, she felt this was good fun. She picked up the chain waiting for Bram to tell her what to do with it.

"Okay Mosey. Play, girl, play!"

That did it. What good fun! She picked up the heavy chain that held the traps and started to shake and rattle them. Dirt, leaves, debris flew everywhere. On her own she let out a thundering trumpet! Perfect, thought Bram. If that didn't do it, nothing would. He waited fifteen minutes for her to do it again.

Bram heard voices. They were coming. A few minutes went by, then a large group of men crept through the fog. Bram was shocked when he counted two dozen! Far more than they had anticipated. They all looked like the local tough, nomad renegades, dressed in sisal wrap and rags. They were creeping quietly; each carried a machete at the ready and a dagger tucked in a sash around their waist. Bram was worried they might step on one of the people hiding in the trenches. The man in front was whispering directions to the others. As they got closer, the poachers became excited. They must have thought their fortune was made when they saw Modoc who appeared to be an elephant struggling to get out of the traps. As they approached Bram panicked as he saw one of the men pull out a small handgun and was aiming it at Modoc's head! Of course, they had never thought how they planned to kill the elephant!

"Modoc!" he yelled.

As he launched himself out of the tree, Mo swung her head toward Bram as the gun went off. The bullet whizzed by and just barely nicked Mo's ear. Ahmed immediately jumped out of his hiding spot and together he and Bram tackled the man with the gun and knocked him to the ground. From out of their hiding places came the rest of the sanctuary men, charging into the poachers, machetes raised, blood splattered as they met them with full force.

The poachers were not going to go down without a fight. Their own machetes were ready before the sanctuary force came swinging. Knives drawn, machetes flashing, they met the Shangari people head on. Modoc, seeing what was happening, reminisced of the farmers' episode, and grabbed one of the poachers slamming him into the ground. But the poachers were professional at this game of war. They knew how to use the machete, not for cutting trees but for people! The opposing forces' blades flashed and clanged briefly Ahmed saw his men falling one by one, fighting to the last. The poachers had the upper hand.

No! no! It cannot be, he thought. To lose the battle with the poachers they would lose Shangari.

From the forest then came a loud ear piercing shrill. From the trees and through the bush came the forest people, both men and women, yelling in their own language, the men carrying small machetes, the women waving sharpened sticks, kitchen knives, some with pots and pans; they came leaping through the brush to jump on the poachers beating and stabbing them like angry bees on an intruder.

Their women were hitting and beating the poachers with river stones and frying pans. Their children came, biting the ankles and stabbing their legs with forks!

The Sangari people with renewed energy came at them. Their machetes were finding their marks more often now and the poachers' numbers began to dwindle. It wasn't long before most of the poachers lay on the ground. Outnumbered and in shock, the remaining handful threw down their machetes and knives and raised their hands and dropped to their knees.

"Asifminfadlik aghfir," (sorry please forgive) they said over and over.

The battle was won, the enemy was defeated.

The end of any battle is never a place of joy. All suffer from it. The loss to the victors can sometimes be greater. Comrades had fallen, their families left in tears, heartache, and grief would be endured for years to come. The trap battleground lay in ruin. Machetes, knives, forks, pots, torn clothes, pools of blood lay where people had fallen. Modoc stood bewildered. The men she threw down still laid there groaning from the broken bones they suffered.

The forest people were busy picking up their weapons: bows and arrows, stones, pots, kitchen knives, poles. Some were carrying out their wounded, the women already caring for their wounds. All were guided to the infirmary. So many, so quick, the poachers where dumbstruck from the surprise attack. A few Shangari people, like the poachers, lay injured. There were losses. Not many, mostly cuts, but some deep. The women came with stretchers and medical supplies. Poachers and staff alike headed back to the house infirmary. Those that couldn't walk were put on stretchers as were the seriously injured and the few that were dead. The injured on both sides, the poachers, the staff, the workers all would get medical attention.

Vashu, the leader of the forest people, came to Ahmed. Under five feet tall, with bushy hair and a goatee, he came dragging his machete on the ground. Blood ran down his shoulder that Bram sensed was not his.

"They will not come back," he said in broken bush English.

"No, they will not," answered Ahmed.

"The house in the bush is safe."

"Yes, it is safe."

"And the birds and deer will live."

"They will live."

"Then we are good?" (Achcha) said, the little man looking up at Ahmed.

"Very good," (Batuta Accda) said Ahmed.

Ahmed didn't know what to do. He was overwhelmed with gratitude. They would have lost the battle were it not for Vashu and his people. He would have hugged the man but thought better of it. He lifted a gold chain from his neck and placed it around the little man's neck. A large ruby medallion hung from the chain.

"Thank you, friend," (Dhan'yanada) said Ahmed offering his hand.

"Very good." (Batuta accha) The little man smiled as he grasped Ahmed's hand.

The little man's eyes glistened with pride. He turned and with a very broad smile lifted the presentation for all to see. A joyous uproar filled the air. Two of the three musicians started to play their flute-like instruments. The drum man joined in as the little people of the forest filed out. The forest was safe, as was the 'house in the bush.'

The Shangari people gathered around Modoc.

"Good girl, well done." Bram stretched his arm around her. Many others joined in patting and hugging her best they could.

"Thank God you yelled to her," said Ahmed. "It caused her to look around at you as the bullet grazed her head."

Bram noticed that the bullet was fired low. Apparently, these men knew where to kill an elephant! Bram dug the bullet lodged in the trunk of the tree he was hiding in. He showed it to Mo.

"See this, girl, this was meant for you."

She puffed a billow of air on it and went back to eating some fruit still on the ground.

She had no idea what he was showing her.

Bram gave Ahmed a look. "No gun, huh?"

"Sorry, Bram, I guess they use it for the 'coup-de-grace' shot. It would have never been lethal at any distance against the herds."

"Coogan, you're going to have to fly to town and let the police know what has happened and to come for the prisoners."

"I'm on it," he said. He left to prepare his plane. Those that were not injured were kept tied to one of the large redwood trees and given food and water and watched closely by some of Ahmed's men.

The afternoon of the following day, the police finally arrived in a beat-up field truck used for hauling produce. The police, having no vehicle of their own, had confiscated it for the haul.

"What will happen to the poachers?" Bram asked the police captain.

"Once we get them to the station and file a report, they will be held for a week or so, and then off to Big Daddy, the state prison in New Delhi."

The poachers were crammed into the truck and, after Ahmad settled their bill, off the policemen went.

"Why do they come now when before they couldn't be bothered?" asked Bram.

"A dead body wasn't worth their while. I am sure they will take credit for capturing the poachers. And then there is the payment. They come for the money and the credit."

The poachers turned out to be nomads from a small village some twenty miles from the forest. They had hidden their small vehicle just on the edge of the forest. Bram remembered seeing a dot for a town on the map some twenty miles from the forest. It was probably the same one. The police had said it was a center for selling skins to traders. Somehow, they learned of elephants in our forest; the thought of getting ivory was a chance to make a fortune. None of them had ever trapped an elephant and one was to pay for it with his life.

"What kind of penalty will they receive?" asked Bram.

"If they're the same ones who broke into the Federal buildings last year, and I think they are, they will get probably fifteen to twenty."

"Months?"

"No, years."

CHAPTER 32

In the months that followed, the sanctuary was a beehive of activity. It was time to harvest. The earth had yielded a bumper crop, and the workers were filling their baskets with an assortment of the many fruits and vegetables.

Gertie and Latika were in the garden from dawn till dusk organizing the pickers and the planters. While the pickers were gathering all the near-ripe fruit and vegetables and putting them in their designated baskets ready for storage, another group was tilling the soil, mixing fresh manure, and pressing the new seeds into the earth.

"Would you like to see where we store our perishables?" asked Latika.

"Yes, I've often wondered what you do with all the nursery food. There is so much of it."

"Come, I'll show you."

Latika led the way ahead of a line of workers all carrying baskets. They entered through a back door into the kitchen, then down a stairway to a large candlelit room.

"This is our storage room. Because it stays so cool, it also acts as our refrigerator where we keep all the perishables." Gertie was amazed at the array of produce. Meat, cheeses, milk, lettuce, corn, tomato, strawberries, spinach. So many kinds of fruits and vegetables were laid out on wooden shelves it appeared much like in a market. Another area housed the medical supplies, some of which had to be kept cool.

"Our wine is brought in from Jodhpur to Goajai where Coogan picks it up. We put it in racks in the storage room far from the freezer section where it's kept at a constant temperature. One trip to Goajai keeps the family in wine for many months.

"While working down here we found a trap door in the floor that opened down into another room." She waved to a worker who threw back a rug uncovering a trap door with a brass handle. A strong pull and the door swung up to uncover a second flight of stairs.

"Come."

Gertie followed her down into the dark. Candles on the wall were lit to reveal another smaller stone walled room filled with shelves holding all kinds of frozen food.

"And this is our freezer." Gertie pulled her light wrap over her head to keep out the chill of the cold air.

"Did you build this?"

"No. The room was here. It was a prison. Look here."

Cemented in the wall hung six iron rings connected to short chains.

"Ahmed told me in the 'bygone days' there were no jails other than the ones in the big cities, so families built these rooms to hold criminals. For minor offenses they were kept in what is now our storage room till the owners of the house felt they had learned their lesson. For major offenses they kept them down here in the freezer room till the police came and took them into custody. I'm sure some of them froze to death while waiting.

"So now we have a cooler/freezer. The 'prison' was perfect. The temperature down here is always constant. We built storage racks to hold a dozen large canvas bags full of large chunks of ice. Ahmed sends the farm workers up to the ice valley where they cut huge slabs of ice, pack them into the canvas bags, load them on our camels and haul them back here.

"We have our own supermarket," said Latika, followed by a laugh.

CHAPTER 33

As time passed, Bandulla became touchable. The natural barriers existing between man and beast were coming down. Although still carrying his air of supremacy, he befriended all who showed him affection. The herd, although still shy, had felt this inner peace as well and had become frequent visitors. Although touching was not permitted, they were no longer aggressive, having lost their fear and surrendered to the warmth of the people. Stale bread or old veggies were the order of the day.

When they came to visit, the workers hand fed them, sneaking in a touch here and there to get accustomed to them and to show their friendliness. Even old Mama let down her protective ways and was the first to push her way through the others to get her share of the goodies being offered.

However, when Modoc was around, she tended to ease back as if not wanting to get into a confrontation like before. The children wanted to play with the herd's young punks, but their mothers gently moved them between their legs. It was just too soon. So they took out all their anxiety by caring for Modoc by

picking dodos (bugs) that had set up house in the folds of
Modoc's skin. An energetic scrub was followed with forest
leaves with antiseptic value, so the intruders didn't return.
Modoc was in her glory.

"Strange we never heard any news about North,"
commented Ahmed. "That rag of a newspaper that comes out
every month in Jodhpur never mentioned anything about the
'lost elephant'."

"That was quite a while ago," replied Bram. "The last
time Coogan flew into Jodhpur to pick up some documents for
you, there was a small article in the back of the local paper that
mentioned the government had called off the search. I still wake
up in the middle of the night after dreaming he has come and is
taking Modoc."

"Well, those days are over. So let it be," said Ahmed.

Adult male elephants didn't spend much time around
the herd. They were solitary animals and preferred to be on
their own; they only joined the herd when nature called, and
they were compelled to service the females. But then, once done,
they moved on and went back to their solitary life in the forest.

But with Bandulla it was different. Instead of going back
into the wild, he preferred to be with Modoc. Most strange. Was
it her gentle way of life and relationships with people? They
came from two different worlds. She, a world of humans,
touching, handling, caring, loving. He, on the other hand, had
never been close to humans and, in fact, had considered them
his enemy. But now all that was changing. His relationship with
Modoc had brought him into a world that before was
completely foreign to him. He found these two-legged creatures
to be gentle, friendly and in no way aggressive. When Modoc
was given a treat, he was given one as well, when she was
bathed, he was sprayed by a hose. He had a choice to stay with
her or go back to the wild. He chose her.

Bram had just come in from helping the workers pile up
Modoc's food supply for the evening. Ahmed sat at the bar
sipping a scotch.

"I've made a decision," Bram stated.

"Well, congratulations."

"No, really, I have decided to let Modoc free to eat her
meals out."

"Which restaurant?" Ahmed said with a smirk across his face.

"Ahmed, come on, I'm being serious."

"Okay, what?"

"Modoc is eating three to four hundred pounds of food each day."

"Well, it's not like we're going to run out of the food supply."

"It's not that. It's a chore for the men to cut and haul it into her pen every day, plus it would be nice for her to choose her own food. So, what do you think?"

"Yeah, well, I think it's fine. You'll need someone to keep an eye on her," said Ahmed. "There's a worker who has taken a liking to her who I think will be just fine," said Bram.

"But there is something else that concerns me," said Ahmed.

"What's that?"

"Mama. Ever since she confronted Modoc there have been hard feelings."

"You mean she's jealous?"

"Whatever, but the threat of another standoff is always there. You know, Bram, there are other dangers in the forest. India is famous for having an abundance of cobras and the forest has its share. Their poisons are lethal enough to bring an elephant down and they're difficult to see in the thick foliage. And then there is the Bengal tiger. Although rarely seen, they have been known to crossover through the mountain passes during the hot summer months and have been seen in the forest."

"You're trying to scare me."

"No, just making you aware."

"Well, Bandulla won't be far off, and I couldn't ask for better security than that."

Bram slowly weaned Modoc from the garden vegetables and let her get her food from the forest. It didn't take long. Each day he would put out less and less of the garden food for her. She would come and pick out her favorites, then off she would go to get her fill in the bush.

A woman worker while in the field picking carrots had brought her child with her. Modoc and Bandulla were standing nearby patiently waiting to get a carrot treat when the toddler, some four years old, probably bored watching her mother unearth carrots, wandered off heading toward the elephants.

Having played with Modoc, she had no fear of Bandulla. She walked right up and wrapped her arms as far as she could reach around Bandulla's leg, then she jumped on his foot not to let go. Totally surprised, Bandulla reached his trunk down gently wriggling it around the child, circling, the tip of his trunk gently prodded her trying to figure out how to lift her away. But as children do, she giggled and hung on not to be dislodged. His nervousness made him blow puffs of air that blew the child's hair causing her to laugh all the more. All this, till the child's mother, shocked to see her with Bandulla, called her away. Perhaps this was a small breakthrough for Bandulla that would edge him a little closer to being touched. And a child shall lead them was never truer than at that moment. They had touched, and it was good.

Gertie and Bram sat on the veranda later that evening.

"Did you hear about one of the worker's children playing with Bandulla. She was playing with him! Can you believe it?" Gertie was ecstatic.

"The innocence so inherent in children should be embedded in us adults," said Bram.

"You're jealous!" Gertie said between laughter.

"What do you think Bandulla would do if I went and hugged his leg? HUH! You would have to peel me off the nearest tree!"

"The day will come, my love, when you will be accepted in Bandulla's life."

Bram yearned to be able to touch Bandulla. It wasn't just the touch; it was befriending him. He needed to build trust. All good friendships are based on it.

What a magnificent elephant he was. Standing far higher than Modoc and a good thousand pounds heavier with tusks that swept within inches from the ground. He could only imagine running his hands over that enormous body, to feel the smoothness of his tusks. What a thrill that would be.

He had once walked under his belly and his head was still inches below his underside. He looked forward to the day he would be able to ride him. Good Lord, way up there! He envisioned it. But he knew to do that Bandulla would need to know the choon, and that was, for now, beyond his imagination. But that was the way it had to be. There were barriers that species never integrated. It had always been so. Never had he ever seen two different wild species touch intimately. Not once! Perhaps it was nature's way of not having them interbreed.

Bram's thoughts were interrupted when—

"You guys want to see something unusual?"

"Sure, what's up?"

They followed Ahmed to the edge of the forest.

"Over there."

Far off in the bush were Bandulla and Modoc. He was gently pushing her away from the compound to go deeper into the forest. She didn't want to go, but his insistence finally won, and she followed him out and away until they were lost from view.

"What do you think?" asked Ahmed.

"I don't know. Strange. Maybe he sensed danger here or he just wanted her to go with him."

"He can be demanding at times. Like most men," voiced Gertie.

Ignoring the dig, Bram said, "But it's most unusual."

"Don't worry, love, Bandulla won't let anything happen to her," said Gertie.

The days passed into weeks, but they were nowhere to be seen.

"I'm really worried, Gert. She's never been away from me for this long a time. If she doesn't return by tonight, I'll get a search party together and go out tomorrow morning at first light and look for her."

Morning came. Bram had organized a mixed group of staff and nursery people to look for Modoc. They were just about ready to leave when a loud rambunctious trumpeting of many elephants was heard. Ahmed left his office, Latika her gardening, all ran out to see what the commotion was.

Coming through the forest down the path was Modoc, Bandulla and yes, a wobbly, little baby male elephant. Modoc had given birth to her baby and was bringing it home. The little guy was hugging his mom's leg as best he could. Bandulla, the proud father that he was, steadied it with his trunk so it didn't fall. Behind them came the 'family' herd, the whole herd all trumpeting, bellowing, pooping, and dancing around.

Modoc brought the baby to Bram, who as usual, was in tears as he knelt and cradled the punk in his arms. He couldn't weigh more than a couple hundred pounds. So small from so large a parent. Its little trunk flapped as the baby had no idea what it was doing out there hanging from its face. His eyes twinkled with long eyelashes that fluttered in anticipation.

If only he knew he was born to a mother who had met the challenges life had to offer and had won. And his father, a mighty king who ruled all of his kind through strength and gentle leadership. What a wonderful combination. He would be taught the best of these two worlds other elephants would never know. He would instinctively be shaped by the love and guidance his parents would give him.

Gertie, Ahmed, Latika and Coogan all crowded in to join Bram, wanting to touch and pet the baby. Bandulla towered over all keeping his trunk close by. If anyone was too pushy, he would gently move their hand away.

Here, for the first time, the herd and the Shangari family came together in a mishmash of touching and petting a new baby. The females in the herd gathered around to touch the baby. Their trunks meshed with human hands for the first time. A jumble of twisting, chirping. clicking, belly rumbles, trunks, hands, and arms all intertwined. How wonderful. Then a scuffle was heard as the herd backed off. Big Mama was coming.

Slowly she came, being the matriarch of the herd, all respected her and moved aside as she came through followed by her own baby not much bigger than Modoc's baby. Never had Mama been this close to any humans. But it didn't seem to matter; she reached her trunk first to Modoc and blew a puff of air into her trunk. Then a moment later, Modoc did the same to her. It was surely an acceptance.

The rivalry was over. Mama's trunk left Modoc and was now allowed to touch her baby. Hands and trunks eased back while she moved her trunk all around feeling the baby's ears and mouth. For a brief moment, the tip of Mama's trunk touched human hands. It hesitated, then moved slowly around feeling others till one of the hands stroked her trunk. She froze as it moved up and down her trunk feeling the firm sensitive tip. Then Mama's baby pushed her way through the many arms and hands and bumped into Modoc's baby. They entwined trunks and squealed. When the baby squeaked, the whole herd squealed. Such a moment!

Big Mama blew dust in the air like saying time to go. Her baby wanted to stay and play, but perhaps another time. Mo's baby started to follow them, but Modoc gently held him back.

Tomorrow, baby. Big Mama moved out; the herd seemed reluctant to follow. Mama's life would never be the same. She had crossed the line into a world she had observed but never entered and experienced. And it was good. The herd followed her up the trail, her baby just behind, squeaking and playing with his trunk as though it was a newfound friend.

They left behind a family in joyful tears at the wonderful experience of being accepted by the herd. Some of the men had wet cheeks and were quick to wipe them off. They were all having kittens. The two families were now one. Bandulla stayed behind. He would be staying close to his new family.

Early morning found Bram and Gertie putting a new sign on Modoc's pen. It read—

'MODOC AND SON'

"What do you think?"

"We didn't put Bandulla's name. He is the father, you know."

"Yeah, I guess I should have put his name up there also, but he's a big boy; he'll understand."

Sanjoe arrived with a pitcher of milk which he handed to Bram.

"What's that for?" asked Gertie.

He dodged the question.

"You know, love, it's time to choose a name for the little one. A name that would be used over and over again for the next umpteen years."

"Everybody's pushing for Modoc Jr. or Bandulla Jr."

"No way," said Bram. "No junior."

"I agree." She thought for a while. "I have a name."

"You do?

"Yeah, I really like it but maybe you won't."

"Maybe I will," he retorted.

"We need a cute name while he's a baby but a name that can change over time. Remember, some day he will be as big as his daddy, so the name has to fit a Monarch. I think I have it," said Gertie.

'Wow! You have it all figured out, do you? Okay, let's have it."

She closed her eyes and crossed her fingers. "The name I love while he is a baby is Bandie! What do you think?" She kept her fingers crossed.

"And when he's older?" asked Bram.

"Bandor!"

Bram looked concerned. Teasing.

"You don't like it?"

Bram's face turned into a smile. "Honey, I love it! Bandie is perfect for him now and Bandor, well yes, it is fit for a Monarch."

"So, it's agreed?"

"Nope," said Bram.

"Why, you said you liked it."

"I do, but I wanted Mo's name in there somewhere. After all, it's her baby, too.”

Gertie thought about it. "You're right, honey." She thought about it for a moment more.

"How about Bandor Modoc Gunterstein? "

"Really? It doesn't sound weird?" questioned Bram.

"No, I don't think so," she said, hiding her real concern. "Besides, who's going to call him all three names at once?"

"Yeah, okay, so be it."

He took the pitcher of milk Sanjoe had brought and held it over the baby's head.

"We christen you, Bandor Modoc Gunterstein,” and with that, he poured the milk over the baby's head!

When her laughter subsided, she said, "Bram, you're crazy."

CHAPTER 34

Two old Indian codgers, Ajay and Godal, sat at an outdoor table
in front of a dilapidated, raunchy bar called the 'Hilton' in the
dusty small town of Baszer on the edge of the Sinar Desert. Both
were dressed in shabby Lungi (Sarongs) and dirty brown
turbans. A beat-up rusty temperature gauge hooked on a nearby
post read 102 ^{0}. Beer bottles were scattered on the table, most
were empty. A half dozen fly-infested 'rock hard' biscuits in a tin
can sat uneaten. The flies were feasting on them, and the men
kept swiping them off. Six scrawny kids, wearing old sisal bags
for clothes, and their scrawny dogs sat eying the biscuits and
slobbering but said nothing.

Ajay had enough of the buzzing. "God damn flies!" he
yelled and dumped the biscuits into the street. A mad dash took
place as the kids and dogs scrambled for them. Dust flew,
bickering started, a fight ensued. Local birds darted in and out
snatching a few of the hard crumbs.

A small, wooden radio screeched iconic Indian music,
the static making it nearly impossible to hear. This was what the

local men of Baszer did. Nothing. Just sit and listen to the radio and drink beer. A scratchy voice came on with the local news:

<u>Morning Talk Show</u>

"This is your host, Jim Dutton, bringing you the latest news from Northern India and our dry, but beautiful and intimidating Sinar Desert. I am, as always, joined by my co-host Bert Huston riding the air waves."

Bert: "Yes, Good morning, Jim. Well, the first topic of the day is this story about bones being found in the upper region of the Sinar."

Jim: "Yeah, they were quite large and believed to be the remains of that elephant lost in the desert a number of years ago."

Bert: "That was what everybody thought until they sent them over to the museum where, on close examination, they were found to be camel bones."

Jim: "Apparently some thief stole a camel and took off into the desert. But he never

made it. So, the pile of bones is what remains."

Bert: "On the subject of bones, they never found that elephant that wandered off in the

desert with his trainer?"

Jim: "Na, never did. Probably never will."

Bert: "Wonder what happened to them?"

Jim: "Probably died climbing one of those two-hundred-foot-high dunes."

Bert: "Yeah, poor guy."

Jim: "Poor elephant you mean."

Bert: "I hear the governor is offering a reward for anybody having information as to

their whereabouts. Dead or alive."

Just then the radio went dead.

"Ah! Stupid radio," bitched Ajay banging the table.

An old grey-haired bearded fellow sat nearby at another table sipping a nearly finished bottle of beer. He was dressed in a tattered kaki outfit and wore a cowboy hat with a tag that said "Walmart." He looked like a skeleton the skin had dried on. He was illiterate, yet sometimes he would come out with things that were quite sharp. The locals treated him as the village Looney and because of this they called him Lou.

Hey, Lou, if you know where the elephant is, you could
get the reward. It would buy us a lot of beer," Ajay said,
then snickered.

Lou was mumbling to himself.

"So do ya?" asked Godal jokingly.

The old man never looked up. "Nope. Maybe."

"Yes or no? Do you?"

"Nope, maybe...gonna buy me a drink?" asked Lou.

"Well, yeah sure. We'll get you one."

They beckoned to a fat, aged woman in a torn, too-short
cotton dress to get the old man a beer. Without getting
up, she reached into an old, dilapidated Coca-Cola chest
and pulled out a hot beer.

"So did you, man?"

"What?"

"See a man and an elephant?"

"Yeah, sure, yeah, betcha."

Godal didn't know if he was telling the truth or just
wanted another beer.

"Saw them some years back, I did, heading towards the
Kruki Forest. Yeah, doubt if they made it though. Yeah.
Looked pretty worn out. Yeah, worn out."

"Never heard of it," said Ajay. "Where is this Kruki
Forest?"

He pointed over his shoulder. "That way."

"Is it far?"

"Yep."

"Could you show us?" said Godal.

"Nope, I'm busy. Got meetings to go to."

"Is it difficult to get there?"

"Yep."

"Can you take us?"

Hesitant. "Got ah meeting."

Neither Ajay nor Godal had ever heard of that forest,
and they had lived their lives in the desert forever. But their
patience was wearing thin. Maybe, just maybe, this old fart was
telling the truth. They had known old Looney for many years.
"He may be a little off center, but he never lies," Ajay muttered.

"You know, Godal, Looney may have a lead. Let's check
it out. It's not like we have a 'meeting' to go to," he smirked. "I

could get word to the Governor's office we're looking for the elephant so we will get the reward if we find it. They would give us something, even if we found the bones."

"Wow! Wait a minute. You want to go traipsing out across that god-awful desert on Looney's word? You're as crazy as he is. Even if we get to this forest, what then? They're not going to be standing there waiting for us."

Ajay pulled his chair over close to where Lou sat slouched. "Lou, look at me." Lou struggled to open his blearily eyes. "You sure you saw them?"

"Who?"

"The guy with the elephant."

"Uh huh. Plain as night."

"You saw them go into this forest?"

"Uh huh."

"That's it? So, then what? Where did they go?"

"Don't know."

"Hey, Lou. Where were you?" asked Godal.

"Uh huh. Yep. Twice. Hunting."

"Hunting what?"

"Stones."

"What kind?"

"Pretty ones. They're in the mountains, they are."

"Find any?"

"Nope, yes, few, not many. We saw a house there."

"Where?"

"There's a house in the forest, kinda spooky house there."

"In the forest?"

"Uh huh."

"Did you go in?"

"No. No. Scary, didn't go there. It's in the forest, yeah old one."

"Did the man go there?"

"No. Don't know. Maybe."

"That does it," said Ajay. "I'm going. You on board?"

"You sure you want to go trekking out in that godforsaken desert on that old man's word?"

"I've known Lou for many a year. He knows, I tell ya. It's not like we have a 'meeting' to go to." He laughed. "Let's do it, Godal."

"Yeah, shit, okay, why not?"

"What about the guy who owns the elephant? What's his name? North, South?"

"I don't know."

"It's North. Anyhow, I'll bet he would pay a lot to find them. More than the governor." "You're right, I'll put through a message before we go. You never know, it might be worth it."

North was engrossed in reading the newspaper and smoking a cigarette when Jake rushed into his office.

"Hey, boss, I think we might have found them."

"Jake, I'm busy. What are you going on about?"

"The guy and the elephant."

"I thought that was old news. How many people have called saying they found them or their bones just to get some money out of us? We already got paid the insurance money."

"This is different. This guy left a phone message that they know where they're at. He's from that same area where the crash took place."

"How close?"

"Probably fifty miles."

"What? That's close?"

"In the desert, yeah. I think he's the real McCoy."

"Well, drop my cookies, wouldn't that be something. So, tell me more."

"The message says he was told that they're staying at an old house far up in a forest on the upper end of the Sinar Desert. Near the mountains. They want to know if you will pay them to check it out."

"Well, lordy yes, make a deal. Ha! Would you believe it! After all this time. Tell this guy to go for it and get back to us. Move, man, move! If it's true, saddle my horse. I'll be on my way for the 'coup de grace'."

For a couple of cases of beer and with a promise to split the reward if they found the elephant, they got the old man to agree to take them where that forest was. Ajay borrowed his friend's broken-down old lorry that the owner swore would 'take you to the moon and back.' "It's got camel wheels."

"What the hell are camel wheels?"

"You've lived here all these years, and you don't know what camel wheels are?"

"Uh! Just tell me."

"They're bigger than most. Way bigger. You can let some of the air out until they're near flat, so they become like a tractor. Go anywhere with them. I promised to cut him in on the reward if we find the elephant."

"Won't be any money left if you keep giving it away."

"It's a long reach, Ajay, and we're crazy to try. But what the hell. We're still young, kinda, only pushing sixty."

"You wish. But there's still enough in us for a bit of adventure. Huh? How long a trip is it?

"How far is it, Lou?"

"Dunna know, maybe five or six days."

"If we find them, the payoff will be worth it."

"And if we don't?" challenged Godal.

"Ha! Shit! Man, think of it like digging for gold. It's the quest that counts, man!"

He laughed. "Okay. Let's get with it."

They loaded enough petrol to go to the moon, packed up a bunch of bread, pretzels, hard sausages, bags of peanuts, cheese, chips, five jugs of water, five crates of beer, and with the old man in tow, they took off.

Each day, with the help of the moon, they traveled the few hours before sunup and the few hours after, all to avoid the heat. Lou slept a lot. On and off, he would wake up, point if they were off course, and go back to sleep.

"How does he know?"

"He just knows."

At night they would pitch a small tent, eat some of their grub, then early the next morning move on. Sometimes they would just sleep in the lorry. Early on day five, the forest came into view.

"Hey, Godal. Wake up. The old man was right! We got forest. Ha!"

When Lou saw the trees and the edge of the forest, he was overjoyed. "Didn't I tell it right? Huh? Huh?"

"You sure did, old man."

Within the hour they were in the forest. The lorry was doing all the things that cars do when they have had enough.

Steam billowed up out of a hot, dry radiator so thick they couldn't see the engine.

"What now? It's dead," said Ajay.

"At least we made it to the forest. So, give it a rest. It just needs water for the radiator."

"We can use some of our drinking water. How are we going to get through the forest? There are no roads."

"Nope. It's here," said Lou.

"Where?"

Lou pulled some brush aside showing what looked like an old road. "Looks like it hasn't been used in years. It's totally overgrown."

"Think the lorry will fit going through the forest?" asked Ajay.

"Looking at the forest, I doubt it. It's really thick."

"If not, we walk. Probably best, if they are there, they won't hear us coming."

"So, in the morning we'll follow the road. Let's see where it goes. Look for the house."

"If the house is as old as the road, it's probably disintegrated by now."

"Well, it's almost dark. We'll crash here until morning, then we'll head in."

At sunup, Lou was the first one up, scouting here and there, kicking foliage off the old road.

"Forget the truck, Lou, the trees have grown over the old road so it would be impossible to drive on it."

So, the three with their morning beer in one hand and a chunk of sausage in the other took off into the forest following the old road hoping it would take them to the house. Within an hour they found themselves deep in the forest; everything looked the same. trees, bushes, streams of water, but no house. They were ready to go back when they heard voices. Coming through the brush were a couple of men carrying buckets of ice. They crouched down so as not to be seen.

"What the hell? Where would they get ice up here? Couldn't come from here?" Godal whispered.

"Whatever, we need to follow them. They have to be from the house."

Sure enough, within fifteen minutes the minarets of the temple appeared over the tops of the trees. The three were bursting with excitement for finding it.

"Do you think the man and his elephant are there?"

They hunkered down in the brush and waited. Hours went by till they saw a group of people come through the gate. Some were carrying equipment, others food baskets. Then he saw a man dressed like a maharajah walking with a white person. Behind them was an elephant!

"That's them! That's them!" squealed Lou.

"Shush! They'll hear you."

"Yep. Sure is..."

Lou was giggling. "Told ya. Told ya. By golly!"

"Let's get the hell out of here, we got work to do!"

They couldn't get back to the lorry quick enough. All talking at once, laughing, throwing their empty beer bottles in the brush. The old lorry, once filled with water, oil, and a little love perked right up. Off they went singing an Indian ditty about an old man and his beer.

CHAPTER 35

Ten days later Ajay wired North that they had made the trip back to town and were anxious to wrap up the deal. North put through a direct call to them.

"They're here, Mr. North, we saw them."

"Yes, yes! Good job, my man. Now look, Sonny, what's your name?"

"Ajay.

"Okay Ajay . . . what the hell kind of a name is that? But whatever, don't scare them off. We will arrange a flight to meet you in this town you're in. Meanwhile, organize some men, tough ones, to go with us. And we have to figure out how to get an elephant out of there."

Godal, overhearing the conversation, took the phone from Ajay. "Hey, boss, I'm Ajay's partner. No problem. Let me handle that. We can haul your big guy in a camel trailer. They hold a dozen camels at a time."

"So, get one and stand by," said North.

"How much you going to pay us?" asked Godal.

"Well, ah yes, how much?" mimicked Ajay.

"How about $1,000.00 and you split it with whoever helped you?"

The phone went dead.

"Hello, JJ, you there?"

Ajay's voice came back on. "You come and get your own elephant," said Ajay. "It's worth a lot more."

"Hold on now. What were you thinking of?"

North figured he would be asking a huge amount, so he started low. But whatever was asked, he was prepared to pay it. He would have paid any amount to get them. He heard voices quibbling back and forth. Then Ajay got back on the line. "Double," he said. "That's final. No less."

"Double?... well, okay, but you're breaking the bank, ya know," North said as he held back a snicker.

"Cash, not check."

"Fine, fine, see ya there."

Ajay ended the call. "Well, glory be, we got a deal."

Ajay was all over the place jabbering a mile a minute. They went over to a secluded corner of the kiosk and sat.

"We're getting two thousand dollars."

"Two thousand dollars! Jesus!"

"You crazy man, keep your voice down. If Looney hears us, we'll have to split the money three ways."

They went over to the beer joint to Lou. He was always there sipping his beer.

"Hey, Lou, my man. Guess what? You're a rich man. You're gonna be drinking a lot of beer."

Lou was impatient to know. "How much, how much?"

"The elephant people are gonna pay you $300.00 dollars for finding their elephant. That's a lot of beer money, Lou."

Lou looked up from his beer glass. "Yeah, that's a lot of money, huh. To bring my daughter so, ah, she can get out ta hospital, huh. She wants to come live with me." He giggled. "$300.00. Wow. My daughter. Huh? huh?"

"Didn't know you had a daughter," said Godal.

"Yep. A nice one. She can take care of me."

"Shit," said Godal. "I didn't know he had a daughter." He whispered to Ajay, "Now I feel bad."

"Why? he's happy. We're happy."

"Yeah but—"

"So, give him some of your money. I'm keeping mine."

North and Jake, along with a cameraman and equipment, boarded a flight to New Delhi, India, via Jodhpur. From there they hired a private plane to take them the rest of the way. During the Jodhpur flight, North was having a withdrawal seizure from not being able to smoke.

"Jake, gotta have a smoke."

"Can't have one till we land. It's illegal."

North looked around to see if there were any flight attendants in the cabin. Seeing none he got up and headed for the toilet, then locked the door. A flight attendant, walking by the toilets, saw smoke seeping under the door. She banged on the door.

"Open this door immediately!" she yelled.

Jake, hearing the commotion, leapt from his seat, and headed for the toilet. North was franticly trying to put the cigarette out under the faucet while waving his hand trying to clear the smoke. The stewardess, using her emergency key, unlocked the door and opened it to have a puff of smoke envelop her.

"Sir, what are you doing? You are breaking a federal restriction. Discard that cigarette and come out here right now!"

"Look, honey—"

"What did you call me?" she said.

He pulled her blouse close to read her nametag. "Look, Miss Libershits… " He'd read her badge wrong. She smacked his hand away. "It's Liberashitz, and I'm calling the captain."

"No, no, miss whatever. Look, how about," he pulled some money out his wallet, "I'll contribute a couple of hundred to your best welfare."

"You're offering me a bribe?"

"Yeah, for just one more quick puff."

That did it. She called on her phone for the captain to come and deal with the passenger.

"Sir, I have a man here who is offering me a bribe to allow him to smoke in the lavatory."

"Oh shit," North murmured to himself as he put his wallet back in his pocket.

The captain arrived and was quite disturbed by what the flight attendant said on the phone. "What's going on here?"

The stewardess told the captain about the cigarette, misspeaking her name and attempting to bribe her. Jake noticed North reaching for his wallet, worried he was about to offer the captain a bribe, so he grabbed North's hand.

"I was just trying to tell Miss Liber," North started.

Jake interrupted. "Ok, boss, we know her name."

Jake tried to explain North's abusive behavior to the captain. "Please, Captain, he's been under a lot of strain lately due to a recent loss and has been delusional," he lied.

"Who are you?"

"His friend. I was sent to take care of him."

"You're not doing a very good job of it."

North looked at Jake like he was off his rocker. "Delusional?" he murmured. "Jake, where in the world—" he started to say.

"Please, sir, with your permission, let me just calm him down, and get on with the flight."

"Look, Mr.?" said the captain.

"Jake will do."

"Mr. Jake, I have the authority to handcuff him to his seat or turn him over to you to keep him under control. Which will it be?"

"Sorry, Captain, no need for restraints, I'll keep a close watch on him. He's just a bit overwrought."

"I will have to report this to the authorities when we land. So, get to your seat and stay there, no more of this."

Once back in the seat Jake asked, "Mr. North, what is wrong with you?"

"Well, I was just a bit disoriented." He smiled.

"You what?"

North just shook his head, crunched down in the seat, and was snoring in minutes. Jake had been with North a long time and had noticed a change in him over the years. Where before, although ruthless, he was sane enough to reason and logically work things out, now he would do anything on the spur of the moment, unconcerned whether it was right or wrong.

His vengeance against Bram had turned him into a psychotic tyrant. He had reached a point where getting back at Bram was more important than running the circus. Jake was concerned about what was going to happen when he found Bram and Modoc. Would he be irrational or sane, although come to think about it, for him there wasn't much difference. Jake wondered if his habitual smoking habit had anything to do with his neuroses. It was hard to say. But he did know it would eventually kill him.

Sure enough, upon arriving at the Jodhpur airport, they were approached by an airline representative and two federal agents who took North into custody. They kept him in their observation room for hours questioning him. Jake could see they were perplexed by his irrational behavior.

"Your friend needs help," said the representative from the airline. "We don't want him on our planes anymore. If you're his friend, see that he goes to a doctor."

North was given a stern warning and a year's penalty barring him from flying on their airline. All the time he was being reprimanded, Jake was afraid North was going to offer the officers a bribe, so when they returned from the security office, he was relieved that the reprimand wasn't worse. North was trying to hide an 'I told you so' smile.'

"Hey, you the people who ordered the rover?" said an Indian fellow dressed in the customary Dhoti (loincloth) with an old Western shirt. He wore a soiled white turban and looked like he needed his beard trimmed a month ago as it was scattered all over his face. Remnants of his last meal were still on his shirt. A sorry representation for the leasing company. "I've been waiting a long time, what's up?"

"I beg your pardon," said North in his usual uppity manner. "No need to be rude."

"Yeah well, my instructions are to pick you up, which I'm doing, and take you to the town of Baszer to meet up with some guys called Ajay and Godal at the Sinar Hilton."

"Can't we drive it ourselves?" asked North, not looking forward to riding with him.

"Sure, get lost like your elephant friend. And what about knowing where the water wells are? There are no roads in the desert. It's all by instinct or compass. Anyhow, company policy forbids it. Apparently, someone ripped them off by not coming back with the Rover. So is it a go or not?" he asked.

"Yeah, yeah. It's a go," said North. "What your name?"

The driver, never a fan of Westerners, thought for a minute. "Call me Phaarat (Fart)," he said, putting North on.

"Phaarat! That's your name?"

"No, but you foreigners couldn't handle my real name so Phaarat will do."

"What does it mean?"

The driver smiled. "It's just a name."

"Okay, Phaarat, what's the plan?"

"First we go to the town of Baszer which will take half a day travel, if we're lucky."

"What can happen if we're not?"

"Well, Rover breakdown, Nubian robbery, dry wells, things like that."

"Alright, then what?" said Jake.

"We'll meet your friends who are going to show us the way to the forest. Anyhow, we'll spend the night there. It will be late, and we don't want to be alone in the desert at night."

"Why?"

"Same reasons I just gave."

"Yeah, what else?"

"We'll need to buy enough food and drinks for the trip." Jake made a mental note to buy a few cartons of cigarettes and some cigars for the trip. "Also, we'll need fuel, refillable water jugs, eats, sleeping items. Should I go on?"

"No, that's enough."

"Then in the morning we leave for this forest which I have never heard of. Your 'friends' know the way, right?" asked Phaarat. "I hope so, driving in the desert can be a bit risky. Robbery, motor problems, dry wells—"

"You already said that!"

"Yeah, we'll just need to be prepared. So just sign here and we'll be on our way."

"Jake, handle it," said North, feeling this guy was not one he would get along with. Two cigarettes later, all the transactions were done. They rented the Land Rover for a couple of months, including Mr. Rude as the driver. Morning came and once loaded, they were off across the Sinar Desert headed for Baszer.

By late evening they arrived at the Hilton, the same place Ajay and Godal met Lou at the outside bar. The hotel was as rundown as the bar. It featured four rooms and one toilet.

It was the only 'hotel' in town. Once North saw it, he went back to the car and wouldn't get out. It took Jake several hours to have people clean the room they were to stay in.

"Wait till he sees that nasty toilet," laughed Phaarat.

North would only eat the food they had brought in the car.

"But it was part of our deal," said Jake. "They're to give us three meals."

"You can have my half," said North, as he put together a cheese and tomato sandwich from the cooler box. North slept in the car that night.

The next morning, they met Ajay and Godal. Ajay didn't want Lou there, but in a small town everybody knew when white men were coming; so, Lou was there. Over a coffee and biscuits, they told North about seeing the elephant and its trainer.

"There your guy was, walking out of this huge temple," said Ajay.

"And right behind him was this huge elephant following along like a big dog," added Godal.

"Yeah," said Lou, "right there, they were."

"Well, sounds like we have them, Jake," said North, a big smile crossing his face.

"What about hauling the elephant out of here?"

"I've arranged for this big camel carrier to come. He should be here by early morning to follow us—that's providing nothing goes wrong."

"Yeah, right!"

"And where are my tough guys?" asked North.

"We had to get them out of another town. None like them around here. They're coming with the camel trailer. Providing nothing goes wrong."

"Yeah. Right. I hope they're tough enough to do what's necessary."

'Oh, yeah, no problem. Wait till you meet them."

"Okay. Let's go get my elephant."

"Not till we get our money," said Ajay.

"You know you should get paid after we see them," said North.

"Uh oh!" murmured Jake. "Here we go again."

"Ha! You people are always afraid to let go of your money." Ajay stood and said, "You go find them yourselves." They walked away.

"Boss, what are you doing? After coming all this way, come on, pay the man." North was in one of his Psycho moods. "If you want to get Bram, now is not the time to argue."

"Yes, of course," said North, coming out of his stupor.

"Jake, take care of the good man." "Oh boy, oh boy, yeah, the money," said Lou, dancing around now.

As Jake was handing out the money, Lou couldn't control himself. "OK OK, my 300, yeah ok."

"What does he mean, his 300?" said North. "Our deal was for $2,000.00 total. Has the deal changed?"

Lou seemed to stop in midair. "Huh?" he said.

Godal butted in. "No, no, we're all sharing so Lou gets his share which is $666.00, right?"

Jake handed each man the $666.00 plus and an extra $30.00 dollars to make up for the missing $2.00. "Here's a bit extra," he said.

Each man got an extra $10.00 dollars. Lou was ecstatic when he was given the $666.00. He left mumbling to himself about bad people and his sister. Ever since Godal had found out about Lou's daughter being in the hospital, he felt bad about the deal Ajay had cut and was happy when Lou got his fair share. Ajay gave him a dirty look.

"So that's it?" said North.

"Yeah. Let's rest up and in the morning make our move." He turned to Phaarat. "When do you think we will get there?"

Phaarat looked at his watch. "Sunday, Sunday afternoon unless something goes wrong."

CHAPTER 36

Sunday was always the day for their family picnic. Bram and Gertie with Ahmed, Latika, Coogan, Sanjoe and a few children from the staff all gathered. Another 'family' was to join them. Modoc with her newborn Bandie and, of course, big papa, Bandulla. Since the birth of the baby, Bandulla had become touchable, and Bram couldn't keep his hands off him. A friendship that Bram had always wanted had formed. He had put a rope around Bandulla's neck to help him climb to his spot to ride. Bandulla didn't understand about raising his foot for Bram to get aboard. That would come in time. All the food was put into cold containers to keep fresh, including a basket of fruit and vegetables for Modoc and Bandulla. Modoc was heavy in milk for Bandie when the need arose. Everything was loaded in large leather saddlebags that Bram, together with Gertie, had made for Modoc to carry. Slung over her back, one on each side, they fit her body comfortably. A heavy blanket was put on her first so the bags wouldn't chafe her hide. And of course, a bigger one was made for Bandulla. He had become a 'big' part of the family and seemed to enjoy doing his share. Gertie made one with a similar design for Bandie. Made of sisal, it set over his little back with a pocket on either side. In it were his bottle, bib, hairbrush, and nail file for his toes. It took a while before he would keep his trunk off it.

With Bram astride Bandulla, all the men, Ahmed Sanjoe and Coogan wanted to ride him.

There was no way Bram could guide him. He hadn't learned the choon yet, so his guide was Modoc. Wherever she went, he followed.

"Hope there are no low tree branches we have to go under," Ahmed said as he grinned.

Gertie sat Modoc so she could watch over the baby and behind her was Latika and a row of smiling, jittery staff children.

And so, on a sunny June morning through the Kruki Forest they came. At peace with the world, all dreams fulfilled, their laughter rang out in tune with the birds of the forest. Life was good. The forest people who made the music for the wedding, although still quite shy, walked behind. They wanted to be included in the picnic but didn't know how. Occasionally, one would play a melody on his flute with the sound of the drums accompanying him. A strange combination that seemed to work.

The walk to Lake Namaste was part of the fun. Some of the children slid down Bandulla's back and hung onto his tail, others chose to walk with the forest people mimicking their playing on their drum with forest sticks, others used a stick as a flute. Picking berries, telling stories, nibbling out of a fruit basket along the way. Bandie was given a line of bells to play with. Each a different size, each sounding a different chime. He would play with them as he walked. One would swear he had figured out his own melody to play, at least it sounded that way. But it wasn't long before he got them tangled in his feet.

On the approach to the lake there was a cove where the water washed small shiny pebbles on the shore. The shore itself was covered with bright green grass, and a sprinkle of daisies bordering the glen. A perfect place for a picnic.

Huge pine trees shaded the cove from the desert sun. A sacred joyous spot of tranquility that God must have surely bequeathed to Bram and Gertie.

Modoc crouched so they could unload the containers, blankets were spread out, rocks held them in place, food set out and a mixed case of beer and wine was put in the shade to keep it cool. But first, a dip. A race to the water, elephants as well, all plunged into the cool water, splashing and swimming. Some used Bandulla as a diving platform. Bandie stayed at the shore with his mother playing in the shallow water, swinging at the small minnows with his trunk. The day would come when he would be out there swimming with his parents. Games were played, couples smooched, Bram and Gertie fell asleep under a nearby banyan tree.

Mo, full of all the goodies, leaned against a tree and closed her eyes, content to doze in the solitude of the moment. Bandie folded his little legs and slept at his mother' s leg. Bandulla stood at Modoc's side, his trunk lay on her back and as the day slipped away, all dozed in the serenity of the lake.

It was afternoon when Modoc came out of her solitude. She had heard something not heard before. There it was again. This time so did Bram and Ahmed. Out of the bush came men, strangers, armed, and tough. The family stood and came together.

"Who are you? What are you doing here?" Ahmed spoke.

One of the men walked over and hit him with the butt of his rifle, knocking him to the ground. Latika screamed and ran to him.

"Shut your mouth and just stay quiet," she was told.

The other men, all mumbling, circled the family. There were six in all. Four carried guns, another a machete and Jake who carried nothing. Modoc had sensed the danger and was in a stance of defense while Bandulla, feeling the unrest, was confused, and kept his trunk up in the air searching for the vibes that would tell him what was happening. Bram and Gertie went to Mo.

He didn't want her being shot for doing what she did best, protecting them.

Out of the bush came North, dressed in old-fashioned jodhpurs boots, pants, and a pith helmet, and smoking a corona. He carried a small horse whip.

"Well, well, well. Finally, after all these years, I got ya." He made a move as though catching a fly.

"Bram, who is this?" asked Ahmed.

"I will answer for him," said North. "I am the rightful owner of the elephant Modoc. Always have been, always will be."

"Not true," said Bram.

"What do you want here?" said Ahmed, as with the help of his wife he staggered to his feet, blood flowing down his head.

An uproarious laugh erupted. "Hahaha! What do I want? I want them," he said, pointing a tobacco-stained finger at Bram and his glorious elephant. "That's what I want. I have chased after him for many a year and spent a good deal of money. Now it's payback time." It was then that he noticed little Bandie laying against Modoc's leg. "My my, what do we have here? A baby elephant. You have done well for yourself, huh, Modoc."

She grumbled hearing her name.

"Surely we can settle this amicably. Come to my place where we can sit and discuss this matter," offered Ahmed.

"Who is this man?" North asked Bram.

"He is my father."

"Your father? No, your stepfather perhaps. Well, well. Pleased to meet you. Yes, of course, we will follow you back to your house to get refreshed. That desert trip was exhausting. But no tricks. My men will shoot you if need be."

"We have no intention of playing any tricks on you," said Ahmed.

With the guns at their back, the family walked down the trail toward the house. The forest people, not understanding what was happening, quietly slipped into the bush.

"Let them go, they are of no value to me," said North. Walking just behind North was Bandulla. "Good Lord, you're a big one. I wish I had you in my show." He quickened his step so as not to be stepped on.

North threw his corona stub on the beautiful soft loam pathway as they approached the sanctuary, squashing it with the heel of his boot only to light another. Upon arrival at the compound, the staff gathered, unsure what to do.

"Go back to work all of you. Nothing to be concerned about," Bram told them.

"Jake, put a couple of the men outside around the wall in case our friends try to leave. Then you and the rest join me—inside."

As they approached, Ahmed told the guard to open the gate. Bram put Modoc and Bandulla into Modoc's pen. The baby stayed with Mo. As they entered, North was amazed at the house.

"My, my, such an establishment and all this out here away from everything." A man entered bringing drinks. No one except North took one. He continued. "That's why it took us forever to find you."

"Now then, Mr. North, what can we do to bring this to an amicable conclusion?" asked Ahmed.

"You can't. Modoc and this bastard son of yours will come with me. There will be no dickering. We will drive back to Baszer. Once there, I will fly to Jodhpur and on to New York while my people will continue with Bram and the elephant to Mumbai. From there, it's only a matter of taking a ship from the port to New York."

"Jake and two of these men will accompany you all the way back. So, you see, you are mine. Ha!"

"See here, old man," said Coogan, who stood and confronted North.

The next thing he knew he was flat on his back looking up at a rifle pointed at his head.

One of North's men had hit him in the stomach followed by another punch to his jaw.

Bram stepped up. "Please. Enough." Bram helped Coogan to his feet. "Father, I'll have to go with him."

"But there's got to be another way."

"There is no way. Let's not have one of you die over this."

North pulled out a piece of paper. "Bram is right. This is the Bill of Sale. I own all the animals at my circus, including Modoc." He handed the paper to Ahmed.

"And Bram. Do you own him too?" said Ahmed.

North laughed loudly.

Bram said, "Actually, I own Modoc, not Mr. North."

North spoke loudly. "He has a contract with the circus to perform and he has breached his contract."

"It's not true," said Bram, "neither of his papers are legal. They are fake."

"So, what will happen to him?" Ahmed asked, indicating Bram.

"He'll go to jail, of course. I'll have police waiting at the gate when we arrive to take him away. He has caused me nothing but trouble and has to pay his dues."

"And Modoc?" Ahmed continued.

"She will be assigned another trainer."

"But I told you, she won't work for anyone else," argued Bram.

"We will see when we return. The new trainer will be able to handle her after we give her some pills to quiet her down and if not, there are other means."

"You can't do that! If you let me, I will work with her."

"Where, from jail?" laughed North. "Dear boy, you want me to risk you running away again?"

Bram put his head down. "No, I, too, am tired of all this. I promise to stay and train her as I always did. If I am not with her, she will die. She has never let anyone else handle her and wouldn't know how to adjust. Would it be better if she dies or hurts someone? Let me work the act and I will promise to stay."

"Boss, you need him for the show," said Jake.

"And I will be there to help him," added Gertie.

"Gertie, my dear, I see you have found your way here. Yes, of course, do come. Well, well, I didn't know you got married," he said, eyeing her ring. North was silent for a while as though he was considering what Jake said. Then when it looked like he would agree he said, "No, no, no, I cannot trust him.

"But do come, Gertie, you can mourn him as he rots in jail." North was doing what Jake was afraid of, switching back and forth not knowing what he would say or do next.

Ahmed spoke. "You are one mean son of a bitch." He stood. One of the toughies approached and pointed his gun at him.

"Father, please, there is nothing more that can be done."

"Yes, so true, or we can shoot Modoc." North snarled, "That would be one way out."

"What good would that do you?"

"Satisfaction. But being a money man and having her perform, plus the huge amount of P.R. of finding her and bringing her back will reap me a fortune."

Jake, trying to bring him back to the reality of the situation said, "Boss, you'll need Bram for the tribute and the parade."

"Hmm. So, this I will think about. It is getting late. I have a vehicle waiting at the forest border that will carry Modoc. There is nothing more to be said."

Gertie was resigned to the fact that they would have to go. "I will have Mirer pack some things for us," she said.

"Let me help. She won't know which things," said Lakita.

"Yes, please do, because you won't be coming back," said North with a devious smile. "All you women can go, I have your husbands, so if you do anything to mess up my deal, I'll just shoot them. Another drink, please." He waved to the man holding the tray of drinks. Fifteen minutes passed.

"Time is up, dear ladies, time to go."

Two pieces of luggage were brought out. The staff stood bewildered.

"Mr. Bram, where are you going?" asked many.

"When will you be back?" asked another.

Many of the women wept aloud.

"Someday, perhaps. I will miss you all," he said, knowing he would never return. "I leave with a heavy heart. My time spent here with you has been the happiest time of my life. God be with you."

Bram gave a namaste. All did likewise. There was sobbing and tears as they walked out to Modoc's pen. Bram opened the gate to her pen. Modoc along with Bandulla and baby Brandie came out in a somber mood. They sensed something was up. The big gates closed behind them as the group moved down the trail heading to the edge of the desert. The gunmen walked behind them followed by the elephants.

They rounded a corner and from out of the thicket appeared the forest people, several dozen or more. Men and women alike carrying their weapons of pots and pans. Some stood with bamboo poles cut from the forest, others held large rocks at the ready. Their children hid in the bushes, others crouched up in the trees. All stood quiet, their pots tinkling against each other. They had seen the guns and witnessed Ahmad and Coogan being knocked to the ground and remembered the poachers' attack. Something was wrong. They waited for Ahmed to tell them what to do.

"Who are these little people?" voiced North.

Ahmed, worried they would try to stop North and his men and get themselves killed, said, "They are just the local people. They mean no harm."

"Yeah, well, best they keep their distance. Let's go!" yelled North.

North and his men walked through the forest people shoving them out of the way.

Standing in the middle of the trail appeared the Chief, Vishnu. As small as they were, they stood as giants in their determination to protect their friends.

"Now what?" yelled North. "You better tell them to get the hell out of our way or we'll shoot the little bastards."

Bram yelled, "Vishy, it's alright, they are friends!"

Bram knew he neither spoke nor understood English other them a few words picked up at the compound and there was no one here to translate for him.

The chief stood defiant. All he knew was his friends were being taken somewhere with bad people who had guns and they didn't want to go. Bram stepped forward to try and convince him to leave but was stopped by North's men.

"They don't understand. Let me try to talk to them," he said.

He pushed the man's arm aside and began walking to the chief. One of North's thugs leveled his gun at the chief. When he did, the forest men, thinking their chief was in danger, ran at North and his men. Shots rang out. Two forest men fell to the ground. The chief fell in Bram's arms.

"Stop! Stop! What are you doing?"

Some of the forest people seeing their Chief fall dropped their weapons and ran to him.

Others went to the men who had fallen.

"Oh! My God, what have you done?" cried Bram.

He knelt by the chief. His little body lay limp, blood seeping from an open wound in his side. Bram took his shirt off, bunched it up and pressed it onto the wound in hopes of stopping the bleeding. He grabbed two of the forest people showing them to pick up the chief.

"Shangari! Shangari," he pointed. Bram knew the only hope would be to get him to the compound. "Sanjoe, go with them. Take the others also."

The chief's eyes flickered open. A smile danced across his face. He grasped the red crystal in his hand, his eyes sought out North.

In his broken forest tongue, he spoke: "I Vishnu, you cannot kill God."

North, oblivious to the pain he had caused, yelled, "Let's move it, now!"

"Dear Vishy," said Gertie, "I hope he will be alright."

Bram and Gertie walked as one, holding each other knowing they would never see Shangari again. All Bram was and would ever hope to be was there, and to leave it behind shattered his world. He felt Gertie's body tremble as her hand tightened in his.

The forest wore a shroud. No birds flew that morning. The water in the brooks turned cloudy, the deer stayed in the thickets not to be seen. The energy once felt was gone. There would be none for evermore. The forest was in mourning.

CHAPTER 37

They arrived at the desert's edge. Waiting there was a large, dirty truck and trailer. Phaarat was there, as was Ajay, Godal, and Lou all standing quiet, their heads down like naughty children caught in the act of doing a wrong.

Bram remembered; this was the spot where Modoc and he had rested after surviving the desert. It had been so long ago. They were so thrilled to have made it across the desert. And then Ahmed, the man to be his father, appeared from out of the vastness of the sand dunes. He came like an earth god to take him into his life to love, to care for.

Bram touched the giant oak where they first met. His father came up behind him and wrapped his arms around him.

"My son, keep us in your heart as we will you. I will do everything in my power to set you free. Whatever your needs, we will send them to you."

"Father, there is nothing I can say that will tell you how much I love you. I have been so fortunate to have found you."

With this, he hugged the man who had been his father, his mentor, his teacher. They couldn't talk; their throats were too dry with grief. Gertie came as did Lakita. The family gathered around them in a circle of love, hugging, and kissing with tears of sorrow. Everybody spoke at once.

"How could this have happened?"

"We thought those times were past."

"What will we do without you?"

"Come, come now, we need to move on," bellowed North.

"I need to speak to my wife, alone," said Bram.

"Ah! Well, yes, of course. I am not a thoughtless person but do it quickly."

Bram took Gertie aside. He brushed the hair that had fallen on her face.

"My love, I need to go. Our dream is no more but how wonderful that we have had this time together. But now, you must stay. There will be no future for you to come with me. I will be in jail, and we will not be together."

Gertie trembled and burst into tears. Then, trying to control herself, she said, "Bram, Bram, my love, listen to me. I cannot leave you…ever. You are my soul, my life. I can only survive being near you. I'm going with you." She buried her head in his shoulder and sobbed. "Please, Bram. Please, at least we will be together. If you have to be in…she couldn't bring herself to say the words "…that place, I will stay close by."

"But what about your life here with all your friends and family?" asked Bram.

"I will miss them each and every day. We will always have Shangari in our hearts and the memory of what once was. It will be so very painful. But my life is with you, Bram. I will never leave you."

He held her tight. "If you go, our lives will be one of misery," he reminded her.

"Then let us suffer together," she mumbled between sobs.

Bram knew she would not stay. They went over to North.

"My wife will come with us."

"As you wish. See, I am not a cold-hearted person. But now we must go."

"Bram, what about little Bandie?" she cried.

"He is too young and too fragile to make the trip. He would die," reasoned Bram. "And Modoc? How can you separate a mother from her baby? Gertie, what am I to do? I have no choice. He will have to stay with his father."

"You will have to tell Modoc. How do you do that?" sobbed Gertie.

Bram hesitated. "It will be difficult, but she will have to understand."

"What if she won't go?"

"Then North will shoot her. He is that evil."

North was having a coughing spell while lighting another cigarette.

"Enough! Load Modoc, now!" he ordered in his sternest voice. He was impatient. His other self had reared its ugly head again. He leaned over and yanked the choon from Bram's belt.

"Let's go, let's go, move! Move!" yelled North. He was having one of his fits.

He took the choon and began jabbing Modoc with it. The point, although blunt, was pushed hard enough to puncture her skin. She howled in pain as blood poured from the wounds. Bandulla, standing close and seeing what happened trumpeted his fury and grabbed North. He swung him up in the air far above his head ready to throw him to the ground and probably step on him. The thugs raised their guns ready to shoot Bandulla.

"Wait, don't shoot! The fall will kill Mr. North!" It was Jake running to stop them. Bandulla, his body shaking from the anger he was feeling, bellowed his rage. Bram jumped in front of him raising his hands shouting, "Bandulla, no, no! Put him down!"

Bandulla held him as far up as he could, not about to let him go. His eyes were as red as the blood seeping from Modoc's wound.

Bram lowered his voice. "Come now, set him down."

Bandulla had no idea what Bram was saying. All he knew was he wanted to dash North to the ground, but Bram, his friend, stood in the way. His hesitancy gave him time to cool down until finally he eased North to the ground. Bandulla stood, shaking from the ordeal, but Modoc was his mate and he would never allow anyone to harm her.

Bram went to North. Gertie was there as well and together they dragged him out of harm's way. No one else came to help. He was in shock and shaking. They got a blanket from the Rover and wrapped it over him.

North's first words were, "Give me a cigarette." He couldn't stop shaking.

"You should have let Bandulla kill him," said Coogan. "It would have solved all our problems."

In a weak voice, North said, "Load her."

The men opened the trailer gates and lowered the ramp. It was time. Bram needed to talk to Modoc. How to do that? How do you tell a mother she will have to leave her baby behind and she will never see her mate again? You don't. Once parted, they don't know they will never see each other again. Maybe tomorrow. Next week. There is no 'never' in the mind of the wild heart. They can only wait and suffer.

But there is something else. Something that guides them. Unconditional love.

An emotion so strong that it can overcome their instinct.

And so, it was for Modoc's love for Bram.

Their instinct may tell them one thing but their love for another may be stronger. So the choice is theirs. It's deeper than humans can understand. In the wild it happens naturally.

Ironically, all could be for naught with psycho North and his hoodlums standing by. Bandulla had calmed and was running his trunk over Modoc's cuts where the choon had punctured.

Bram walked Modoc over to the trailer, Bandulla and the baby followed.

"Stay here, Mosey," he said.

Bram took hold of one of the massive tusks and guided Bandulla over to where the trail back to Shangari began. Then he gently eased Bandie over to join his father. He took Bandulla's trunk and laid it across the baby's back pressing gently. He spoke to Bandulla.

"Big guy, take your newborn, care for him, bring him up as the son you wish him to be. We're going on a big trip and will never see you and the little one again." The words he spoke were for him. He knew Bandulla didn't understand his words, but he hoped Bandulla would sense the feeling they projected.

Bram bent down and hugged the baby to his chest. "Go with your father, little one."

Bandulla stood slowly rocking back and forth as through contemplating his options. Then, turning towards Modoc he stretched his trunk as far up and high as it could go toward Modoc. She swung her trunk up as well to form an invisible arch. The low guttural trumpet they shared was one of remorse. Was this their way of saying goodbye?

"You have to go home to Shangari," Bram told him patting him on his leg.

"Go. Now."

Bandulla knew the word "Go". The staff had used it quite often at the compound shooing him and the herd away. Bandulla started up the trail a bit confused yet knowing this was the right thing to do. Baby Bandie followed his father while glancing back at his mother. Why wasn't his mother coming? At the top of the trail, before it disappeared into the thick forest, Bandulla stopped and looked back from where he had just come. Tomorrow they would go to the sanctuary. The staff had probably put out some veggies for him and they were always happy to see little Bandie. Mama and the others in the herd would have to share their milk.

Bram went to Modoc. He spoke to her as he would a father to his daughter. "Mosey, we have to go now, it will be difficult, but we must. Your baby will stay with his father to be raised in his world, to learn the ways of the wild as well as feel the love from those at the sanctuary. We have to leave, or North will shoot you."

Voices convey feelings and Bram could only hope his feelings would reach out to her.

Bram stepped into the trailer. "Come along, girl." He didn't want to force her. If he did, she would always resent him for taking her away from her baby. No, she had to decide of her own free will. Modoc looked at her mate and Bandie as they moved away on the trail. Then at Bram waiting in the trailer. Bandie stopped on the trail and looked back squealing for his mother.

Bandulla draped the tip of his trunk across the little one's back and gently urged him on.

"Modoc," said Bram.

It wasn't the word; it was the emotion that was wrapped around it. It wasn't a question or a command but rather a calling to decide. Modoc shook her head, thumped the trailer floor with her trunk, sprayed the earth and put her foot on the trailer floor. She had chosen. Somewhere deep down in her being came a sound not heard before, akin to a gut-wrenching sob. She hesitantly walked to the front of the trailer to Bram and cradled her head against his chest. He shared the sorrow of a mother's sadness to leave her baby behind.

The evening light cast its shadows as Bandulla raised his head and trumpeted his goodbye to Modoc. It was heard through the forest all the way to Lake Namaste, to the ice canyon and to the sanctuary. Little Bandie raised his trunk to mimic his father but only a faint squeak could be heard. Maybe someday. Then they disappeared into the forest.

Gertie and Bram got in the car alongside Jake. North rode in front with Phaarat. The rest rode in the back of the truck. The remaining family stood under the giant oak holding each other and trying to console one another.

"Let's go," said North.

Phaarat threw the Rover in gear and off they went into a world of the past that Bram knew quite well. Far out in the desert only a trail of dust was seen until the vehicles disappeared over the dunes. All that could be heard was the woeful trumpet of a mother mourning the loss of her baby.

CHAPTER 38

Many years had passed since Bram, Gertie, and Modoc left their beloved life at Shangari. There wasn't a day that went by when the pain and sorrow of remembering didn't bring Gertie to tears. It hurt so much. Modoc had lost a considerable amount of weight and Bram attributed it to her having to leave Bandulla and her baby. Her jolly way of finding joy in everything she did was extinguished. There were nights when she would raise her trunk high in the air and trumpet a long sorrowful plea. Bram knew it was her longing for Bandie. When he heard it, a feeling of guilt coursed through him. Had he made her choose? Of course, but the final decision was hers. She didn't know North wouldn't have allowed her to stay. Bram hated to think what would have happened if she had decided not to go. Just how far would North's vindictiveness have gone?

North had kept Bram and Modoc together when he learned that what Bram had said was true. Even under duress, Modoc would not work for another and if the trainer became too aggressive, she would show her other side. She would not allow herself to be mistreated. Since their return to the circus, they had adhered to the stress and hardship under the strict rules of North, obediently doing what was asked of them while suppressing their unhappiness. North was in his glory having Bram kowtow to his demands.

Ahmed had come trying to figure out a way to get Bram and Modoc back to Shangari. It was all in vain. The legal battles and cost of getting Modoc back were prohibitive. Even Ahmed's numerous resources couldn't overcome the hurdles North had set in his way.

Bram spent most of his time with Modoc brushing her skin, cleaning her ears, checking her teeth for any ready to fallout. Her nails were filed, drops of cool medicine dripped into her ageing eyes to clear away the mucus that gathered in the corners.

Some days were better than others. One of the harder ones was when Gertie and Bram were sitting on the fence that made up Modoc' s pen talking about the old days when Gertie happened to mention Bandie. Modoc's head jerked up, her eyes flashed, a low guttural sound was heard, and her whole body trembled. She had heard the word Bandie. Bandie was here! At least, that's what she thought. That was Gertie calling him! She took off, knocking over the chairs and tables, ran around the pen looking for him, squealing, searching each nook for her baby. But it was all in vain. She tired after an hour with Bram trying to soothe her. Gertie burst into tears.

"I'm sorry, Mosey, so sorry. She remembers Bram, oh! My God, she remembers. She will never forget."

Finally, one day, North had his final smoking seizure. The usual spittle was replaced by blood, which poured from his mouth. He collapsed in agony gasping for breath. Jake called an ambulance and North was rushed to the hospital where he was pronounced dead on arrival. He had died from his smoking addiction. The sideshow people and performers saw to his burial. A box of Cuban stogies was thrown into his coffin.

"For his journey downward," someone said.

It was a fitting end for someone who had caused everyone around him so much pain and strife. Although it had taken literal years, the reaper had come for North, and with it a small sense of justice. Bram never spoke of it, but the years of the chase and animosity were finally over and with a small sense of relief.

It wasn't long after the funeral that bankruptcy was filed, the tents, bleachers, floodlights, all that made up a circus came down and were to be sold at auction. But even with North's death, the circus would live on, continuing to provide joy and laughter for so many. Although many had worked at the circus over the years, coming and going on their own respective journeys, those that remained decided to pool all their resources. They bought as much as they could at the auction and set up a new, albeit smaller, circus at an abandoned lot down the road from the original. It was a fresh start for many of the performers, and the chimpanzee and lion trainers approached Bram to join them in this new endeavor, but the years were catching up to Modoc.

"We would love to join you," Bram said, "but Mo is getting up there in years, and I think it is time we rested a bit. But Gertie and I, along with Mo, wish you all the love and happiness to get you where you are going."

"How about one last farewell show then? You've been the heart and soul of this place for so long, Bram. Your fortitude kept many of us going during the worst days with North," offered the chimpanzee trainer.

Bram eventually agreed. It wasn't a month later that the 'new' circus opened to a rousing crowd of spectators. The first show for the new circus would be Bram and Mo's last. It was a special night as the performers who would continue with the circus each paid a small tribute to Bram and Modoc and Bram could swear the crowd had never been louder in this bittersweet moment.

Shortly afterwards, Bram, Gertie, and Modoc found solace at a wild animal ranch that furnished exotic animals to the motion picture studios of Hollywood; it was an atmosphere that was familiar to them, if not far less stressful and unique in its own ways to what they had experienced before. The family who owned the ranch had given them a home where they could spend their days in quietude not afforded to them since Shangari. If a call came in from the studio for an elephant, Modoc was available.

When she wasn't being pampered on a movie set, Bram would sit on a stool in the barn for hours picking and grooming things on Modoc that were not there. He just wanted to be with her.

She loved to hear him speak of the good old days at Shangari.

"And remember when we went fishing and you got caught up in the line," he said with a smile. She liked it when he smiled and laughed. It made her feel good. She would do her clicking or belly rumble. Sometimes she would do her back leg dance. Bram was careful never to mention Bandulla or Brandie.

"And the farmer," he continued, "boy, that was some battle, then Malcolm came running in and you had to pick him up on the run. Wow! And then, there was climbing up the pass and," Bram stopped and burst into tears. It brought back memories of Sian. Modoc put her trunk around his shoulders.

"We have to stop going to these places, Mosey," said Bram after blowing his nose. "Memories can hurt."

Bram spent his days caring for her. Too many baths, cutting her nails too short, and scrubbing her wrinkled skin till it became pink. Modoc was starting to show her age. Her years since leaving Shangari had taken their toll. She couldn't lift heavy things with her trunk. Her eyes were failing, and she had lost her tusks which gave her a toothless old woman look. Many elephants lose their tusks as they get older. It doesn't hurt; in fact, not having the weight to carry around must be a relief. But she didn't seem to care and neither did Bram. She had been one of the rare female elephants to have them. But like so many Hollywood starlets of the past who saw roles lost as they aged, Modoc started getting fewer and fewer calls as time went on.

One day, Gertie baked Bram's favorite pie. Cream cheese smothered with gobs of raspberries, strawberries, and a few slices of bananas to top it off with whipped cream around the sides. A slice was set off to the side for Mosey. The phone rang.

Bram had been racking his brain about the future. Although he, Gertie, and Modoc were always welcome at the ranch, he worried they'd overstay their welcome and his thoughts always drifted back to Shangari. As he ate, he recounted his survival in the desert, for the millionth time it felt like to Gertie. But this time she prompted him with a question.

"Whatever happened to those nice army fellows who covered your tracks from North?" she pondered. And in an instant a lightbulb exploded in Bram's brain. He dropped his fork and ran towards unpacked boxes of his belongings. He never wanted to unpack them as they were the few things they could take from their days in Shangari, and he feared the memories would be too much. But now, like a madman, he dug through the boxes until he found what he was looking for. A card. A beat up, worn out old card, that had miraculously remained legible after all this time.

"I can only hope it still works," he thought out loud as Gertie shadowed him as he ran around with a vigor he hadn't shown in years. He then picked up the phone and dialed the number. It rang for what felt like an eternity until a voice on the other end picked up. It wasn't the one he was hoping for, but when asked, they said who Bram was looking for was simply out at the moment and Bram left a message.

"What's gotten into you?" Gertie asked bewildered.

"Hope," was his simple reply as he kissed his wife and then went back to eating his pie with a smile on his face.

The next morning, Bram was again filing Modoc's nails, and she could feel Bram's more upbeat attitude. She playfully nudged him with her truck as he went to work keeping his best friend happy. Finally, the phone rang, and Gertie called for him.

"Bram, it's for you."

"Bram, my good friend, how are you?"

The voice was a familiar someone from the past.

"Captain?! Is it really you?! How are you?"

"Doing well, Bram. And you?"

"We're okay. Hearing your voice brings back so many memories."

"Yeah, I can imagine. How is my favorite girl?"

"Modoc? She's fine, getting old as we all are."

"Listen, Bram, I caught her last performance at the circus. It was just brilliant."

"Yeah, it was a special evening."

"Say, I got your message, if you're around, I would love to see you."

"Well, that would be wonderful. In fact, why not come for dinner? We'll have a lot to catch up on."

"Sounds great."

"How about tomorrow, say 8:00? I'll give you the address."

"I'm so looking forward to it. Is it okay to bring a friend?"

"Of course, more than welcome. I'll tell Mo about you coming. She'll have kittens!"

"Oh! My God, yes. See you then."

"Gertie, that was my good friend, the captain who was the pilot of our plane that crashed in the desert.

"Of course, honey, you've told me that story a hundred times."

"Well, he's coming for dinner tomorrow night, okay?"

It was late Saturday afternoon when the captain arrived. Walking in with him of all people was Jack, his co-pilot. What a wonderful surprise.

"Hey, Bram, how ya doing, buddy?"

There were hugs all around. Both guests wore their uniforms.

"We're still on duty."

"I see there are more stars on your epaulet."

"Yes, I'm now a Colonel."

"So now I will have to call you Colonel."

"Na, everybody still calls me Captain."

"Well, congratulations. That's a very high position and so well deserved," said Bram.

"And, Jack, you have a few new ones as well."

"Yeah, just made it to Lieutenant. It was slow going but worth the wait."

"Honey, come and meet my good friends from the cras—"

"Yes, yes, I know, the plane crash. Hi, I'm Gertie, he tells that story every chance he gets. So pleased to meet you."

"Yeah, that was quite an experience. We're the only people he won't have to repeat it to," he laughed.

"Before you get settled, come and meet your old friend."

"Do you think she'll remember us?"

"We'll see, it has been a long time."

As they rounded the corner, the captain called her name. "Hey, Mosey. Remember me?"

She stood quiet for a moment, as though she was recalling the voice. Then yes, she remembered! Bram opened the gate and out she came her belly rumbling and squeaking.

She wrapped her trunk around them both and pooped.

"That's a sure sign she remembers you," said Bram, smiling.

The captain hugged her as he did that day, stretching his hands across her head pressing his face to hers. He held it there a moment as a wave of emotions showed on his face. Mo didn't move, she knew what it meant. It seemed it was as important to her as it was to him.

The captain wiped his eyes, a bit embarrassed. "Those were harrowing times, yes they were," he exclaimed. "I never thought she would remember, but she did. I've been told that elephants have an extraordinary sense of memory, but I thought that was just a myth."

"Not true," said Bram. "She remembers things that happened long ago, things I had forgotten."

Gertie had prepared one of her special dinners that evening and once all had finished, they retired to the porch where small talk took over the conversation. Catching up was both fun and sad.

"I hear North died."

"Yeah, rumor has it he was buried with a box of Coronas in his coffin."

"That's as it should be. He could have a smoke on his way down."

"I wish I had kept my hair like you," said Jack, taking off his cap to reveal a smooth, bald head.

"And your hair isn't grey, it's silver. What kind of hair gel are you using?" asked the captain.

Bram laughed. "I had nothing to do with it. It is what it is. Gertie is the one who never changes. How's that?"

Bram told them of the Varuna Falls. "She dipped her hand in the water and has never aged since."

"You mean you found the 'Fountain of Youth?'"

"No, it doesn't exist. It's a myth, but Gertie is the same now as when we married."

"Really? Maybe it's your love for her. She will never change in your eyes."

Bram smiled as he nodded.

"Look what I found in a store in town," said Bram. It was a bottle of wine from India marked 'New Delhi.'

Gertie brought four glasses and Bram did the honor of serving.

He held his glass high. "A toast to…" he hesitated…
"Shangari."

This time it was Gertie who shed a tear.

"Sorry, honey, I didn't mean to bring up the past."

"It's alright. I was remembering the celebration and the toast to our marriage."

He leaned over and gave her a kiss on the cheek.

"Those were wonderful days, but it hurts to think about them now," said Bram.

"Have you ever thought about going back?" asked the captain.

"Ha, to God's ears. Every day, my friend. But that's what hurts, knowing it can never be. Not without a miracle. Or a lot of help."

The colonel put down his glass of wine.

"Would you go back if you could?"

"In a heartbeat, but we would never leave Modoc and there is no way to get her back."

The captain and Jack went over to the couch and sat by them.

"Bram, what you and Modoc did for us the day of the crash has stayed with us all these years. Jack and I will never forget it. We would not be alive. Our wives would not have a husband nor our children a father." He hesitated. "And after we got your call a couple days ago, we immediately decided this injustice needed to be rectified. Bram, you're going back. You and Gertie and Modoc are all going back."

"What did you say? What? Why would you say that? Please, don't joke…we…"

The captain and Jack put their arms around them.

"You're going home. I have arranged with the Army and the powers that be to supply the transport of a plane big enough to hold the old girl and you guys. You can pack your bags. Just tell us when you're ready."

Bram was in a state of shock. Gertie burst into a heart wrenching sob. She let out all she had held back all those years. She grabbed Bram and was shaking so much the colonel had her lie down on the couch. Jack brought a glass of water. Bram sat there pouring his heart out in tears that had been held back for so many years. He let it all out. There were no words to speak; it was all too much. All they had hoped and prayed for was going to happen. Through his breathless tears he got out, "Mo's going to have kittens."

CHAPTER 39

That night when their guests had left and the house was quiet, Bram got out of bed slowly so as not to awaken Gertie and sneaked downstairs. Gertie heard him get up and knew where he was going. It was a balmy night, and the moon was showing off her new outfit as it shone bright and clear. As he approached Mo's pen, he whispered, "Mosey, are you awake?"

"Unhhhgh," came a reply.

Elephants rarely laid down but with age creeping up on her and her past injuries it was best to save energy. She lay on the soft bed of straw. Bram knelt by her head and stroked her face.

"Got something to tell you, girl." A sleeping gurgle could be heard. "We're going home Mo, back to Shangari."

It was one of the few words she remembered being used a lot from those days. She tried to get up when she heard it.

"We are. Do you believe it?"

She put her head down and let out a sigh that seemed like she had been holding in forever.

"Uuurrrggggg."

"You're going to see your little one. Well, I hear he's grown up and looks just like his father. And your mate will be so happy to see you. Everybody will be. And we can go have a swim in Lake Namaste."

"Zeeeee."

"Mo, are you asleep?"

"Zeeeee."

"You didn't hear a word I said."

Bram laid down beside her and curled up in his special place at the wrinkle of her neck.

Going home, back to Shangari. Imagine.

"Dear God, I…I… can't find the words to tell you how grateful I am. You have been there for me every step of the way, teaching me to make the right choices, guiding me to take the right path. Sometimes the path was so hard to travel but you got us through. And now to go back home is more than I can imagine."

The realization of going back was too much for Bram.

Like a giant wave of emotion, it washed over him. He burst into tears sobbing his heart out waking up Modoc.

"It's okay, Mosey. They're tears of joy.

"Sleep well. This night I need to be with Gertie." He wiped the tears from his face, hugged Mo, and headed for the house.

Gertie had breakfast prepared when Bram came in. He was sprouting straw from having laid next to Mo.

"How's our girl?" she asked.

"She's fine. Just fine," he said. "I'm hungry."

They spent that day and the following night basking in each other's love. Few words were spoken. Their love for each other was all that was needed.

A week later all was arranged. Bags were packed, Mo wore her best ankle bracelets and the chains Ja and Bram had given her. Bram was dressed in an Indian outfit topped off by a white turban. His silver hair was curled in a ponytail, and he looked most elegant. Gertie, beautiful as always, was dressed Indian style with her golden hair showing flecks of grey. They were an elegant pair, older perhaps, wiser for sure.

Their excitement was unprecedented. They had sent a dozen messages to Ahmed and Latika and Ja of their coming.

Their mailbox was stuffed with their answers. Letter upon letter of questions and thoughts, mostly repeats flowed back and forth.

They thanked the ranch owners for giving them a home. "We owe you a debt that can never be paid."

"It's not a debt but a gift. We will miss you all," said the owner.

The day arrived. A large Army storage van pulled up. There was fresh straw on the floor and buckets of goodies, all favorites of Mo's. The van backed up as close as it could to Mo's enclosure and a ramp was put in place. Once in the van, Bram put only two chains on her. More to help her balance and keep her in one place rather than to bump against the sides of the van. Her moving forcefully could tip the van over.

A limousine arrived and who was driving but Jake from the circus! He had hired the limo to take them to the airport. Jake never did feel the way North did. To that day he felt bad; it was his way of apologizing for taking part in the raid. He wanted to do something for them to show he had mended his ways. On the way to the airport, he apologized for his behavior. They realized working for North would have been most difficult and they graciously accepted his apology. The limo followed the van into and through the airport to the private Army airstrip. At the gate a big sign said:

UNITED STATES ARMY POST 482
AUTHORIZED PERSONNEL ONLY

A guard opened the gate and saluted as they passed. Parked just off the runway was a 385-cargo plane. A modern version of the one they had flown in before, only bigger. There was no ramp but instead men were loading supplies onto a hydraulic lift that was taking them up into the cargo hold area. Both the captain and Jack were there overseeing the operation. They signaled for the lift to be lowered that would take Mo up to a large open hatch in the center of the plane. The captain came over to the limo.

"Morning all, we're just loading supplies that will be dropped off in Calcutta on the way back. Thank goodness they needed them. It was the only way the Army would authorize the plane to fly into India. Carrying the elephant was a humanitarian endeavor. You've made a lot of friends and admirers over the years." The van backed up to the plane. The doors opened and Mo walked out onto the airstrip. When she saw the plane close-up, she became quiet and nervous. She didn't want anything to do with it. She remembered. Bram spent an hour convincing her it was all right. It took another hour for her to check it out. She only had to step on the hydraulic lift that would carry her up to the large opening at the side of the plane. The lift was far better than the ramp. Bram doubted she would have entered the plane by way of the ramp. Finally, with coaxing from all her friends, she stepped onto the lift that raised her up to the large opening at the side of the plane. Once there she stepped off into the huge cargo section. The captain and Jack had spent a lot of time preparing for her anticipated arrival. They knew Modoc's traumatic experience might deter her from wanting to be inside the plane. Too many memories, all bad, so at the suggestion of Bram, they did things to take her mind off it.

They had the air conditioner turned on emitting a strong scent of jasmine. An assortment of flowers was spread against the walls. Baskets of fruit and her favorite berries were lined up for her to enjoy during the flight. They even had drum music playing like the forest people's music. All these things to help take away the bad memories of that day. It worked. In front of her was the cockpit wall, only like the fuselage walls, it was covered with baskets of fruit and flowers. Anything to take her mind off the past traumatic experience. Bram took her to her spot where the chains had been put in. She stood a bit further from the window but close enough to see out. She stood for a few minutes as if remembering.

Bram could only imagine what Modoc was seeing in her mind's eye. His thoughts took him back to that horrible time reliving the smoke and fire and experiencing the panic. The jeep crashing into the cockpit wall narrowly missing him, Modoc falling against the cabin wall, crashing into the cockpit, carrying Jack out, and finally breaking through the fuselage to the outside. It was so vivid.

"Coffee anyone?"

It was Jack, playing host. He was sitting in the spare seat behind his co-pilot seat and was acting as their host. He would be bringing them dinner and wine and taking care of all their needs.

It jolted Bram back into the world of reality. He had broken into a sweat.

"No thanks," he said, not wanting Jack to see his reaction to his thoughts.

"Bram, are you okay?" Gertie asked. She had come in from the passenger door and was putting on her seatbelt.

"Yeah, I'm fine, honey, just fine."

The big cargo freight door was closing. Mo put her ears out expecting the loud engine to turn over. There was nothing but a high-pitched whine as the jets were almost silent. As the plane began to lumber onto the runway, she started a rocking motion, a sign of anxiety. Surely, she, as was Bram, was reliving the crash—the plane in a dive, her being chained, the smoke, and fire, crashing through the cockpit door all brought back the memory of that terrible experience. Bram got up and went to her.

"It's okay, girl, nothing to be concerned about."

He stroked her head, rubbed her tickle spot, and fed her some of her favorite berries from the basket.

The cockpit door opened wide to show the captain and Jack at the controls.

"Comfortable, are you?" said the captain.

"Yes, quite, thank you."

"Just like the old days, huh," joked Jack.

"I hope not," Bram said with a frown.

There were two seats set close to Modoc for Bram and Gertie. They held hands as the plane taxied down the runway. There were no engines turning over, no popping noise, only the whining of the jets as the plane raced down the runway and lifted into the sir. So quiet, thought Bram. Once the plane was in the air, Modoc settled down and watched the clouds drift by. But the least noise, even a rattle, made her stand alert until it passed.

Gertie never let go of Bram's hands. "Bram, is it all really happening?"

"Yes, my love. We're going home."

The hours sped by. Jake brought them their dinner with a bottle of wine to 'take the edge off.' Modoc spent a lot of time looking out the window and was enjoying all the wonderful food lined up for her.

Gertie fell asleep with her head in Bram's lap. Modoc dozed with a bunch of hay hanging from her mouth.

"We're over India now," Jack said, popping his head out the cockpit door. Gertie woke an hour later as the sand dunes of the Sinar Desert appeared. The captain brought the plane down low as they swept over the dunes. Bram broke into a sweat as the vivid memory came to him of when they had reached the river below, the memory of when he and Mosey were at God's gate and Rakesh found them. He envisioned the dilapidated ruins where they met Vinod. He wondered if the man ever recovered.

"Put on your seatbelt, we're about to land," announced Jack.

"Oh! BRAM, BRAM!" yelled Gertie as she squeezed Bram's hand.

The anticipation of seeing his father and all their loved ones was overwhelming. The captain did a flyby to check out the new extended landing strip that had been put in for the big plane to land. He dipped his wings as a welcome to the waving crowd below.

Bram and Gertie knelt by the window as the plane swept down close to the airfield. They were all there. All waving and cheering. The staff had turned out, even the shy forest people were there.

"There's Father!" Gertie cried. "And Latika and Coogan."

And standing close by was Bandulla. They looked for a baby elephant, but none was there, only one half the size of Bandulla stood near him.

"Could that be Bandie? Surely he hadn't grown that big."

But it was Bandie looking so much like his dad.

"You mean Bandor?" said Gertie with a smile.

"He will always be Bandie to me."

Modoc was looking at all the people waving and shouting but she had no idea what it was all about. The captain went high into the sky, did a 180, and came back using every bit of the new landing strip. He roared down the runway coming to a stop far enough away from the crowd to shut the engines down before they arrived.

Jake opened the doors to a group of running, yelling, screaming, howling people. He put down the steps. First to come down was Bram and Gertie who were engulfed in a mob of friends. All were crying and screaming their welcome.

Confetti was in the air. Bram searched in the crowd for his father, where was he?

"There, Bram, there!" pointed Gertie.

Standing over by Bandulla was his father, the Czar, his mentor, the man who had given him a new life. Bram ran through the crowd yelling, "Father, Father!"

Ahmed met him halfway, picked him up and swung him off the ground.

"Bram, my son."

He danced in circles, kisses were flying everywhere, holding tight, never wanting to let him go. Latika was the first to grab Gertie and smother her with kisses. A mass of women swarmed over her hugging, screaming. Little Vishy stood in the back, shy as usual, but looking as healthy as ever. Around his neck was the necklace Ahmed had given him, but hanging next to the jewel was the bullet that had pierced his side all those years ago, worn now like a literal badge of honor. You can't kill a god after all. Coogan and Sanjoe smiled and waved.

"Vishy! Bram yelled. He ran to him picking him up to Vishy's embarrassment. The crowd broke up laughing.

Amid the excitement Bandulla burst out a trumpet. Bram grabbed Gertie's hand and with Ahmed walked over to Bandulla and Bandie. Bram couldn't hold back another minute.

He wrapped his arms round Bandulla's huge head.

"How I've missed you."

For a moment Bandulla was wondering who this human was till he smelled his odor, and above all, Modoc's scent on him! His mate. He looked around. Where was she? He trumpeted and wrapped his trunk around Bram. Yes, of course, now he remembered.

They went to Bandie.

"How big and strong you are," said Gertie.

He was too young to remember. There would be time, lots of time. He was a perfect match to his father.

"We have a lot of lost time to make up for."

A loud trumpet came from the plane.

Bandulla moved to the plane, careful not to step on anyone.

Bram jumped on the lift and up he went to untie the chains around Mo's legs.

"You're home, Mosey."

She knew! She danced a jig to the exit.

She grumbled, chirped, and pooped! She had heard the crowd but didn't know who they were till smells of the forest came in the air and mixed with Bandulla's odor on Bram. She was home! She stepped out on the lift to a rousing cheering crowd of friends. She stood tall looking like she had in the old days and bellowed a trumpet greeting. As the lift touched down everybody surrounded her. Hugging, crying. The kids wrote "Welcome" in chalk on her body and threw confetti on her. Flower leis were draped around her neck.

Then a moment of silence went through the crowd as Bandulla approached Mo.

Elephants did not kiss or hug, but they did their own thing with their trunks intertwining, making a sucking noise; but this time was different. Modoc grabbed Bandulla around the neck, their trunks encircled each other, their bellies rumbled. Bandor squeezed in between them getting his share. Perhaps he knew it was his mother. It was only for elephants to know such things.

And so, the forest awoke that day. It had remained dormant since they had left. The flowers bloomed; the deer pranced in the glade. The springs sparkled with cool, clear water and Bram's energy was felt throughout the forest. Time seemed to have stood still at Shangari, perhaps waiting for their return. And like the forest, Bram was complete. His family was whole again, his heart filled with indescribable joy and love. Surrounded by the friends and family he had made along the way; he was finally back where he was always meant to be. No more running. He was finally home.

THE END

www.ingramcontent.com/pod-product-compliance
Lightning Source LLC
Chambersburg PA
CBHW061554310726

48972CB00008B/2746